DRAGON
BY
MIDNIGHT
KAREN KINCY

This is a work of fiction. names, characters, places, and incidents either are products of the author's imagination or are used fictitiously. any resemblance to actual persons, living or dead (or any other form), business establishments, events, or locales is entirely coincidental.

ISBN-13: 978-1-7379251-0-1

Cover Designer: Psycat Studio
Editor: Jennifer Rees
Copyeditor and Proofreader: Laura Helseth
Interior Design and Typeset: The Illustrated Author Design Services

DRAGON BY MIDNIGHT

ONE

CINDERELLA

Before she became a dragon, the night had been a dream.

Cinderella traveled through the woods as darkness fell. She leaned out the carriage window and inhaled the scent of loam and nocturnal flowers. Stars glittered above, a handful of diamonds scattered across the black velvet sky. Even without a coachman, the dappled gray horse knew its way. Part of the enchantment, she supposed.

Tonight, Prince Benedict Charming would hear her confession.

No matter how much the carriage jostled over ruts in the road, the thought couldn't be knocked from her mind. She tugged at her white gloves, which came to her elbows, and wished she would stop sweating. Best not to dampen the prince.

Knightsend Castle perched high on a cliff. Golden light spilled from hundreds of windows, shimmering in the waterfall that plunged into a ravine. Mist cloaked the lake below and chilled the air. Cinderella shivered and hugged herself. The Fairy Godmother hadn't given her anything as practical as a cloak.

The dappled gray horse trotted higher on the zigzagging road. As they neared the gates of Knightsend, snippets of music and laughter escaped into the night and punctuated the endless rush of the waterfall over the cliff.

When they stopped, she quite forgot how to breathe.

The carriage door opened, no footman required, and she peered up at Knightsend. Towers of pale granite soared heavenward. The castle rivaled any cathedral in grandeur and majesty, flaunting the royal family's wealth.

What if Prince Benedict didn't recognize her? After all, she had deceived him when they first met. He knew her only as Cinderella, the servant girl from Umberwood Manor, and not as the rightful heiress to her childhood home.

What if her stepsisters discovered her? Worse, her stepmother?

She shrank away from the castle, the memory of rags clinging to her skin despite her marvelous gown, shimmering in starlight blue. It wasn't too late to turn back. Remembering to breathe, Cinderella picked up her skirts and stepped delicately from the carriage. Her ankles wobbled in her crystal slippers until the enchantment steadied her step.

Guards opened a groaning door. Red-coated footmen ushered her into the ballroom.

She needed no invitation, which meant that Prince Benedict truly had invited all the maidens in the land tonight.

Would he even care that she had come?

Mirrors reflected a kaleidoscopic whirl of gowns, chandeliers, and gilded candelabra. Ladies and gentlemen waltzed under a ceiling of celestial blue. My, how beautiful they were! Envy twisted her stomach. She could never dream of affording such glamours: magic to make skin as smooth as alabaster, and hair outshine gold.

Then she saw him.

Prince Benedict Charming strode across the ballroom with the easy confidence of someone who had never been poor or ugly. Someone who knew the world adored him and bent to his will. His wheat-blond hair glinted under the glow of the chandeliers. His blue eyes outranked the clearest summer sky.

The prince needed no enchantments to look so stunningly handsome.

"Benedict," she whispered.

Their stares met.

Her heart fluttered in her chest, a caged bird, as she waited for him.

Benedict's gaze traveled from her hair down to her slippers. A slow smile brightened his face. "You look better."

A blush scorched her cheeks. "Thank you." Surely he meant it as a compliment.

"Dance with me."

She followed his lead to the dance floor. He held her close, one of his strong hands clasping hers, the other resting at the curve of her spine. This close, it was impossible to ignore how tall he was, or the way his eyes sparkled.

Were princes ever born less than perfect?

"Lost in thought?" Prince Benedict said.

"A little," she admitted. She had to tell him who she was, and what had been stolen from her. "Your Royal Highness?"

"Please, call me Benedict."

"Benedict?"

"That's better."

"You don't know why I'm truly here."

"Oh?" He smirked. "Not to win my heart?"

The musicians launched into a polka, a rather unromantic dance that left her panting and laughing. She clung to Benedict's shoulders, lightheaded, and fought to catch her breath. Her corset restricted her allowance of air.

"Goodness," she managed. "I feel as if I might swoon."

"My apologies." He winked. "I didn't mean to be so breathtaking."

She lowered her gaze. The crown prince was altogether too charming for her. She had so little experience with flirtation.

"May we sit?" she said.

"Of course."

Benedict led her onto a balcony perched over the waterfall, which muted the music. Red roses clambered over the castle. He twisted one from its vine, knocking a few petals loose, and presented it to her. She took it with a polite smile. When a thorn pricked her thumb through her glove, a tiny dot of blood stained the white.

Hopefully, it wasn't a bad omen.

"Please," Benedict said, "rest your feet."

Her heartbeat still hammered against her corset. She gathered her skirts and lowered herself onto a granite bench, which was less comfortable than it could have been. Were cushions not majestic enough for the castle?

"Benedict." She sucked in air. "I haven't been entirely honest with you."

The corner of his mouth quirked in a smile. "How intriguing. You lied to me?"

"No! Well, yes." She fidgeted, the granite hard beneath her derriere. "When we first met, I told you my name was Cinderella."

"I thought it was unusual."

"No more than a nickname." An inescapable one, from her stepsisters. "My name was once Ginevra Darlington."

Benedict blinked a few times. "Darlington?"

"Yes. I'm the last of the Darlingtons. The true heiress to Umberwood Manor." She struggled not to sound bitter, since that would, of course, be unladylike. "You know of Umberwood, don't you? Of its history?"

The prince tilted his head, a few strands of his wheat-colored hair slipping over his face. "If I remember correctly, it was a gift."

"To my mother, Lady Vivendel Darlington, for a great service to the Queen of Viridia."

Benedict frowned. "I can't recall why."

"My mother never told me before she…" She swallowed past the ache in her throat. It had been years, but it still hurt.

"I'm sorry for your loss." His blue eyes glimmered, luminous in the moonlight.

Cinderella twisted her fingers in her lap. "My father remarried before he passed away. My stepmother claimed the title of Lady Darlington and squandered the family fortune. She spent it all on gowns and glamours."

Benedict's frown deepened. "You were wearing rags when you found me in the forest."

"Not *rags*, exactly."

"I meant no offense."

"My wardrobe is the least of my concerns." She picked at a loose thread on her gloves. "We are on the brink of losing Umberwood."

Benedict gazed at the eternal plunge of the waterfall. "What a shame."

Lord, how direct could she be while maintaining some semblance of modesty?

"Long ago, your mother gifted mine Umberwood," she said. "I would hate to lose such a precious gift from the royal family. I came to the ball tonight, Benedict, in the hopes that you might help me save my childhood home."

"Might I suggest marriage for a lady of ambition such as yourself?"

Her lips parted in surprise. "Marriage?"

When he turned to her, a smile shadowed his mouth. "Why come to Knightsend tonight, and not any other night?"

"Because the royal family doesn't grant audiences to girls dressed in rags."

He laughed, the sparkle back in his eyes. "But I invited you to the castle. Even when you hid your identity from me."

"You invited all the maidens in the land."

"Ah, but you are the fairest of them all."

Heat scalded her cheeks. "Even in rags?"

"They can't disguise your beauty."

"Such flattery!" She waved her hand as if shooing away his compliments. "My stepsisters dream of marrying royalty."

"And you?"

Never had she dreamed of Prince Benedict Charming. What a lie that would be! Especially after she had found him utterly naked, swimming in a pond, a memory so scandalous that she willed herself not to stare at him now.

She glanced at him through her eyelashes. "It depends if you believe in love at first sight. Your future bride might be at this very ball. Heaven knows how you will find her, though, if you don't dance with all the maidens in the land first."

Benedict smirked. "An impossibility."

Should she ask him about Umberwood Manor again? But no, that might seem as though she was begging for royal gold.

Was marrying rich much better?

"I hear the hors d'oeuvres are delicious." He held out his hand. "Shall we investigate?"

"Yes, Your Royal Highness. I'm famished."

Her stepsisters would never dream of expressing a bodily need such as hunger, especially not around an eligible bachelor. How unrefined to want food rather than subsisting on pretty little dreams. But Cinderella often wanted too much.

She followed Benedict into a dining room laid with a grand buffet. Tables bristled with candlesticks and centerpieces of exotic fruits. A thief would be rich from a few pocketfuls of cutlery in silver and gold—she was just poor enough for the thought to occur to her. And the food beggared belief: deviled eggs, smoked ham, lobster salad, liver pâté, sugared grapes, crystal bowls of punch, and tiny pink cakes iced with roses.

Benedict stabbed a cake with a fork and wolfed it down whole. He knocked back a flute of champagne. "Delicious."

"Heavens!" Cinderella touched her fingertips to her mouth.

His grin looked feral, as if he would lose more of his manners after drinking more champagne. Attempting to be dainty, she nudged a deviled egg onto a silver plate big enough for a dollhouse. Likely worth only half of a commoner's income. Benedict wasn't paying attention, his gaze fixed somewhere over her shoulder.

"Excuse me for a moment," he said.

He disappeared into the crowd. Cinderella nibbled the egg with significantly more decorum than he had devoured the tiny pink cake. If all royal cuisine tasted this good, she might not terribly mind living here.

On a fireplace mantle, a gilded clock chimed half past ten.

Cinderella finished the deviled egg. Less than two hours of the enchantment remained. Her Fairy Godmother had warned her the spell would break at the stroke of midnight. She would return to nothing more than a girl in rags.

This could be her only chance to save Umberwood Manor.

Her mouth went dry. Swallowing hard, she helped herself to a cake, which left her mouth sticky-sweet. She washed it down with a swig of punch. Rum scorched her throat all the way down. Good lord, that was strong. She had only ever been tipsy once before.

Perhaps she was a fool for believing Prince Benedict would help her without repayment. Marrying the Crown Prince of Viridia would save her from her stepmother, but she doubted he would choose her for his bride. Princes like him had a reputation for deflowering pretty girls before marrying a more acceptable lady.

Could she barter her virginity to save Umberwood Manor?

Such a shameful thought. She banished it from her mind, even though she knew she had little else of worth to the prince.

Maybe that was all he wanted.

The rest of the night passed in a blur.

Benedict found her, danced with her, told her things to make her laugh. He flirted and flattered her until she hoped for more. She sampled the lobster salad, smoked ham, and a single sugared grape, since her corset wouldn't allow her to indulge. When she drank more punch, the rum left a pleasant heat in her belly.

By the buffet, Prince Benedict looked at her as if he had told another joke, one she had missed. She forced herself to laugh again.

"Are you quite all right?" he said.

"Pardon me. I would like to powder my nose."

She slipped away from the hubbub of the ball and entered a cool hallway. Mirrors, suits of armor, paintings of royalty with smug smiles and bored eyes. Where was the bloody lavatory? She giggled, since she would never say such vulgarity out loud.

Finally, a footman trotted down the hallway. "May I help you, milady?"

"I'm trying to powder my nose," she whispered.

"Of course." He had a placid demeanor. "Down the hallway, the first door on your left."

"Thank you."

Hadn't she already tried that door? Perhaps this was a test devised by Prince Benedict. Whichever maidens could find the lavatory in this labyrinth of a castle were worthy of his affection. The rest simply perished.

When she found the door unlocked, she swept inside with a sigh of relief. Her ball gown hadn't been designed for this inconvenience. Perhaps Fairy Godmothers never powdered their noses, so to speak. That must be awfully nice.

Someone rapped on the door.

"One moment!" She hurried to wash her hands.

When she stepped from the lavatory, she stifled a gasp.

Eulalia.

Her stepsister regarded her with a poisonous glare. "Cinderella."

Eulalia's emerald jewelry glittered across her chest. Her green silk gown plunged daringly low, and her dark hair had been glamoured to glow under perpetual starlight. All of it cost a fortune. The Darlington fortune, to be more precise.

What a detestable wench.

Cinderella faked a smile. "Fancy seeing you here."

Eulalia did not seem to find this amusing. "You reek of rum." She wrinkled her nose. "And your hair…"

Cinderella hadn't even glanced in the mirror. "My hair?"

"Disheveled." Eulalia sneered, as if she looked like a harlot.

"Oh," Cinderella said, brightly. "I was dancing with the crown prince."

"Enjoy it while it lasts."

Eulalia brushed past before slamming the door to the lavatory. Cinderella snickered. Of course, Eulalia would be envious. She wondered where her other stepsister, Delicata, was at the moment. Undoubtedly lurking in a dark corner, kissing a duke. She never did share her mother's aspirations for a royal wedding. Lady Darlington planned to auction off both Umberwood Manor and her daughters to the highest bidder.

Cinderella wandered back to the ball. If she imbibed enough rum, she might be better at flirting with Benedict. She might even think about letting him kiss her. Maybe he did believe in love at first sight, and she could pretend.

"Bother," she muttered.

She had forgotten her white gloves in the lavatory. But Eulalia must have thrown them into the refuse. No point in going back.

By the punchbowl, Cinderella's skull began to ache, probably from the rum. Forgoing the punch, she nibbled another sugared grape. Blood rushed into her face. She fanned herself with her hand, though it did nothing to cool her down.

"Cinderella!" Prince Benedict emerged from the crowd. "There you are."

She swallowed the grape with difficulty. Her skin prickled like she had run naked through a field of nettles. She hugged herself, trying to surreptitiously itch her arms. Pain stabbed her stomach and doubled her over.

"Cinderella?" Benedict was at her side in an instant.

The gilded clock on the mantel began to chime.

Midnight.

Benedict held her by the elbow, but Cinderella broke free and fled into the ballroom. Dancers whirled across the parquet, slowing her escape. She teetered in the crystal slippers, her footsteps sloppy as the enchantment unraveled.

Was that Delicata, smirking at her disgrace?

Cinderella tripped over her gown. She fell to her hands and knees.

Her skin was on fire, the stinging intensifying from nettles to wasps. Her hands splayed on the polished wood of the parquet floor. Even her nails burned. Claws scythed from her fingers, each a crystal blade.

Distantly, she heard the last chime of the clock.

Her fingertips turned purple, as if twisted with a tight string, before darkening to blue. The indigo color rushed from her hands to her arms. Her skin shattered into glass-sharp scales. Spine twisting, bones crunching, she shuddered into another shape. Her gown fell from her in tatters while her body swelled to a gargantuan size.

When Cinderella screamed, the noise wasn't human.

The spell had broken.

TWO

SIKANDAR

Sikandar was late to the royal ball.

Ladies fluttered throughout Knockingham like butterflies. Tonight, their crown prince would choose one of them as his bride. These Viridian royals didn't value political alliances, since their monarchs kept marrying commoners for love. Viridia's economy seemed equally frivolous, exporting wine, clocks, and cheese.

Sikandar couldn't care less about the royal family of Viridia. He wanted—needed—what they had locked away in their treasury.

His one chance of redemption.

Knightsend Castle perched high on a cliff above Knockingham, its towers peeking over a bristling forest. Mist shrouded the dark pines. Sikandar left behind the cobblestoned streets of the city for a road paved by ancient conquerors, the stones a thousand years smooth. Horses and carriages rattled past at an alarming speed.

It took him a small eternity to climb to Knightsend. The fortress looked more ornamental than impenetrable, all stained-glass windows and pretty little towers, though gunpowder had rendered castles obsolete. A waterfall churned over the cliff, tossing mist into the dusky evening. When he stepped through the wrought-iron gates, a peacock wandered past. He raised an eyebrow. Shipped from Azurum?

The guards at the door wore shining plate armor. Also ornamental.

"Good evening, gentlemen." Sikandar spoke to the guards in his most formal Viridian. "I'm here for the ball."

The left-hand guard sneered. "You aren't a maiden."

"Astute observation."

Behind Sikandar, a girl giggled. He looked over his shoulder and saw three of them lingering behind him. They whispered behind their hands, their jewelry glittering in the lamplight. His woolen shawl hid his best Azuri formalwear. With a flourish, he stripped off the shawl and tossed it over his arm.

That got them staring.

He hadn't worn his brocade coat since his sister's wedding. Golden embroidery twisted over shimmering midnight blue silk. His tailored trousers matched, a shade of muted gold. His sister had teased him, calling him a princeling.

He blinked away the memory like a bad dream.

"Who are you?" the right-hand guard demanded.

"A sorcerer from Azurum."

The girls behind him gasped at this revelation.

"Sorcery!" one of them said in a stage whisper.

"Will there be magic tricks at the ball?" asked another.

"Perhaps." Sikandar forced a smile. "But first, I must speak with the king."

"You have an appointment?" the right-hand guard said. "His Majesty doesn't grant audiences to strangers off the street."

What a pain. He could teleport inside, but he didn't want to sound the alarm.

"My name is Sikandar Zerian."

The guards glanced at each other. Surely, they knew of his family's reputation. A Zerian at the door was never welcomed, though never rejected. Nobody wanted their name written in his family's meticulous list of enemies.

"Speak to His Majesty's steward first," said the left-hand guard.

"Thank you, gentlemen."

Before they could change their minds, Sikandar breezed past them into the castle. He paused in the entrance hall. Impressive. Crystal chandeliers shimmered from vaulted ceilings painted like the night sky. The royal family had to be fabulously wealthy. Maybe cheese, wine, and clocks weren't such bad exports, after all.

"Sir." A footman materialized by his elbow. "Might I unburden you?"

Sikandar swung his pack from his shoulders. "Thank you."

To his credit, the footman didn't flinch at the considerable weight. Unbeknownst to him, the pack contained an assortment of sorcerous supplies.

Nothing *too* dangerous.

"And your shawl, sir?"

"Of course." Sikandar straightened, feeling a little more like a gentleman.

"Pardon me!" One of the girls caught up to him. "Mr. Zerian?"

"Yes?"

"Are you truly from Azurum?" The doe-eyed young lady stared at him as if he were a special treat, imported for the night.

Obviously, she hadn't heard of the Zerian family. Or she had, and found danger thrilling.

"I am. And I'm afraid I'm busy."

"Oh, but I would love to speak with you more! I've read so much about Azurum. Tigers and rosewater and harems with captive maidens…" The girl clutched her hand to her bosom, looked heavenward, and sighed.

He raised his eyebrows. "You have read so much, haven't you?"

Before she could elaborate upon these fictional harems, he slipped out of the entrance hall and found his way to the ballroom.

Gods, had they really invited all the maidens in the land?

A morass of dancers blocked his way. Ladies outnumbered gentlemen. Many unmarried girls clustered in the corners, fanning themselves vigorously and eyeing their competition as one does before entering into ritual combat.

Wonderful. Now they spotted *him*.

Sikandar retreated to a dining room with a buffet table. He grabbed a silver plate and loaded it with sugared grapes, to avoid making conversation. He tracked down the nearest servant, who was refreshing an empty punchbowl.

"Excuse me." Sikandar raised his voice. "It's urgent that I speak with the king."

The servant had a placid, almost mulish look. His large ears didn't help. "Do you have an appointment with His Majesty?"

"No, but—"

"Sorry, sir, I'm afraid an appointment is required."

"Could I speak with your steward?"

"The steward is indisposed at the moment. The ball is a rather hectic occasion."

"That's an understatement."

"Enjoy the refreshments."

Sikandar sipped some of the punch. It scorched his throat on the way down. Grimacing, he set aside the glass. He didn't drink alcohol. No wonder so many of the guests here tittered stupidly and stared at him for too long.

Gods, he had to attract the attention of the King of Viridia. But how? Magic tricks?

He needed the Jewel of Oblivion before it was too late to redeem himself. Was it worth trying to steal it from the Viridian royal vault? With his luck, he would fail miserably.

"Might I ask why you are guarding the punch bowl?"

A young lady confronted him. Her burgundy hair clashed with her yellow ballgown. Her skin reminded him of porcelain, too white and flawless, as if she were an imaginary woman from an advertisement selling high-end perfume.

Glamours. The magic scented the air, almost imperceptibly, with lilacs and lightning.

"Pardon me," he said. "The punch bowl is all yours."

She refilled her glass and swigged a drink. "Better." She sighed. "I hate these horrid balls. Mother wants us to marry into money."

Sikandar glanced sideways at her. "Isn't that the point?"

"Perhaps." Her gaze traveled over his brown skin. "Where are you from?"

"Azurum."

"I thought so. Do they have balls like this in Azurum?"

"The equivalent."

She curled her lip slightly. "I suppose it's unavoidable." Her gaze sharpened. "Who are you, anyway? It's horribly improper for me to ask you myself, without being introduced by someone, but you have my curiosity."

"Sikandar Zerian."

"Zerian. That sounds awfully familiar."

He kept his face blank. "Does it?"

"Aren't they a *bad* family?" She whispered it like a scandalous secret.

"Do I look bad?" he deadpanned.

She arched her eyebrows. "Not particularly."

"Nice to meet you. Though I still don't know your name."

"Delicata Darlington."

"Do you know the royal family?"

Delicata laughed. "If only! Then I could simply marry Prince Benedict Charming and make all of Mother's dreams come true."

The sound of applause echoed from the ballroom.

Delicata followed his gaze. "Speak of the devil." She poured more punch into her glass. "Until we meet again, Mr. Zerian."

Fortified by alcohol, she sauntered back to the ballroom.

Sikandar followed at her heels. Gasps and laughter rippled through the room. Prince Benedict strode by, a glimpse of fair hair and a grin, before he vanished into a sea of eligible maidens. Sikandar doubted the crown prince would come up for air any time soon. He would have to dive in after him and drag him out.

One of the young ladies collapsed on the floor.

Down on her knees, she shuddered before sprawling across the wood. Her skin turned blue as her body twisted into another shape. Guests crowded around the grotesque spectacle. A predator's shriek tore from her mouth.

Heart hammering, Sikandar lifted his hands, bracing himself to summon defensive magic. He lost sight of her until she unfurled over the ballroom.

His stomach lurched. "Dragon."

Candlelight glimmered on her armor of blue scales. Wicked horns curved from her head. Her jaws gaped, saliva dripping from her fangs, and breath scented with brimstone fouled the air. When she spread her leathery wings, she knocked down a chandelier, which plummeted and chimed into a thousand shards of crystal.

From beauty to beast in less than a minute.

The power hit Sikandar's gut like a sucker punch.

Screams echoed in the ballroom. Ladies fainted while gentlemen scrambled for the doors, throwing aside dignity and chivalry.

Prince Benedict drew his dress sword, the gilded blade useless against such a monstrosity. The dragon slithered away, claws gouging the floor. She whipped her head, searching the ballroom. Her fiery eyes looked wild.

The dragon lunged.

Instead of taking off the crown prince's head, she crashed through a magnificent window, scattering chunks of masonry, and fled onto a balcony. Prince Benedict bounded over shards of glass and chased his foe outside.

Sikandar would prefer not to be burnt to ashes. He didn't want the royal family of Viridia dead, either. Not when he needed them and the contents of their treasury.

Swearing, he followed the prince.

The dragon barely fit on the balcony. Her wings and tail scraped the granite castle walls. Cracks spiderwebbed through the stone underfoot. Sikandar leapt back, stumbling, and caught himself on the rubble. Prince Benedict, rather ridiculously, brandished his sword while balancing.

The dragon reared onto the railing. Between one heartbeat and the next, she perched on the brink of flight.

Half the balcony crumbled.

The dragon plummeted into the ravine, twisting in the air, a serpent with useless wings. Mist shrouded the lake below. She vanished.

The impact punctuated the waterfall's roar.

Silence.

"Dead?" Sikandar said.

Prince Benedict glanced back. "Who are you?" He raised his gilded sword. "Did you conjure the dragon?"

"No!" Sikandar raised his hands. "I'm not that kind of sorcerer."

"But you *are* a sorcerer?"

Maybe he shouldn't have worn brocade silk tonight. Playing the part of a mysterious stranger could get him killed.

"Answer the question." Prince Benedict pointed the sword at his neck.

Sikandar kept his face emotionless. "I'm a sorcerer from Azurum, trained at the University of Naranjal."

"And?" The prince's blade edged nearer. "State your name."

"Sikandar Zerian."

"I know who you are." Benedict's knuckles whitened around his sword. "The Zerian family banished their sorcerer son. Murder, wasn't it?"

Rumors had reached Viridia already. "I won't deny it."

"I'm not surprised." Prince Benedict sheathed his sword grimly. "Father!"

King Archibald Charming of Viridia.

He didn't look like a king, regardless of his crown and velvet clothes. More like a woodcutter who enjoyed tavern brawls. He had a grizzled beard, meaty arms, and a nose that must have been broken at least once.

Sikandar dropped into a low bow, his hair falling into his eyes, hoping he remembered the correct etiquette here.

"Rise," said the king, as if commanding a dog.

Sikandar gritted his teeth, but didn't risk disobeying. "Your Majesty, I—"

"Benedict, what the hell happened here?"

"Father." Prince Benedict's throat bobbed as he swallowed. "She turned into a dragon."

"Who?" King Archibald thundered. "A witch? An assassin?"

"Just a girl."

"Clearly not *just a girl*, you imbecile." A vein bulged on the king's temple. "She destroyed half the castle!"

Benedict rubbed the back of his neck. "But she seemed so sweet and innocent."

King Archibald sneered like he had smelled a cesspit. "Don't be distracted by tits and a pretty face. I would place my bet on a dragon in disguise. She wouldn't be the first to hide her wicked nature with feminine wiles."

"Like a werewolf?" Prince Benedict asked. "Or that siren princess?"

"Precisely." King Archibald stroked his beard pensively. "That scaly abomination left your poor cousin Edgar with demon spawn instead of heirs." He curled his lip. "Benedict, tell me you didn't kiss that girl."

"I only thought about it," the prince stammered.

"Thank god." King Archibald grunted. "That's how they ensnare you with their diabolical enchantments."

Wonderful. Laymen coming to their own conclusions about magic.

Sikandar cleared his throat. "Excuse me."

"Who the hell are you?" King Archibald rounded on him.

"Sikandar Zerian of Azurum."

"Zerian?" The king retreated a step, his nostrils flaring like those of a bull. "What do they want?"

"Don't ask me, my family banished me."

"For murder," Prince Benedict interjected, unhelpfully.

"Irrelevant." Sikandar shook his head. "In my expert opinion, the dragon girl was cursed."

A woman's voice echoed across the broken ballroom. "What was her name?"

Queen Eira of Viridia glided to them in a wine-red gown. She stopped where the dragon's claws had ruined the parquet floor. She wore no glamours. Her silvery blonde hair glinted, frosted by age, and she had eyes of palest gray. She looked almost colorless, like she had faded away over time.

Sikandar bowed again. "Your Majesty."

"Cinderella," said Prince Benedict. "She told me her name was Cinderella, before she confessed her true identity."

Queen Eira traced a claw mark with her gaze. "Which was?"

"Ginevra Darlington."

The queen's stare froze in place. "Darlington," she murmured.

She knew more that she wasn't telling them. Sikandar sensed an opportunity.

"I can help the royal family," he said, "by ridding you of the dragon."

King Archibald snorted. "For free?"

"For the Jewel of Oblivion."

The king held out his hands as if weighing the magical gem against the dragon. "It seems rather coincidental that you arrived at the same night the dragon did, then offer to make it all go away for a very specific price."

Sikandar's mouth went drier than the deserts of Azurum, but he forced himself to smile. "That would be too obvious. Surely my family has a reputation for more cunning than that? I'm offering my expertise in curses and hexes."

King Archibald turned instead to his son. "Benedict, you will slay the dragon."

The color drained from the prince's face, but he squared his shoulders and gripped the hilt of his sword. "Yes, Father."

"Wait," Sikandar said. "Magic can be cleaner than a blade."

King Archibald sliced his hand through the air. "There's no time to wait. Not with a monster rampaging around my kingdom."

The dragon was hardly *rampaging*. She had fled the castle.

"No," Queen Eira interrupted. "We should send the sorcerer. The Zerian family understands how to kill with discretion."

King Archibald glowered at her. "You would deny our son the honor of a dragon hunt?"

"Honor matters less than a swift resolution."

"Fine." The king folded his thick arms. "Let them both try."

Sikandar touched his hand to his heart. "The dragon will never darken the skies above your kingdom again. On my honor as a sorcerer."

Which wasn't much.

The queen met his gaze with her unsettlingly pale eyes. "Sikandar Zerian, if you win, the Jewel of Oblivion is yours."

"Thank you, Your Majesty."

"Save your thanks for your victorious return."

THREE

CINDERELLA

Hitting the lake knocked the air from Cinderella's lungs. She sank deep below the inky water, twisting, trapped in an unknown body with claws and wings. Her heart raced with panic. One constant remained.

Breathe. She had to breathe.

Cinderella's tail scraped rocks. The bottom of the lake. Kicking, she surged upward and burst into the air with a gasp. She half-swam, half-scrambled onto the shore, stumbling over boulders. Her limbs felt loose and disjointed, like an unfamiliar puppet. Not even her eyesight was the same. The night looked too stark and bright.

High above, overlooking the cliff, Knightsend glittered in the moonlight, ruined by broken glass and scarred masonry.

She had done that. Her dream had become a nightmare.

Screams still echoed in her memory. She crawled along the shore, her belly and tail dragging on the gravel. When she straightened to her full height, the distance to the ground dizzied her for a moment. She had to be twice as tall as before, and rivaling a draft horse in weight. What *was* she? But that was a foolish question.

Dragon. There was no other word for it.

Only hours before, she had been dancing and laughing with Prince Benedict, feeling a glimmer of hope that she might save Umberwood Manor. Why hadn't the Fairy Godmother warned her that her spell came with a curse?

Dragons could still cry. Scalding tears streamed down the scales on her face.

She fled from the castle. Brambles tangled the edge of the forest. She crashed through the thorns, her wings clamped along her back, her claws gouging the muck. Teardrops sizzled as they landed on the damp leaves underfoot.

Prince Charming would find her. Not to win her hand, but to slay her.

Deeper and deeper into the forest she ran. God, she had to stop. Just to let the choking in her throat subside. Endless trees hid the castle from sight. The wind shattered and reshaped the canopy of maple leaves overhead. She was lost in the wilderness. Where she belonged.

Her sobs faded to sniffling. Puffs of steam escaped her nostrils. Her gaze fell to her claws. They shone in the starlight, even brighter than her crystal slippers had been, once upon a time. Her eyes blurred once again.

No. She had to stop blubbering. Dragons didn't do that. They lurked in caves, alone, where no one but princes dared venture. Maybe Benedict could save her. Maybe true love's kiss would turn her back. But he had already attacked her with his sword. He would find a nice girl, a pretty girl, who would never betray him by becoming a monster.

Even Delicata and Eulalia were better candidates for his wife.

Cinderella's heart tightened into a knot. She lashed out at a tree. Her talons shredded bark and splintered wood. Destruction felt surprisingly good. She had never destroyed anything before, except her own hopes and dreams.

She was a monster. They would never let her return to Umberwood Manor. It didn't matter where she went now. She wandered into the night.

What had she done to deserve this curse?

When she first met Prince Charming, one enchanted twilight, had she doomed herself somehow?

Cinderella had been working in the garden, a chore she found secretly satisfying. Lady Darlington kept threatening to tear it out, since the roses and rosemary belonged to Cinderella's late mother, but she was a miser to the bone. She would never waste coin on mere herbs or vegetables, so long as she never dirtied her own hands growing them.

Cinderella stooped over the soft, dark earth, yanking out clumps of clover, buttercup, and yarrow. She would have left the prettier weeds, since they were simply misplaced wildflowers, if not for her stepmother's certain wrath.

Lady Darlington did enjoy wrath more than the other seven deadly sins.

Cinderella rested her hands upon her aching back and stared at the sapphire sky. Evening was falling upon Umberwood Manor. Robins peeped and rustled in the hedgerows. Above her, swallows returned to their roosts. A hint of winter's chill touched the wind. Soon, summer would be forgotten, and autumn would be no more than a memory.

Umberwood brought a sweet ache to her heart. She loved her childhood home dearly.

Weeds vanquished, Cinderella bent over the carrot patch. She tugged a dozen twisted roots from the dirt and brought them inside the kitchen, onto the battle-scarred table, before washing her hands in the scullery sink.

There was time before dinner to bake a dessert. Cloudberry scones were one of her childhood favorites, though she would never tell her stepmother or stepsisters. Neither would she confess to the quiet joy of baking, alone in the kitchen of Umberwood Manor, imagining that this great house could one day be opened as a bed and breakfast.

Cinderella snatched a basket and escaped through the garden gate. Lingering too long in the manor was dangerous. Lady Darlington could always think of some horrid task, since she had a vivid imagination for punishments.

She crossed through a wizened old apple orchard. Ripe fruits hung like cabochons of ruby and topaz. Beyond the orchard, apple trees gave way to wilder forest. The path wound among gnarled roots and dark hollows. Sometimes, in the dead of night, she heard wolves howling. Her stepsisters would never dare venture this far into the woods, but Cinderella knew wolves to be shy creatures who avoided people.

She could hardly blame them, considering her own acquaintances.

Evening's last light sliced through the forest. Picking up her skirts, she veered from the path and climbed a hill. Wild cloudberries favored dappled sun beneath birches. She scuffed her boots in the leaves, enjoying the rustle and crunch.

"Victory!" she muttered to herself.

Golden berries gleamed against velveteen moss. She ate the first one, a guilty pleasure, the taste almost too sweet. The rest of the cloudberries went into her basket. When she stood, a flash of silver caught her gaze.

Below the hill, waist-deep in a glimmering pond, a man shook the water from his hair.

A very naked man.

Rivulets trickled down his shoulders and back. His muscles flexed in a fascinating way. When he waded toward the shore, she sucked in a fortifying breath, gripped her basket, and turned her back on the stranger. How horrendously improper!

"Wait!" he said.

She froze. "No, thank you."

"I'm nearly decent."

Against her better judgment, she stole a glance. He shrugged a shirt over his shoulders, the linen clinging to his wet skin. When he lifted his gaze, his eyes were bluer than forget-me-nots. Heat scorched her cheeks.

He buttoned his shirt. He had beautiful wrists, every tendon and vein chiseled like a statue. "My apologies. I didn't mean to startle any fair maidens."

She arched her eyebrows. "This pond is rather close to a path."

"Are you accusing me of premeditated nudity?"

"I never said that."

His hair was starting to dry, turning the color of wheat. "What's your name?"

She couldn't tell him the truth. Not dressed in rags and streaked in dirt. "Cinderella."

"Where are you from, Cinderella? A little cottage in the woods?"

"Umberwood Manor." Of course, he would believe her to be a servant at such a grand house. She clutched her basket of cloudberries in both hands. "And you are?"

"Benedict."

"Like the prince?"

A grin crept over his face. "Like the prince."

Her fingers flew to her mouth. Lord, had she been blind? Prince Benedict Charming, the heir to the throne of Viridia.

"Your face isn't on any coins," she said.

"Yet." Benedict coughed as if hiding a laugh. "Why haven't I seen you before?"

"In the forest? Have you been bathing here often?"

"Swimming. And no."

She shrugged. "It's getting late." She glanced at the angle of the sun. "I must return to Umberwood for dinner." If she didn't cook it on time, her stepmother would be furious.

Benedict stepped closer. "Will you come to the ball?"

"Which?" Her stepsisters talked endlessly of soirées and dancing, mostly to spite her.

"Tomorrow night. Knightsend Castle."

The heat returned to her face. She had no time to spare from her chores, and nothing to wear, but she could hardly complain to the Crown Prince of Viridia.

He smiled again. "All the maidens in the land are invited. Come. Dance with me."

"Perhaps," she said.

She walked away without a farewell.

Against all better judgment, Prince Benedict Charming ruled Cinderella's thoughts. When she closed her eyes that night, she saw him swimming in the pond, the water sliding over his skin. She could stare at him in her dreams.

But she dreamed of more than just beautiful princes.

If she went to the ball, she could go not as Cinderella, but as Ginevra Darlington, the heiress to Umberwood Manor. Her mother had once served the queen herself.

The royal family *must* know Umberwood was rightfully hers.

Certainly her stepsisters would attend the ball. They never missed the chance to preen like a pair of oversized peahens. She envied the quantity and quality of their wardrobes. One could get lost in their closets for weeks.

In the middle of the night, before dawn even considered getting out of bed, Cinderella kicked off her threadbare sheet. Her cot was in the attic, conveniently. Her late mother's possessions hid among the dust and cobwebs.

Shivering in her nightgown, she tiptoed across the creaky floorboards, not wishing to wake her stepfamily. Outside the window, beyond rippled panes of glass, the moon sank beneath a sea of clouds. An owl hooted, lonely, from the old pear tree.

Cinderella knelt beside an antique trunk. Slowly, she unbuckled the latches and lifted the heavy lid. Tissue paper rustled inside, yellow and brittle like onionskin. Beneath the paper, a glimpse of pink silk glistened.

Her mother's dress.

Rose perfume still clung to the silk. Cinderella held it close to her face and blinked fast to avoid tearstains. Her mother had been a petite woman, smaller than Cinderella, but she could let out the seams and alter the bodice.

It would be enough. It had to be.

By candlelight and moonlight, she sewed all through the night.

A cockerel crowed near sunrise. Her eyes gritty, Cinderella blinked. She stepped out of her nightgown in favor of a chemise, then put on her corset, hooking the busk in the front and tugging the laces tight in the back.

She slipped the dress over her head. A cracked mirror leaned against the wall. She swept off the dust cloth, sneezed, and looked her reflection in the eye.

Pink silk shimmered at the first touch of dawn. She turned this way and that, noting a crooked seam here and there. She combed her strawberry blonde hair with her fingers before twisting it above her head. A slight improvement. Prince Benedict Charming might not even laugh upon her arrival.

Cinderella hid the dress beneath the crumpled tissue paper.

Before her stepmother or stepsisters woke, she dressed in a shapeless brown frock and hurried down to the kitchen, where she stoked embers in the iron stove. Her stomach rumbled as she cooked porridge, scrambled eggs, and fried thick rashers of bacon. She could have wolfed down most of the food herself, but she ladled porridge into a bowl, served eggs and bacon on a plate, and carried the breakfast upstairs on a silver platter.

Outside her stepmother's bedchamber, she set down the tray and rapped twice on the door. Rapping thrice was unacceptable. Lady Darlington demanded unobtrusive servants.

"Enter," her stepmother said.

Cinderella pushed open the door, holding it with her toe while she balanced the tray upon one hand. Lady Darlington lurked in bed, leaning against a pillow. She pursed her lips at the tray. No doubt she expected Cinderella to drop her breakfast and had a plethora of insults at the ready.

Cinderella tread carefully. "Good morning, Stepmother."

Lady Darlington jotted down a note in her book of household finances. Enchanted, her hair shimmered an inhuman color between silver and violet. Her eyes, too, were violet. Each of these everlasting glamours flaunted her wealth.

She didn't deserve to look so beautiful. Like a rotten apple painted gold.

God, her stepmother should have been the most hideous woman in the world, but instead she wielded her beauty like a weapon.

"Where shall I set your breakfast?" Cinderella said.

"Upon the side table."

She obeyed. The sooner she was done here, the sooner she could escape down to the kitchen.

"Eulalia and Delicata will require a lady's maid this afternoon."

"Of course, Stepmother."

"They need to look their finest for tonight's ball. Rumors have been swirling about Prince Charming."

Cinderella kept her face blank. "May I ask which rumors?"

"Why, the crown prince hopes to find a bride."

Her stomach fluttered. Under her stepmother's gaze, she attempted a docile nod. "How wonderful."

"We shall take a splendid carriage to the ball. An indulgence for a night."

"We?"

Lady Darlington smiled icily. "Everyone with an invitation."

"All the maidens in the land will ride in your carriage?"

The brittle smile cracked. "Impertinence will not be tolerated."

"I'm sorry." Cinderella sweetened her voice. "Surely, a carriage would have room for four. Might I come with you?"

"Don't be ungrateful for the roof over your head."

"I'm not, I—"

"You should be thanking me, not asking for more."

"I *am* grateful," she said, before she could stop herself.

Lady Darlington's lips twisted into a glacial smile. She closed her book and set it by her cooling breakfast. "When your father passed away, I didn't have to welcome you into my home. He willed Umberwood Manor to me and my daughters. My dear, you should be thankful that you don't live in the poorhouse."

Her words clawed a scab from an old wound. Why hadn't Cinderella's father given her Umberwood Manor? Had he truly loved her stepmother more?

"You shan't ruin tonight with your selfishness."

Unspoken words burned in Cinderella's throat, but she forced herself to swallow hard. She put on a docile smile instead of baring her teeth.

"Understood," she said.

"You are excused."

As she gripped the doorknob, however, Lady Darlington clucked her tongue. "You have soot upon your gown. What filth. Make yourself presentable."

Cinderella glanced down at her shapeless frock. Black smudged the ragged hem. She was the one responsible for the household's mending and washing.

"No," she whispered.

Lady Darlington sneered. "Stop mumbling."

She bit the inside of her cheek. "Yes, Stepmother." Anything else would have been dangerous.

Quietly, she left her stepmother's bedchamber. She curled her hands into fists, her nails biting into her palms so hard they left crescents of pain behind.

Tonight, she would go to the ball and win back her voice.

FOUR

SIKANDAR

Prince Benedict swaggered from the ballroom with high arrogance, demanding that his stallion be saddled and his armor polished. But Sikandar stayed behind, even as it neared one o'clock. As maids swept away shattered glass and fragments of chandelier, he hunted among the rubble, careful not to cut himself. He toed aside chunks of masonry with his shoe. When he found what he was looking for, he couldn't help but smile.

"Perfect," he murmured.

Among the stones, a glass claw glittered, as long as a dagger. He noted the jagged end. The dragon had broken a nail while making her dramatic exit from the ballroom.

Sikandar retrieved his pack and tucked the claw inside.

Striding from the castle, he swallowed a yawn. Stars winked in the deep night sky. He longed for a bed with featherdown pillows, but he couldn't afford to rest.

At least he wouldn't have to pay for tonight's lodging.

He did, however, require a place suitable for sorcery. Somewhere he wouldn't be interrupted.

Sikandar followed a well-worn path to the castle stables. Bizarrely, some sort of rodent gnawed upon a pumpkin by a hitching post. Perhaps this was a festive decoration. He shrugged and kept walking. Beyond the stables, a pasture glinted with dew in the moonlight. Horses lifted their heads as he approached, their eyes dark, their breath fogging the chill air. He didn't want to spook them, so he circled around the fence.

Behind the pasture, the grass yielded to pines. The claw glinted silver in the moonlight. Sikandar knelt on the fallen needles, which were thankfully dry. His silk coat and trousers had endured enough abuse tonight.

"Where is she?" he murmured.

He closed his eyes halfway, his sight dimmed by lashes. Magic rushed through his blood. His pulse throbbed in his ears. Gripped between his fingers, the crystal claw began to glow. The claw, while broken, still had enough resonance for him to sense the rest of the dragon. Dangerous magic, which demanded utter vulnerability from the sorcerer. He couldn't shield himself while working this sorcery.

Fear.

It gripped his heart like a cold hand. It wasn't his own emotion.

Forest. Darkness. A place to hide.

That was enough.

Shivering, he let the magic drain from his blood. The claw went dark. He stood, his knees unsteady. The jagged teeth of mountains shone white in the distance.

Deep in the pit of his stomach, fiercer than an intuition, he knew where to go.

He found her in the dark.

Fireflies darted around his head, not flying too far away, as if even they sensed danger ahead. He had summoned them upon entering this forest. Ancient trees sheltered a deep gloom. Moss glittered underfoot in the firefly-light, bejeweled by dew, and steam misted the cold night air.

"Strange," he muttered.

He touched his fingertip to a dewdrop. Warm. It tasted salty.

Dragon's tears.

A ravine cleaved the forest ahead. He followed the glow of fireflies and the gnawing in his gut. Shadowed by ferns, a cave gaped in the ravine's underbelly.

Sobbing drifted from the shadows.

Was there a preferred way to approach a cornered dragon? Particularly one crying as if heartbroken? He squared his shoulders, reached into his pocket, and stepped into the cave.

The dragon lurked within, a shape in the dark.

"May I offer you a handkerchief?" he said.

She lunged to her feet, her talons scraping stone. Her eyes glowed like cinders.

"Who are you?" Sorrow choked her voice.

He froze. "You can speak?"

"I think so."

"You think so?" He frowned. "I heard you crying."

Her tail lashed like an angry cat's. "Tell me your name."

"Sikandar." She didn't need to know he was a Zerian.

"How did you find me?"

He pocketed the handkerchief. "Magic."

She sucked in her breath through her teeth. "Are *you* the one who cursed me?" Smoke curled from her nostrils.

Sikandar didn't want to discover his flammability. What was her name? "Cinderella." He lifted both hands. "I'm not a threat to you. But Prince Charming is looking for you."

"To save me?"

"To kill you."

"God." She sobbed. "I thought he might marry me."

"Prince Charming is less than charming."

"And you?"

"I promised the royal family that the dragon will never darken the skies above this kingdom again."

She glared. "What a poetic way to say something so cruel."

"Note, however, that I didn't promise to slay the dragon."

"Excuse me?"

"I'm a sorcerer. Easier to break the curse instead."

Which was definitely a lie, but he didn't like killing. He was, by all metrics, a terrible murderer.

Her smoldering eyes narrowed. "Would you?"

"I can try."

"Why should I trust you?"

He couldn't resist a smirk. "Why shouldn't you trust a stranger from Azurum?"

"You aren't a very good salesman." Her claws clicked on stone. "What's stopping me from simply biting off your head? Or toasting you alive like a marshmallow?"

"Marshmallow?" He repeated the word with care. "What manner of horrible torture is that?"

She laughed, surprising him. Sikandar retreated a step.

"A marshmallow isn't torture," she said. "It's a sweet that children roast over fire."

"Let's not talk about roasting anything over fire."

She sniffed. "Really?"

"You might have a shot at becoming Prince Charming's bride rather than a trophy on his wall."

"Shall I reconsider roasting you?"

"Please." He licked his lips. "I have my handkerchief, at the very least. You're free to borrow it."

"In case you haven't noticed, I'm far too monstrous for handkerchiefs."

"Nonsense."

Cinderella let out a shuddering sigh. Her brimstone-scented breath ruffled Sikandar's hair. He locked the muscles in his legs, resisting the urge to flee from the cave.

"Here," he said. "To prove I'm a man of my word."

When he offered the handkerchief again, she crept nearer, her scales rustling against the ground. Her claws flashed like ice as she reached for him. He fought the jolt in his muscles, and the instinct to run, instead refusing to retreat from the dragon. She plucked away the handkerchief with surprising delicacy, though her crystal talons still brushed his hand, as smooth as glass. One of them was indeed broken.

"I'm sorry," she said. "I'm not accustomed to being a dragon."

She blew her nose with a wet sound that made him confident he didn't want the handkerchief back.

"Keep it," he said.

"I haven't any pockets," she scoffed. Her eyes simmered.

"Of course."

He folded the handkerchief and tucked it away, reminding himself to burn it later.

She flicked her tail. "Why won't those fireflies stop following you around?"

"Maybe dragons can see in the dark, but sorcerers can't. Not without summoning illumination."

"So you can't see my hideousness." It wasn't a question.

"I never said you were hideous."

"Because you can't see me."

He shook his head. "I already saw you at the ball."

"Why were you at the castle?"

"That's a story for another night." He couldn't meet her burning gaze. "We should leave this cave."

"We?"

"Unless you would prefer to lurk in the shadows forever."

Without waiting for a reply, Sikandar exited the cave. The muscles in his back tensed as he imagined claws tearing into his spine. Just when doubts wriggled from the crevices of his mind, the dragon slithered into the light.

Moonbeams touched her blue scales with silver. Beautiful, in a draconic way. Though he was the tallest of his brothers, he stood no higher than her shoulders when she unbent from the cave. This close, she had the unexpected scent of burnt toast and a hint of jasmine tea. Was that sweetness all that remained of the girl within?

She licked her lips with a forked tongue. "What now, sorcerer?"

"Sikandar," he reminded her.

She hesitated. "Sikandar." She repeated the syllables of his name with care. "Am I doomed to be a dragon forever? Please tell me the truth."

"Not all curses can be broken. But that won't stop me from trying. You have my word."

"The word of a stranger from Azurum," she muttered.

He stared sideways at her. "Do you have anyone else?"

"No."

"Before we can break the curse, we need to understand it. Are there any schools of magic nearby?"

"Agatha's Academy of Magic." When he cocked his head, she elaborated. "A boarding school for young ladies seeking refinement in enchantment. My stepsisters begged my stepmother for admission, but they simply couldn't afford it, and neither of them was talented enough for a scholarship."

"Where is this Academy of Magic?"

"Grimleigh. I've never been, though. I've only ever seen an advertisement in a ladies' magazine."

"Our next destination."

"Aren't we lost in the wilderness?"

"Ah, but I have a map in my pack." He unfolded it with a flourish. "There. Grimleigh."

Her eyes brightened. "We aren't far, are we?"

"We should sleep first. Away from civilization."

"In the cave?" she protested.

"You're a dragon. That's hardly your number one priority."

Her wings wilted with defeat. "I doubt any bed and breakfasts cater to dragons."

He wasn't sure what a *bed and breakfast* was, but he didn't ask. He should have bought a Viridian phrasebook, though of course banishment had been a distraction.

"We need to stay hidden," he said.

"I'm done lurking in the cave like a monster. I would rather sleep in a meadow."

He frowned. "In the trees. Less obvious."

"Fine," she sighed.

"Will you trust me?"

Her breath caught in her throat. "Yes, Sikandar."

He held her gaze for a moment too long, and heat flooded his face. He had promised to help a dragon. No, to help a girl under a curse.

She had no idea who he was, or what he had done.

One year ago, he made a wish.

He remembered the day like last night's dream. How air shimmered in the heat rising from sand.

Sikandar bit into an apricot, the juice sweet in his dry mouth. The University of Naranjal shaded him, an onion-domed tower blocking the sun. In the courtyard, an oasis glimmered beneath palms. The sorcerers controlled the water here.

Camels grumbled as a caravan lingered near the gates. Traveling merchants, here to haggle over enchantments and sell alchemical supplies from the corners of the earth.

Sikandar finished his apricot and flung the pit into the palms. He dusted the sand from his kaftan, the blue of a third-year student, before striding across the courtyard. Fifth-year students, robed in red kaftans, lounged by the oasis. The older students narrowed their eyes at Sikandar as he filled a flask with water. One of them tossed a globe of scintillating white magic between her hands while gossiping with her friend.

Her mouth shaped the name *Zerian* before she slid a glance at him.

Gods, they always acted like he might poison the oasis or curse them in their sleep. It wasn't his fault his family insisted he study the darkest magic taught at the university. He needed to be the kind of sorcerer who could kill.

He tucked the flask into his kaftan and ducked through a doorway. He hurried down sandstone stairs. Underground, the sun surrendered its power to the shadows. The air smelled of damp rock. No one knew how far the tunnels wandered beneath the University of Naranjal. They resisted the cartographer's pen, shifting like the sands above.

Sikandar followed the way by heart, the only safe passage. When a door of juniper wood blocked him, he laid his hand flat against the silvery wood. When he closed his eyes, an enchantment pulsed like a heartbeat. It caressed his fingers. Curious.

"Open," he murmured.

His bones ached as his own magic answered, heating his skin like a rush of blood. The door groaned open.

Inside, the room was dark. He snapped his fingers, summoning fireflies for illumination. They zipped into the corners, revealing a long-neglected storeroom of cobwebbed shelves.

There, in the corner, he found what he wanted.

A brass lamp, tarnished and forgotten. Sikandar polished it on his sleeve and read the words engraved there.

Slake my thirst.

Fingers a little unsteady, he pried the lid from the lamp. It looked empty. He uncorked the flask and poured a trickle of oasis water inside. When it hit the brass, it sizzled into instant steam. Sikandar jerked back, dropped the lamp, and stared at his fingers.

Unburnt.

A curl of violet smoke crawled from the lamp. From the smoke, the curves of a woman took shape, her skin the color of amethyst, her eyes obsidian. Gold bracelets encircled her wrists. Gold silk twisted around her body like living flame.

She was beautiful the way a viper was, a graceful terror.

"Jinni," he whispered, a dry croak.

She smiled, a hint of fangs beyond her lips, and spoke in a honeyed purr. "What do you desire?"

Sikandar had known from the day he found the lamp. From the instant he knew it imprisoned a jinni.

He said nothing. The words in his mouth dried to dust.

"Fame?" said the jinni. "Fortune?"

Sikandar shook his head, finding his voice. "No."

"Love?" The jinni sauntered nearer, tracing her fingernail between her breasts. "Whatever you wish."

"I want—" He swallowed. "I want you to save someone."

"Who?"

"My grandmother."

The jinni tilted her head, her black-silk hair slipping over her shoulder. "Death cannot be cheated."

Did the jinni know how his grandmother had withered away, the light in her eyes gone dark?

"She's sick," he said. "Dying."

"You have three wishes. Choose wisely."

Wisely? He curled his hands into fists. As if it would be foolish to save someone he loved. But the folktales said that jinn had no hearts, since they were creatures born of wind, fire, and sand. He knew what it meant to be loved.

He banished any emotion from his voice. "I wish for my grandmother's sickness to be healed, and for her health to be returned."

"Yes, master." The jinni's smile didn't touch her obsidian eyes. "Your wish is my command."

His first wish.

His greatest mistake.

FIVE

CINDERELLA

When morning warmed the forest, dew drifting into mist, Cinderella woke in a grove of aspens with lemon-yellow leaves. She remembered nothing, for one glorious moment, until sunlight flashed on the scales armoring her skin and the claws curving from her fingertips. One of the claws had broken in her haste to escape the castle last night.

Dragon. The word transmuted her heart to lead.

Despite the beautiful day, this was all a nightmare from which she could never wake.

The sorcerer, Sikandar, slept in the grass. His wool shawl didn't quite hide his silk jacket, midnight blue glimmering with gold embroidery. Under any other circumstances, she would have been no less than scandalized by waking up next to a stranger in the middle of the forest. Her reputation would have been ruined.

Especially since the stranger was a handsome sorcerer.

She uncoiled from the ground. She still didn't feel like herself, her skin distant, her bones unfamiliar. Sore, she stretched her wings wide.

Could she fly? Could she breathe fire? She hadn't a clue.

Thirst dried her tongue. She hadn't drunk anything since the punch at the ball. Not even a mouthful of water after plunging into the lake. How inconvenient.

When she sniffed the air, it smelled of mushrooms and dirt, overlaid with the woodsy spice of autumn leaves. She didn't smell water. Did water have a smell?

Goodness, she was already terrible at being a dragon.

She wanted to flounce down, cry, and eat her weight in chocolates. Though at her current size, that wouldn't be an insignificant weight. Besides, there weren't any chocolatiers in Grimleigh. The mountains gleamed white with snow, bearing an unfortunate resemblance to ice cream.

She cleared her throat. "Sikandar?"

He blinked sleepily before scrambling to his feet. "How long have you been watching me?" He spoke Viridian with a hint of a lilting Azuri accent.

"Only for a moment," she said, perfectly innocent.

Wincing, he rubbed his neck. "You were right, I'm starting to regret sleeping in the dirt."

To her utmost horror, her stomach growled at a volume resembling seismic activity. Dinner at the castle seemed like no more than a distant memory. She had only nibbled hors d'oeuvres at the ball, constrained by her corset.

Sikandar was staring at her. "Did you growl at me?"

"No." She averted her gaze. "I'm simply a bit peckish."

"Peckish?" he repeated.

"Hungry."

"What do dragons eat?"

She didn't want to know. In fairy tales, dragons consumed princesses and perhaps small children. She shuddered, her tail flicking against nearby ferns.

"Maybe a nice rabbit?" Sikandar said. "Or a pheasant?"

She recoiled. "Heavens, no! I would never hurt such innocent woodland creatures. Poor things!"

He was staring at her again. "You don't eat meat?"

"I do, but I've never killed anything before."

"I believe you." Tilting his head, he rubbed his thumb over his lower lip. "You aren't what I expected for a dragon."

"Well, I'm *not* a dragon, that's why."

"I would love to cook breakfast and brew a nice pot of chai, but we don't have time to linger."

"Chai?"

He raised his eyebrows. "Milk tea? With spices?"

"I've never had it."

"You should." He slung on his pack. "Later."

After glancing at Grimleigh on the map again, they climbed uphill between the white-trunked aspens. Her claws gouged the rich earth. Sikandar kept stumbling on roots hidden in the fallen leaves. His shoes seemed more appropriate for dancing than hiking in the wilderness. She followed at a distance, not wanting to touch him by accident. Because he was a sorcerer, or she was a dragon? She wasn't sure.

Cinderella sighed. "Heavens, I'm famished. What I wouldn't give for mashed potatoes with gravy, salmon swimming in butter and lemon juice, roast goose stuffed with apples, lavender cake with clotted cream..."

"I don't know half of those things." Sikandar paused to knock a pebble from his shoe. "But I'm certain that I haven't brought any of them with me in my pack."

"Couldn't you summon food with a spell?"

He laughed. "Magic doesn't work like that. Better to hunt."

She shuddered. "No!"

"How else do dragons survive?" He squinted. "I doubt they have butlers or footmen serving them breakfast."

"I—I don't know the first thing about hunting. I'm a lady."

"Not anymore."

She gave him a look. A rather effective look, since he swallowed hard. "Don't be rude."

"I'm merely being practical."

She let out a doleful sigh. "If only we could pop into Umberwood for breakfast along the way."

"Umberwood?"

"Umberwood Manor. Where I live with my stepmother and two stepsisters." She clamped her wings along her spine. "It was meant to be my inheritance, but..."

"But?"

"But my father changed his will before he died."

Sikandar glanced sideways at her. "Why?"

"My wicked stepmother soured his mind and poisoned his thoughts against me." She had held this anger for so long it gleamed, the grit turned to pearl.

"Would your wicked stepmother want you cursed?"

She growled. "She hates me. So do both of my stepsisters."

"Are they great and powerful sorceresses?"

"No." She rolled her eyes. "Delicata and Eulalia don't have an ounce of talent between them. There's a reason they spend so much of their time trying to look pretty with the costliest glamours and gowns."

"Delicata." He tilted his head. "I met a Delicata at the ball."

"Darlington?"

"Yes. She was on a mission to marry rich."

Cinderella grimaced. "They tried to stop me from going. They ripped my mother's dress."

"But you went anyway."

"Thanks to my Fairy Godmother."

"Who?"

"My Fairy Godmother waved her wand and cast an enchantment. A beautiful dress and a beautiful carriage all in gold..." Choking up, she dabbed at her eyes with talons. "She warned me that the spell would break at midnight, though she said nothing about turning into a dragon."

He raised his eyebrows. "Had you met her before?"

"I hadn't."

"Might this Fairy Godmother be the one who cursed you?"

Her stomach plummeted. Last night, she hadn't thought of such a thing, too lonely and desperate. But she had trusted a mysterious woman lurking in her garden, purely on the basis of a fancy costume and a few parlor tricks.

A tear rolled down her face, chased by another, sizzling on the grass. "I'm such a fool."

"Cinderella," he murmured. "This isn't your fault."

Why was it so hard to match his gaze? He had impossibly long eyelashes. His eyes were the color of coffee without any cream. She had no business staring at sorcerers, no matter how attractive they might be.

"I'm sorry," she said. "For blubbering so much."

"I would offer you my handkerchief again, though I'm afraid it's too far gone at this point."

She laughed through her tears. "No, thank you."

"Understandable."

"I didn't expect you to be such a gentleman."

"I will take that as a compliment."

She sniffed and wiped her cheeks on the scales of her wrist. "My mother never told me about a Fairy Godmother. But that wasn't the only secret she kept from me."

His eyebrows angled into a frown. "Tell me more."

"My mother did a great service for the Queen of Viridia. In return, she was gifted Umberwood Manor."

"What kind of service?"

"She never told me, and Prince Benedict didn't know."

Sikandar raked his fingers through his hair. "Your stepmother hates you, your Fairy Godmother might have cursed you, and your mother hid secrets from you."

"In a nutshell."

"And Prince Charming wants to kill you."

Her stomach clenched, but she faked a cheerful voice. "Oh, is that all?"

"Are you certain of the way?" Sikandar asked.

They struggled through a thicket of blackberry brambles. Thorns snagged his clothes and clawed his skin. Blood seeped from razor-thin welts. Cinderella held her wings high to avoid suffering a similar fate.

"I'm not," she said. "I have no sense of direction. Besides, aren't you the one with the map?"

"Maps aren't everything."

"A compass would be nice."

"Agreed," he muttered. "If only I brought one."

She exhaled in a huff. "Goodness, I hate blackberries."

"But you have armor."

She glanced down at the scales on her legs, glimmering indigo in the shadows. "Don't remind me."

He whacked a bramble with a stick. "Can't you fly?"

"I've only been a dragon for a day."

They battled through the blackberries, fighting a thousand thorns. He stumbled and nearly fell against her, but he jerked his hand back.

"My apologies," he said.

She averted her gaze. "No, I'm sorry. I can barely walk without tripping over these claws."

"I'm sure you're graceful on a good day."

She laughed. "Are you always this polite?"

"Always." He said it with a straight face. "Especially when talking to dragons."

"A prudent policy."

He untangled a blackberry vine from his sleeve. "Are you certain you can't fly us to Grimleigh?"

"Perhaps we should find a road."

He kicked away another bramble. "That would be more dangerous than thorns. We wouldn't be able to hide a dragon in broad daylight."

"We can't spend all day lost in the wilderness. What if the curse can only be broken within the first three days?" Her throat clenched at this horrid possibility. She talked faster, stuttering a little. "What if—what if we're already too late?"

Sikandar leaned against his walking stick. "Doubtful. Curses take time to root."

She shuddered, imagining dark tendrils crawling through her body. "I don't want to wait."

He slung his pack off his shoulders and unrolled the map. It didn't, of course, mark the spot of the blackberries, but a road cut through the forest nearby.

"This way," he said.

They backtracked through the brambles and turned eastward across the hills. When trees yielded to a road, Cinderella was tempted to kiss the stones.

A gentleman on horseback reined in his horse.

"Good morning," Cinderella said, exceedingly polite.

The gentleman's eyes went as wide as saucers. He tipped his hat before kicking his mare into a gallop. Farther down the road, a goat herder swore at them and chased his flock into a ditch until the dragon passed.

Honestly, the goats didn't even smell tasty. Far too goaty.

Sikandar rubbed his chin. "They didn't run away screaming from a dragon."

"Well, I wasn't rude."

He cleared his throat as if trying not to laugh. "Are dragons common in Viridia?"

"Hardly. Hundreds of years ago, most of the Viridian dragons were slain by knights."

"Why?"

"Dragons are dangerous, of course."

He hummed, a neutral noise. "Are they intelligent?"

"Pardon me, are you implying I'm stupid?"

"Not at all. I'm wondering if wild dragons can also have meaningful conversations."

The thought made her pause. "I haven't the slightest idea."

"We have only legends of dragons in Azurum."

Her mind wandered as they walked. She imagined a land of forbidding mountains and deserts where jinn whirled within sandstorms. But they had tigers over there too, which brought to mind tangled forests thick with shadows and leaves.

"What is Azurum like?" she said.

Sikandar shrugged. "Warmer."

"Why did you leave?"

His shoulders stiffened. "Necessity."

He wouldn't look her in the eye. Was he hiding dark secrets? Maybe that was a required prerequisite for a mysterious sorcerer from a strange land.

After an uncomfortable pause, Sikandar said, "Breakfast?"

"Please."

They stopped at the White Hart Inn, a half-timbered building that must have slumped at this crossroads since medieval times. Cinderella lurked under the trees, hidden from the road, while Sikandar went to the inn to buy food. A barmaid stopped sweeping the threshold to smile at him. She cocked her head and twirled her hair around one finger.

Could she blame her? Sikandar was indisputably handsome.

Not that she would ever admit that to him. Now certainly didn't seem like the appropriate time to swoon over a dark-eyed sorcerer.

Sikandar left the White Hart Inn carrying a wax-paper bag. She sniffed the air and caught a hint of sausage and yeast.

"I asked them for their special of the day."

"What was it?"

"Something called pigs in blankets?"

Her mouth started watering. "Splendid."

They ate in a woodland glade. She devoured breakfast as fast as manners would allow. The sausages baked in dough rivaled any royal feast. She licked her claws clean, inspecting her own forked tongue with a morbid fascination.

"What a lovely little picnic," she said brightly, though it was a brittle kind of brightness.

If this was a picnic, maybe she wasn't a monster. Dragons certainly didn't picnic, did they? At least she could pretend to be a lady.

"Pigs in blankets aren't what I expected," he said.

"Do you like them?"

He shrugged and took another bite. "Well enough."

She sniffed. "That barmaid certainly liked you."

Frowning, he lifted his head. "Who?"

"The girl outside the inn. The one who smiled at you." He was still staring at her blankly. "Don't tell me you didn't notice her!"

"What was there to notice?"

She laughed. "She was flirting with you?"

He rubbed the back of his neck. "I'm often oblivious of flirtation."

Was he always this endearing when embarrassed? She resisted the urge to tease him more, though she couldn't stop smiling.

"How old are you?" she said.

"Eighteen." He frowned deeper this time. "Why? How old are you?"

"Seventeen." She glanced at the sky and sighed. "Though to be honest, I have no practical experience with flirtation myself."

He wasn't listening, his stare fixed on the road.

"Sikandar?"

"Quiet!" he whispered.

Hooves clattered on stones. A white stallion galloped down the road, frothing at the bit, ridden hard by a man in shining armor. Prince Benedict Charming.

The last bite of Cinderella's breakfast tumbled to the ground. "Benedict!"

The prince reined in his stallion. The horse whinnied and wheeled, but Benedict spurred him toward the trees. His hand gripped the hilt of his sword.

"Dragon!" he shouted. "Don't hide from me."

Dread plunged her heart into the depths.

"This way," Sikandar hissed.

He dodged into the forest. She rushed after him. They both crouched behind a fallen log cloaked in moss. She lay low and flattened her wings along her back. Her heart thundered so hard, she was sure it would betray her.

Benedict rode into the woodland glade. He leaned over the saddle as he scanned the ground.

The wax-paper bag.

It lay crumpled among the leaves, alongside the bite of lost sausage. The prince slid from the stallion's back and crouched in the dirt. His fingers traced the outline of an unmistakable footprint: the taloned foot of a dragon.

"God, no," she whispered.

Benedict's head jerked up. Had her whisper been more of a whimper? The prince unsheathed his blade with a flash of steel.

Sikandar spat what had to be a swear. "Hold my hand."

"What?"

"Hold my hand!"

She stopped asking questions.

Her talons linked with his fingers. With his free hand, he sketched in the air, an invisible symbol—they lurched sideways, backwards, out of nowhere.

Between one blink and the next, they tumbled into a forest of shadowy pines.

Where the hell were they? Mist clung to the air here.

"Teleportation?" she said, her voice shaking like her legs.

Sikandar released her hand and staggered forward a few paces. His face was the color of ash. "Are you all right?" he asked.

"Are you?"

"Wait."

He held up a finger, then collapsed in the dirt.

SIX

SIKANDAR

Sikandar tasted blood in his mouth. The price of his mistake.

When he swallowed, he discovered he had bitten his tongue. Groaning, he opened his eyes.

A dragon loomed over him.

He gasped as if a bucket of ice water had been poured on his face. He scrambled back on his elbows and raised his hands for sorcery.

"Sikandar!" said the dragon.

Memories drifted into his mind. Cinderella. Prince Charming. Teleportation.

"How long have I been out?" he said.

"A few minutes. You're bleeding!"

She was right. "I know."

Crawling onto his knees, he spat blood. He always hated this part, how his hands wouldn't stop shaking, how a cold sweat broke out on his skin. He fumbled inside his pack, his fingers clumsy. He found two bread loaves shaped like bugs, only slightly squashed, with raisins for eyes. Absurd, but he needed to eat before he was unconscious again.

If he didn't, he might not wake up.

"Are you all right?" she said.

He tore into the bread with his teeth. "I will be."

"Ladybug bread." She let out a nervous laugh. "You bought it at the inn with breakfast? We bake it in autumn, traditionally. I'm babbling, aren't I?" Her gaze met his. "What happened to you, Sikandar?"

He swallowed the bite. "Magic isn't free. I misjudged how much teleportation would cost me." She was heavier than she looked, though he didn't tell her that.

Or the fact that he had been expelled from the University of Naranjal before graduation.

"How far away are we?" she said. "From Prince Benedict?"

"Unclear."

Some of the fog had cleared from his head. He no longer teetered on the brink of darkness.

"We should go," he said.

Standing so quickly was a mistake. He staggered, catching himself on Cinderella's shoulder. Her scales were unexpected: hotter than skin, polished like mother of pearl. She retreated from his touch and wouldn't meet his eyes.

"My apologies." He coughed. "I'm a little unsteady."

That was a vast understatement. His knees wavered beneath him.

"Let me help you," she said.

"How?"

"Lean on me." She scoffed. "I'm not letting you ride me."

Heat crept into his ears, even though she doubted she meant anything improper. She seemed far too innocent for that.

"Thank you." He let her take some of his weight. "We should check the map. Make sure we're still on the way to Grimleigh."

"That sounds prudent."

He inspected the map longer than necessary, glad for a little distance from the dragon. He didn't know why touching her knocked him off-balance. Was it because he had never met a dragon before? But he was a sorcerer, and sorcerers weren't supposed to blush over monsters or magic. Not that Cinderella was a monster.

Professional. He could be professional.

"This way," he said, pointing ahead.

Together, they wandered through a forest thick with mist-shrouded pines. Mushrooms dotted the ground with pops of red.

Her scales rippled under his hand, interlocking like intricate jewelry. Mesmerizing to the touch.

"Good lord," she said, "I'm still hungry."

He tossed her the second ladybug bread. She devoured it in one bite and looked at him, all but begging with her eyes. Rather like a puppy that wanted a treat. He tilted his head. Was she managing to look *cute* as a dragon? Impressive.

"I bought only the pigs and the ladybugs," he said. "Sorry."

Rain hushed from the pewter sky. Drops rolled down her scales before drifting into steam.

"Thank you," she said. "For saving me."

He nodded. "Of course."

"What do you think Prince Benedict would have done?"

"Tried to slay a dragon."

She sucked in her breath. "Truly?"

"Why in heaven's name are you surprised?"

"Because Prince Benedict knows me." She hesitated. "Well enough to invite me to the ball."

"He's an arrogant prince. I hardly know him, and I hate him already."

"Why?" She blinked a few times. "Jealous?"

He wrinkled his nose. "Why should I be?"

"He's fabulously wealthy and handsome."

"Fabulously stupid and cruel."

Her exhalation clouded the air. "The most eligible bachelor in Viridia. The crown prince. It would be a dream come true to marry him." She laughed, but it was a hollow laugh, her eyes dull. "Happily ever after."

"Was that your dream?"

A long silence passed. She seemed fascinated by her broken claw.

"I went to Knightsend to save my inheritance. To save myself from a lifetime of misery."

"By marrying a prince?"

Her forked tongue flickered. "You wouldn't understand."

"In my experience, marrying royalty never ends well."

"Oh?" She blinked several times. "Are you married already?"

"No." Bitterness darkened his voice. "My sister married a king."

"You aren't joking, are you?"

"I wish I were."

She touched her neck. "Heavens, are you also a prince?"

"I never was and never will be. Just… don't marry Prince Charming."

The spikes along her spine bristled. "I will do what I must."

A beautiful marriage between beautiful people. What could go wrong? But he didn't want to confess to the sins of the Zerian family.

"You need to learn how to fly," he said. "And breathe fire."

She shook her head. "Not if we break the curse first."

After the sun puddled on the horizon, melting into gold, it dripped away into darkness. Sikandar summoned a glittering of fireflies with a snap of his fingers. They circled him brightly until, one by one, they began to flicker out.

His magic was fading. He stumbled in the deepening gloom.

"Careful," Cinderella said.

"Tired, that's all."

How much keener were her eyes than his? Strange that a stranger cared about him, when he was used to nobody caring at all.

She hid a yawn behind her claws. "We should stop."

He nodded, his head heavy, and the last magical firefly winked out. "Here looks like a decent place to camp." He dropped against a tree and kicked off his shoes.

She sighed. "What a pity. We haven't any proper dinner."

"Or lunch."

"Don't remind me." She clucked her tongue. "And how do you have any energy for sarcasm?"

"I don't." He flashed her a smile. "This is my natural charm."

She frowned at him, as if he shouldn't be charming. He wasn't sure he wanted to know what she believed about sorcerers from Azurum.

Shivering, he hugged himself. "Gods, Viridia is cold."

"Is it?"

"You're a dragon."

"Admittedly." She sniffed. "And a Viridian, born and bred."

"Wonder if I have enough magic left to start a fire."

"Wait."

"I won't pass out, I promise."

"But I can breathe fire. Can't I?"

He held up one hand. "Let's not burn down the forest, shall we?"

"I'm not that bad of a dragon." Her tail curled into a knot. "Besides, I tended the fires every day at Umberwood Manor. They called me Cinderella, after all."

He raised his eyebrows. "Cinderella isn't your true name?"

"My name was once Ginevra Darlington." She let out a sad laugh. "I don't feel like her anymore. Sometimes, it's hard to believe she ever existed at all."

"I understand," he said, without thinking. "Sometimes, my past feels like a dream."

"A dream?"

He winced, since he had said too much.

He didn't want to tell her why he had been banished. Couldn't tell her, without risking her trust in him and the outcome of this entire quest. The knot in his chest tightened until it hurt, though he had no way to unravel it.

Avoiding her gaze, he dusted off his hands. "We can collect a few of those stones over there, to keep the fire in one place."

Her talons proved useful for gouging the stones from the dirt. He helped by gathering up some dry branches of pine. Before long, they had constructed a fire pit.

Sikandar stepped well out of her way. "After you."

"Don't look," she said.

"Why not?"

She scuffed her claw in the dirt. "I can't breathe fire with you staring at me."

"Forgive me, but I would rather not turn my back on a dragon breathing fire."

When he smirked, she rolled her eyes. "I won't roast you like a marshmallow."

"Please, don't."

Cinderella breathed in deep. She laughed, the air escaping her lungs with a curl of smoke. "It's the strangest sensation. Fire in my belly."

"I can only imagine."

She inhaled, then exhaled. Flames rushed from her jaws and torched the kindling.

Sikandar dipped his head. "Efficient."

"You're welcome."

Pine smoke perfumed the air as the fire crackled and popped. He held out his hands to warm them. She curled nearby and rested her chin on her tail. Flames danced, reflected in her golden eyes. Firelight scattered when it hit her talons, broken into shards of rainbow.

Lovely. He blinked the thought away.

"How far are we from Grimleigh?" she said.

He didn't bother checking the map. "We should arrive late next morning. If we don't stop for breakfast."

"If we don't stop for breakfast, I will perish from famine." She clutched her chest and pretended to swoon.

"I'm sure we can manage."

"Imagine." Her gaze turned dreamy. "Crispy smoked bacon. Omelets with chives fresh from the garden. Scones with blackcurrant jam and great dollops of cream."

He leaned back against a tree. "You speak so fondly of food."

"I hope to turn Umberwood Manor into a bed and breakfast."

"What's a bed and breakfast?"

Her eyes sparkled. "Allow me to rhapsodize about their many charms. They are far more delightful than an inn or hotel. You would stay with a family, inside their home, and eat a hearty breakfast cooked by them."

He rested his head on the bark. "I'm starting to see the appeal."

"Umberwood has a marvelous garden and an old apple orchard. I could bake scones and cakes and pies for my guests, then serve desserts at breakfast and teatime."

"Breakfast *and* teatime? How extravagant."

She glowered at him until she saw his teasing smile. "I'm sure you would love my baking."

"Perhaps, one day."

"I'm so tired." Her yawn bared every one of her fangs. "Forgive me, I must get my beauty sleep." She laughed hollowly. "Not that I have any beauty remaining."

She was wrong, but he said only, "Good night, Cinderella."

"Good night."

He hadn't believed the jinni.

Death cannot be cheated.

Sikandar lingered on the brink of the grandest cemetery in the city of Zarkona, watching fat raindrops knock purple blossoms from the jacaranda tree above him.

His grandmother loved flowers. When he was a child, he would steal them from the garden and put them in a vase, somewhere she would find them.

"Sikandar!" His mother's shrill voice pierced the quiet. "Don't be late!"

The burial had begun.

Every step felt like wading through quicksand. He couldn't look at his sister's grim face or his brothers' poorly disguised tears. He ignored the stink of liquor on his father's breath. Grandmother was—had been—his father's mother.

On the edge of the grave, Sikandar stopped. His hands hung empty at his sides.

They lowered his grandmother's coffin into the ground.

Goodbye. He didn't say it out loud.

His wish had cured her sickness, but not a month later, she had died peacefully in her sleep.

Perhaps she had already felt death's shadow. The night before she died, she gave him her teapot of engraved copper, with which she had brewed chai for years. She never would have done that if she believed she could still brew him tea herself.

Dirt began to fall upon the coffin.

Sikandar couldn't watch his grandmother disappear. Out of everyone he knew, she was the only one who understood him, who loved him without question.

Damn, he couldn't stop crying.

Father's hand clamped on his shoulder. "Quit weeping," he muttered. "We have guests."

Sikandar knew he was shaming his family, so he turned his face away and unobtrusively rubbed his face on his sleeve.

The funeral guests followed them home, where Mother served them black-as-night coffee and sesame cookies infused with rosewater. Sikandar choked down one cookie, too dry and sickly-sweet, before pretending to drink coffee. He hated how the guests talked about his grandmother, sharing stories that made them look good, especially the ones who pretended they knew her better. She would have hated this whole affair.

Later, after the last guest had gone, he stood in the courtyard under a waning moon. He stared at his grandmother's window. She would never wave at him again.

"Sikandar!" Mother called across the courtyard.

He tore his gaze away from the window. "Yes?"

"Come to bed."

"I... I can't."

Mother's footsteps rapped across the tiles of the courtyard. "Grandmother was old."

He said nothing, not sure how to defend his grief.

"And sick," Mother added.

Pain choked his throat until he wasn't sure he could breathe, much less speak. "I thought I could save Grandmother."

"Save?" Mother's dark eyes shone in the moonlight.

"The jinni's wish," he whispered.

"What jinni? What wish?"

His stomach curdled. Doubt and the desire to please his mother warred inside him, even though he had disappointed her year after year. Sometimes he wondered why he even tried to tell her the truth, when she never wanted to hear it. But he wasn't much of a liar, and he couldn't say nothing, not with her stare drilling into him.

He forced himself to look her in the eye when he spoke. "I found a lamp at the University of Naranjal, deep underground in the tunnels. A jinni's lamp. She told me that death cannot be cheated, so instead I..."

"Yes?"

"I wished for Grandmother's sickness to be healed."

Mother exhaled in a hiss. "You wasted a jinni's wish on an old woman with so little time left?"

Shame bloomed inside him like a bloodstain. "I thought—"

"I don't care what you thought! Gods, how many other wishes did you waste?"

"None." None of them were a waste. "I have two wishes left."

"You still have the lamp?"

"Yes, but—"

"Sikandar." Mother shushed him as if he were still a child. "A jinni possesses unfathomable power. Think of the possibilities. Think of your *family*."

Had Grandmother not been part of the family?

Mother clutched his hand between hers. It would have been a sweet gesture, but her nails dug into his skin. She never knew how to be gentle.

"Your sister!" she murmured. "Your poor widow sister needs a husband to take care of her. Only the best of men. Why not the King of Azurum?"

Sikandar couldn't sleep. He stared at the sky choked with bruise-dark clouds. Rain slid down his cheeks, reminiscent of tears.

Even lying on a blanket of leaves, the hush of rain thickening the night with the scent of wet greenery, he couldn't escape his memories of Azurum. Grief smothered him like a shroud. He rolled onto his side and tucked his knees against his chest.

When he closed his eyes, he knew the jinni would come to him. More sinuous than smoke, she twisted through his mind. He rested not on leaves, but slippery emerald silk. The jinni lounged beside him, a smile curving her lips. Her golden bracelets gleamed against her amethyst skin.

"Sikandar," the jinni murmured.

The muscles in his arms bunched. "Get out of my head."

"One more wish." She traced her fingernail over his lips. He jerked back from her touch. "One more wish, and I will no longer be bound to you."

"Keep your wish. I want nothing from you."

"You want your family to love you again."

"No," he lied.

He hated how she could scoop thoughts from his head like melon with a spoon. What an idiot he had been to ever summon her.

The jinni's skin shimmered. "Tell me what you desire."

"I will never wish again."

Her smile sharpened to the edge of a scimitar. "You want nothing from me? Free me."

"The lamp is lost in the desert. I made sure of that."

"I can help you find it."

Temptation hooked its claws into his heart, but goosebumps prickled on his skin. Once upon a time, he had believed in jinn, believed their wishes were miracles given to mortals by the gods. But he knew now this was a foolish folktale. The jinn's loyalties shifted like desert sand in the wind: unmappable and untrustworthy.

"Come home, Sikandar," she murmured.

Home.

He missed the sun of Azurum, even when its heat soaked into his black hair. He missed the jasmine outside his bedroom window, infusing the night with perfume. He missed his favorite spices, cloves and tamarind. He missed his teachers.

His friends.

Even his family.

But he had been banished from Azurum, and returning would mean death.

"I can't," he said. "Not yet."

"You lack perseverance." The jinni sneered. "Mine has been forged from years of patience."

How long had she been trapped in the lamp? Decades? Centuries? Some said the University of Naranjal taught sorcerers over a millennium ago. He suspected the magic lamp was even older, a forgotten relic of an earlier era.

"Then you can wait." He rolled over. "Now let me sleep."

SEVEN

CINDERELLA

Wolves of hunger gnawed in Cinderella's belly and woke her from slumber.

How late was it? Past midnight? Embers glowed in the fire pit. Nearby, Sikandar huddled under his shawl. Sleeping.

She indulged herself by studying the angles of his face. Her gaze lingered on the curve of his lips. A sigh escaped her.

If she were still pretty, would he want to kiss her? The thought fluttered through her head like a butterfly, as if she were still a girl and allowed to have such girlish fantasies. But this wasn't the time to pine over sorcerers.

This was the time to hunt.

She couldn't stop imagining velvet fur between her fangs, the crunch of tiny bones, and the iron taste of blood filling her mouth.

What was wrong with her? She would never murder an innocent creature.

Never, when she was still human. When she ate nothing but pitiful gruel and scraps saved in the kitchen. She had roasted sausages and fried bacon for her stepfamily to pick at on their plates, while they worried over the sizes of their waists.

Now, she wanted the devour everything in the woodland.

Dragon instinct forced her to surrender.

She slunk away from the dying fire and found a river pebbled with stones. Fat salmon swam upstream to spawn by the light of the moon. She leaned over the dark water before she darted and snapped a slippery fish between her jaws. Twisting, the salmon struggled to escape. She tossed back her head and swallowed it whole.

Bushes rustled across the river.

A doe.

The dark-eyed deer stared at her. Even with the salmon in her stomach, hunger gnawed at Cinderella. She flattened her wings against her spine and stalked into the river. Cold water rushed past her crystal talons. She gripped slick stones underfoot. Another salmon's scales brushed hers as it wriggled past, but she had bigger prey in her sights.

The doe's ears twitched.

Cinderella crouched, every muscle taut.

The deer twisted into a jump and bounded through the bushes. She surged from the river in pursuit. Water hissed behind her as she landed. She crashed through the forest, less nimble than the deer. It zigzagged through the trees, nearly losing her, until it stumbled over a log.

She pounced.

The doe leapt high. She met it halfway.

Her jaws clamped on the deer's neck. It kicked, flailing, but she bit down and pinned it to the dirt until it stilled. Wings flaring, she crouched over her prey. She tore through velvet fur and unwrapped flesh like red rubies, half-closing her eyes with delight, the taste of it luxurious.

She froze.

What had she become?

The doe lay beneath her, an innocent woodland creature. She was a murderous beast. Worst of all, the venison steaming the air looked delicious.

"Cinderella!"

Her Fairy Godmother had returned. Like a ghost, she drifted through the forest, dressed in the shimmering gown of gossamer and amber. Her dragonfly wings quivered as she touched her hand to her mouth.

"Good god," said the Fairy Godmother. "Look at you."

Cinderella shrank back from the deer. "What happened to me?"

The Fairy Godmother's face tightened, exquisite and pale. "My dear, I'm so sorry. On the night of the ball—well, I'm not sure how to phrase this delicately."

"Tell me. Please."

"The enchantment awoke a slumbering curse. Dark, wicked magic deep in your bones."

"I—I'm afraid I don't understand."

"You were born this way."

All the air rushed from Cinderella. Trembling, she locked her legs so as not to fall. "But you can break the curse, can't you?"

She twisted her mouth. "You were meant to be a dragon."

"No," whispered Cinderella. "No!"

"Dearest, I'm so sorry." Pity dripped from her words.

"I refuse to believe it! You must be wrong."

"There's nothing I can do you save you." The Fairy Godmother unraveled at the edges. "You must save yourself. Flee this kingdom and find a home in the wilderness."

"But—but Sikandar promised to break the curse."

"Who?" The Fairy Godmother was already halfway gone.

"A sorcerer from Azurum."

"Be careful who you trust."

Her shape tore apart and vanished into tatters of darkness.

Numb, Cinderella returned to the river. She ducked her face underwater, washing away the deer's blood, before she slunk back to the campfire.

Sikandar was still sleeping. She curled nearby, feeling strangely protective of him.

Should she wake him? Tell him her Fairy Godmother had returned?

No.

If she did, she would have to tell him she had been hunting at night. Worse, she would have to repeat what her Fairy Godmother had confessed. Maybe he would agree that she had been born with an unbreakable curse.

Be careful who you trust.

It took her a long time to close her eyes, the taste of blood and regret lingering in her mouth.

Why had the Fairy Godmother enchanted her before the ball?

She remembered how her stepsisters primped endlessly the day before. Eulalia and Delicata shared a boudoir, a fact that spawned many battles. They vied for the magnificent mirror on the wall, the gilded frame carved with lions and unicorns, sulking when they couldn't see themselves reflected.

"You're doing it wrong!" Delicata glared at her sister.

Eulalia rolled her eyes. "Perhaps you should hold still."

Cinderella focused on sweeping ashes from the fireplace. If she wandered too close, a stray glamour might cling to her, with disastrous cosmetic effects.

Leaning closer to the mirror, Delicata dropped a potion into her eyes. She tilted her head and blinked a few times, then pouted at herself. Her watery blue eyes hadn't changed color in the slightest. They certainly weren't golden.

"It didn't work," Eulalia said.

"Obviously."

Delicata flung a silver hairbrush at her sister, who ducked. It clattered by the fireplace. Kneeling, Cinderella picked up the brush and returned it to the wardrobe.

"Cinderella!" Eulalia snapped her fingers. "Please polish that filth from the silver. Thank you." Her words sounded perfectly sweet, though the sugar disguised poison.

Silently, Cinderella polished the smudges from the silver brush on the ragged hem of her dress.

"Perfect," Eulalia said. "And goodness, look at your face."

"My face?"

Cinderella glanced at herself in the mirror, which was a mistake. Soot smudged the sickly pallor of her cheeks. Her strawberry blonde hair escaped her bun in limp curls. Dark circles shadowed her hollow eyes, much worse than the ones her stepsisters wanted to disguise, but they had been staying out late at dinner parties, not scrubbing dishes in the scullery.

She hated her reflection. Hated that she could never afford beauty. Magic was too costly, especially since her stepfamily was squandering her inheritance.

Humming, Eulalia stroked the silver hairbrush along her flowing locks. They shimmered from mink-brown to copper to cornsilk blonde. For an instant, strawberry blonde.

She met Cinderella's gaze in the mirror. "What do you think?"

Delicata snorted. "Cinderella has no taste."

"You would look better bald," Cinderella deadpanned.

A delighted gasp escaped Delicata. "How wicked of you!"

Eulalia simply put down the brush, her hair fading back to mink-brown, and waved her hand as if swatting a fly. "Cinderella! Lace my corset tighter."

"No," Delicata said, "she's supposed to bring my evening gown of chartreuse chiffon."

Rather than argue, Cinderella rinsed her ashy hands in the wash-basin and hurried to find the chartreuse evening gown. Rejected candidates for the ball had been tossed carelessly on the floor of the boudoir. A fortune in discarded fabric. She tiptoed around a petticoat, stumbled over a crinoline, and earned a glare from Delicata.

"Do be careful," Eulalia said, with a pretty little smile.

Cinderella spotted the gown and helped her stepsister dress. The yellowish-green hue clashed quite violently with Delicata's hair, bespelled to a garish burgundy.

"Perfect," Eulalia said.

Delicata sneered at her sister. "Liar."

"Why would I lie, sweetheart?"

"Because you want me to look ugly tonight. Prince Benedict will be smitten by me otherwise."

Cinderella didn't dare laugh, though she was tempted.

"Take it off," Delicata said. "At once."

Again, Cinderella did as she was told.

Would Lady Darlington throw her into the street the day she stopped obeying? Perhaps she should run away. Find work in Knockingham at one of the taverns or factories.

But she could never abandon Umberwood Manor.

"Have you forgotten my corset?" Eulalia said. "Lace it tighter."

Eulalia's waist was impossibly thin. She would look like a fashion plate tonight. Cinderella yanked the laces even harder, hoping it was at least uncomfortable.

"What are you wearing to the ball?" Delicata said.

Cinderella realized she was being questioned. "Nothing."

Delicata snickered. "Nothing? You plan to seduce Prince Charming like a harlot?"

"I'm not wearing nothing. I'm not going to the ball."

"But the prince invited all the maidens in the land. You mustn't disobey a royal order!"

Eulalia looked coolly at Cinderella. "Are you blushing?"

"She *is* blushing. She's lying." Delicata caught her by the wrist, her fingers bruising. "Tell us the truth."

"What are you wearing?" Eulalia said.

Cinderella yanked her hand free. "My mother's dress."

Delicata squealed. "Show us!"

Refusal would only make it worse. Years of painful experience had taught her that. A cold, hard lump, like the ones found in old porridge, sat in her stomach.

Cinderella left the boudoir and trudged upstairs to the attic. With every step, her feet weighed more and more like lead. She traded her frock for the pink silk dress.

She returned downstairs as if wading through a dream.

When she returned to the boudoir, she recognized the enormity of her mistake. Delicata gawked at her, lips parted in shock, while Eulalia flushed scarlet. Her stepsisters' eyes glittered with envy and longing.

"Where did you get that?" Delicata said.

"I told you," Cinderella said, "it was my mother's dress."

Eulalia shook her head, her earrings quivering. "I could tell. It's so old-fashioned."

"Did you try to alter it?" Delicata said.

"Yes," Cinderella admitted.

Eulalia shrugged. "You might be pretty, if you tried."

"The dress? Hopeless," Delicata said. "Fit for nobody but the rag-and-bone man."

Cinderella crossed her arms and bowed her head. Had her alterations ruined the pink silk dress? Her mother had looked beautiful, once upon a time. She blinked fast. They couldn't see her cry, or they would mock her for weeks.

Eulalia circled her like a vulture. "It's too small."

"Her waist is too fat." Delicata sniffed. "Clearly, she's been nibbling in the pantry like a rat."

Cinderella glared at her. "Stop!"

"Stop," Delicata mimicked. "Your dress needs more work."

She grabbed the sash at the waist and yanked. The pink silk tore with a shredding noise.

"Still not enough," Eulalia said.

Delicata stomped on the gown. The hem ripped as Cinderella fled from the boudoir. Behind her, laughter chimed like bells—Eulalia, who always sounded beautiful, even when she was the ugliest thing in the world.

Cinderella bolted upstairs and stumbled into the attic.

She dropped to her knees, bent over a chamber pot, and wretched. Up came her breakfast of stale bread and lunch of leftover stew. Her eyes and nose running, she huddled by the dust bunnies, willing herself not to sob.

Crying was a luxury. In the back of her mind, she couldn't stop cataloging her chores.

Sweep the cinders from the fireplaces.

Change the bed linens.

Stoke the stove.

Beat the rugs.

Empty the chamber pots.

Mechanically, she carried the pot outside and dumped it into the privy. Nobody stopped her on the way back to the attic. She poured water from a chipped pitcher into a cracked basin. She washed her face, swished water in her mouth, then climbed into bed and dragged a tattered blanket over herself. Everything about her life was second-hand and fraying. Soon her stepmother's voice would shout upstairs.

Until then, Cinderella closed her eyes.

She wasn't sure when she drifted asleep. When she woke, dusk darkened her room. Her heart hammering, she leapt out of bed.

Why had no one woken her?

Tonight was the ball.

Tonight was her last chance to speak to Prince Benedict again.

Of course, they had left without her. She had slept through the pomp and glamour of the carriage Lady Darlington had rented for the occasion. Thankfully.

At least she could finish her chores in peace.

She swallowed hard, her mouth sour and dry, and went down to the kitchen. She brought a dipper outside to the garden well. Halfway through lowering the bucket, she realized she was still wearing her mother's pink silk dress.

Dirt streaked the tattered hem, dangling among the weeds.

"No one cares," she whispered.

It was the truth.

She hauled the bucket from the well, moonlight glimmering on the water, and reached for the dipper.

No. Not moonlight.

Magic.

Raspberry bushes rustled as a stranger glided into the garden. A lady in silver, shining brighter than any moon. The word lingered on Cinderella's tongue, unspoken.

Fairy.

"Good evening, Cinderella."

The lady that outshone moonlight had a mellifluous voice. She shimmered in a gown of gossamer and amber. Her cornsilk hair tumbled past her waist, a few tendrils caught on her dragonfly wings, everything glistening with dew.

"How do you know my name?"

"I have been watching you for quite some time."

Goosebumps dotted Cinderella's arms. "Who are you?"

"Your Fairy Godmother."

"My what?" That sounded foolish. "I don't even have a godmother, let alone a fairy."

The Fairy Godmother smiled benevolently. "My dear, didn't your parents tell you?"

"They never mentioned you."

"Nevertheless, you shan't go to the ball wearing those rags."

"I'm not going."

"Nonsense!" The Fairy Godmother slipped a crystal wand from her sleeve. "All we need is a complete transformation, and then you will be the belle of the ball."

Cinderella smoothed the front of her skirt. She didn't want to lose her mother's dress.

"But I—"

Before the next word left Cinderella's mouth, the Fairy Godmother flicked her wrist. Green light sizzled from the wand and burst like fireworks. Embers of magic drifted down onto Cinderella, clinging to her hair, tingling when they hit her skin. She blinked fast, dazzled for a small eternity.

When the light faded, she gasped.

Gone. The pink silk was gone.

Breathless, Cinderella touched her neck, her heart galloping against her tightened corset. A waterfall of blue organza plunged from her waist to her slippers—and her slippers! They glittered, cut from glass, so delicate and brittle that her knees weakened for fear of shattering them.

"But I can't simply walk to the ball."

"But, but, but." The Fairy Godmother tsked. "Bring me a pumpkin from your garden."

"A pumpkin?" Cinderella didn't usually question orders, but Fairy Godmothers didn't usually waltz into the garden.

Her smile began to look a bit strained. "Yes, dear, a pumpkin."

Cinderella tiptoed in the glass slippers, her ankles wobbling, until the enchantment strengthened her footsteps.

This was madness. She was dreaming. Wasn't she?

She twisted a pumpkin from the vine and only just stopped herself from rubbing her muddy hands on her skirt. She poured well water over her hands, scrubbing the mud out from under her nails. Dirtying the magic wouldn't do.

The Fairy Godmother scarcely glanced twice at the squash. With a flick of her wand, an enchantment spiraled out and transformed the pumpkin into a magnificent golden coach. A startled mouse rustled from the grass. The Fairy Godmother hit the rodent with a bolt of magic and transfigured it into a dappled gray horse. Tendrils uncurled from the coach, harnessing the steed, which tossed its mane and whinnied.

"Perfect!" The Fairy Godmother shooed her toward the carriage. "Waste not a moment more. You have a prince waiting for you at the ball."

Cinderella still had a chance. When she spun in a circle, she watched the starlight-blue gown bloom like a moonflower. Giddy, she staggered to a stop and hugged herself. She swallowed down champagne bubbles of laughter.

"Thank you!" she cried, breathless.

"And remember, the spell will break at the stroke of midnight!"

EIGHT

SIKANDAR

Shivering, Sikandar crouched by the ashes of the fire. It had gone out last night. Cinderella slept nearby, her chest rising and falling slowly. He rubbed his hands together, his fingers numb, and sighed. He wanted a hot cup of tea, but did he want it badly enough to try sorcery? Gods, he refused to embarrass himself by passing out again.

He pried open a tin of loose-leaf tea and spices and inhaled the scent. Cardamom, ginger, cinnamon, licorice, and black peppercorns. Though he didn't have milk to make proper chai, when he closed his eyes, he was back home in Azurum. Like he had never been banished by his family. Melancholy shrouded him, so familiar it was almost comforting.

Blinking away these thoughts, he closed the tin.

He sketched an arcane symbol in the air. His bones ached as he summoned his magic. Fire leapt at his fingertips, heating his skin without burning him.

Cinderella yawned and stretched. "Sikandar?"

"Good morning." He moved the dancing flame to kindling, trying to hide how his hands trembled from even this small sorcery. "The fire went out last night."

"I know."

Was she awake late? He decided not to ask. "I'm making tea."

Cinderella watched him unpack a copper tea kettle. "You brought that from Azurum?"

"It belonged to my grandmother." He rubbed his thumb over the tarnished metal. Half of the engravings had worn away. "It was one of the few things I was allowed to take from home."

"Allowed?"

Damn it, he had to be more careful. "I left in a hurry."

"Why did you leave Azurum?" She studied his face.

He looked away and hugged himself, his hands gripping his elbows. This wasn't a question he wanted to answer. He fed wood to the fire.

"Hear that?" He tilted his head. "Water."

"There's a river. This way."

He followed the dragon through the trees. "You slept well?"

"Enough."

Cinderella stared at the dirt as if it were infinitely more interesting. Perhaps she had nightmares and didn't trust him enough to tell him.

He tried to smile. "We should try to find breakfast."

"That would be nice."

"Sorcery would be too dangerous without it."

When she looked at him, she had a twist to her mouth. "To be perfectly honest, it was quite frightening when you fainted."

He scoffed. "I didn't *faint*."

"You were unconscious."

"I won't argue that point," he muttered.

The river tumbled in front of them, gurgling around boulders. He crouched and poured icy water into the kettle.

"Why are you here?" she said. "In Viridia?"

He focused on the river. "I took a ship." Cold water numbed his hands.

"I'm serious, Sikandar. Why have you come all this way?"

Because he had no one left in Azurum who he still trusted.

Because he had killed a man too important to ignore.

He clenched his jaw. "I'm on a quest."

"A quest," she repeated.

"To find the Jewel of Oblivion."

She shook her head as they walked back to the campfire. "I've never heard of such a thing."

"One of the more obscure magical artifacts."

Did she need to know more? He dragged a flat stone to the edge of the fire, where it would be heated, and set the copper kettle on top.

"Why do you want this jewel?" she said.

He added a pinch of tea and spices to the kettle. "Would you like a cup of tea?"

"Please."

He doubled the amount in the kettle. "Shame I don't have milk for proper chai."

"I'm fond of tea, admittedly, but I would rather talk more about why you're truly here."

"Can't I have at least a hint of mystery?" He forced out a laugh, trying to evade her questions.

"It's far more than a hint of mystery at this point."

He took a dark cotton shirt and trousers from his pack. "Excuse me a moment." He waved at his embroidered coat. "I've been wearing this since the ball."

"That's not a sorcerer's uniform?"

"Hardly." He shrugged off his shawl. "Look the other way."

While she inspected her claws, he turned his back on her. He changed in a hurry, the morning air brisk, and shot a glance over his shoulder. Her head snapped in the other direction.

"You peeked," he said.

"I didn't! Not for more than a second." She crossed her arms. "I was curious about your clothes."

"Of course." He imbued the words with sarcasm. "Sadly, I don't always wear brocade silk."

"That's a shame."

His eyebrows went skyward. "A shame?"

"I liked the color. Besides, don't think you can distract me simply by taking off your clothes."

Heat scalded his cheeks. "That wasn't my intention."

"And you still haven't told me why you traveled to Viridia."

"Cinderella." He rubbed his eyes, gritty with lingering fatigue. "You don't want to know."

She let out a huff. "I very much want to know."

"You won't look at me the same way."

"And yet, I must trust you to break the curse."

His stomach plummeted. He watched crackling flames devour wood, his shoulders tense. Eventually, she would find out he was Sikandar Zerian. And all the ugly rumors would spill out like disemboweled guts. Telling her now would be the most strategic choice. He could control the story and avoid tangling it with lies.

"I want you to trust me," he said. "But I know I need to earn that trust."

"Goodness, tell me!" She clutched her head in her claws.

He swallowed hard. "The Jewel of Oblivion is my only chance at redemption."

Firelight flickered in her eyes. "Why do you need redemption?"

"Have you heard of the Zerian family?"

"No."

Thank the gods. "My name is Sikandar Zerian. I'm the sorcerer son who was banished from Azurum." The words tasted like mildew in his mouth.

"Banished?"

He grimaced at the breathless curiosity in her voice. "Yes."

The distant river filled the silence between them with endless rushing. Steam hissed from the kettle. Thankful for the interruption, he poured some chai without milk for the dragon. Her talons clinked against the copper cup, which looked more like a thimble in her hands.

"Thank you." She sipped the tea. "Sikandar, I'm not a fool."

"I never suspected as much."

"I know you didn't promise to break the curse out of the goodness of your heart. You must want the Jewel of Oblivion in return."

"Correct," he said. It sounded so mercenary when she said it. "The King of Viridia wanted you dead. But the queen promised me the jewel if I could break the dragon curse. They have it locked away in their royal vault. Wasted."

She stared at him over the teacup. "Why the jewel?"

He poured himself chai and scalded his mouth when he drank. Wincing, he put it down.

"Sikandar," she said. "What happened in Azurum?"

Gods, it was unbearable to meet her gaze. Despite her scales and claws, she had such a soft, vulnerable look in her eyes.

"Please," she said, "tell me the truth."

Words boiled over inside him. "I need the Jewel of Oblivion to make my family forget, because they will never forgive me. Not after what I have done."

She said nothing, just watched him without judgment.

Now that he started talking, he couldn't stop. "I found a jinni. I made a wish."

"Those demons in lamps? I thought they weren't real."

"They are very real." He snapped twigs, one after another, and fed them to the fire. "Never trust a jinni."

"Why?"

He wanted to laugh at the innocence in her question. He jabbed at the fire with a stick and flinched as cinders spiraled high. "Jinn prey upon your darkest desires and most secret hopes. They leave you with nothing but ashes."

"Sikandar..."

"For my first wish, I wished to save my grandmother."

Gods, how could he talk about this when his throat kept clenching tight? The pain may have been years old, but it hurt like yesterday.

"And?" Cinderella murmured the word.

"The jinni cured her sickness, but she died in her sleep."

Her breath hitched. "I'm so sorry."

"You don't have to apologize." He shook his head. "I should have never tried to cheat death."

"I understand why you tried. I lost my mother and father."

He glanced at Cinderella, his heart aching. "I remember. You live alone with your stepfamily."

"But I want to hear your story."

He couldn't fake a smile. "I'm not accustomed to that request."

"Why were you banished?" She frowned. "Was it for your grandmother's death?"

"No. Not even my family is that cruel. It wasn't the first wish, or even the second."

"What was your second wish?"

A harsh laugh escaped him. "You will think I'm a fool."

"I promise I won't."

"I wished for my sister to marry the King of Azurum."

She squinted at him. "You told me marrying royalty never ends well."

"My mother asked for the wish. She begged me to help my poor widow sister. But before they asked for my third and final wish, I buried the lamp in the desert." His skin went numb, as if he were drifting out of his body.

"What was the final wish?" Cinderella said.

This was it. The moment she would turn her back on him. But this was also the biggest rumor of all, and she needed to hear it from him.

He met her stare. "To kill the King of Azurum."

She gasped. "But Sikandar… the King of Azurum is dead."

"I know."

"They said it was an accident."

"I know," he said again.

"Did you kill him?" she whispered.

"Not with the jinni."

He waited for her to recoil from him, to sneer at him like the treacherous snake he had become.

"You're a murderer?"

"Yes." The word fell from his lips like a stone. "My family banished me from Azurum. They didn't, of course, declare me the killer. That would have ruined my family's reputation for discretion. But the rumors were enough to damn me."

Cinderella stared into her cup of chai. She said nothing.

"I understand if you no longer trust me. No one in Azurum ever trusts a Zerian."

"Why did you do it?"

He dug his fingernails into his arm. The pain kept him focused. "I didn't want to kill him, but he was hurting my sister."

"Oh." It was no more than a quiet exhalation.

"The jinni's wish would have been so much quicker. Cleaner. Gods, my parents should have asked one of my brothers. Zafar, or Taj, both of them have experience as assassins. I had never killed anyone before the king, I swear."

She rested her crystal claws on his shoulder. "I believe you."

His jaw dropped. "You do?"

"If you were lying to me, you would tell me a story where you sounded much more heroic."

"Fair point." He winced at her accuracy. "I understand if you want to part ways."

"Why would I do that?"

"I'm a murderer."

"Are you planning to murder me in my sleep?"

"No!" He twisted his face. "Gods, no."

She shrugged as if this answered her question. "Is your family truly so infamous?"

"They take pride in infamy. I disgraced the Zerian name by not being a better murderer."

"Thank you for telling me the truth."

"That's it?" he asked, stammering a little. "You don't want me to defend myself?"

"Sikandar." She looked him dead in the eye. "Was your sister's husband allowed to hurt her?"

"Legally, yes. I remember her bruises—" He cut off, his stomach churning.

"You protected your sister when your family wouldn't."

He shook his head. "They asked me to do it."

"To do their dirty work. That was a necessary evil. You aren't an evil sorcerer."

"Aren't I?"

She still had her claws on his shoulder. "You aren't very good at being evil."

"Or I'm a very good liar," he muttered.

"Let's hope not."

His own laugh caught him by surprise. The tension rushed from his muscles and left him weak. He bowed his head and touched one of her crystal claws—the broken one, the edges still rough. She lingered before retreating.

"Thank you for believing me," he said.

"Of course."

The road to Grimleigh climbed high into the mountains, where fall was more silver than gold. Brittle grass crunched underfoot, glittering with a crust of frost crystals. Lingering leaves clung to the skeletal branches of maple trees.

Shivering, Sikandar hugged himself. "At least it isn't snowing."

Snow began to sift down like icing sugar.

Cinderella glanced at the clouds. "You jinxed it."

"Oh, blame the sorcerer."

"I meant it metaphorically!"

He smirked. "Of course you did." He unrolled the map. "We had chai and confessions this morning, but we still haven't had breakfast."

"Are we near a town?"

"Dimmingdale. It looks like a little village."

"I've never heard of it."

"Nevertheless, we should avoid villagers with pitchforks. Hide in the forest until I return."

She sighed. "I suppose you're right."

When Sikandar stepped onto the cobblestoned streets of Dimmingdale, he avoided the curious stares of villagers. Perhaps they had never seen a foreigner here. He wouldn't be surprised if he was the only Azuri boy around. A breeze whirled through the town square, whisking both snowflakes and the warm, yeasty scent of baking bread.

His mouth watering, he followed his nose to a bakery. A bell jingled over the door when he entered. Inside, a glass case gleamed with a beautiful assortment of pies, pastries, cakes, and cookies. One glance, and he knew what to buy.

He paid for his choice, which the baker packed in a box.

When he returned to Cinderella, he found the dragon burrowed into a pile of fallen leaves.

He gawked at her. "What are you doing?"

"Hiding."

He laughed. "Not very well."

She shook herself off, scattering leaves, and peered at the box in his hands. "What is that?"

He cast a small spell with one hand. A glorious chocolate cake rose from the box and hovered in the air. Cinderella gasped, her expression awestruck.

"Don't let it fall!" she breathed.

"I won't. I have found this spell handy before."

"Quick, it's getting snowed on."

He let the cake float while he took a knife from his pack. "I don't have any forks, I'm afraid."

He cut a thick slice for her and served it on the flat of the blade. With her claws, she plucked the slice from the air and nibbled it. She moaned and swayed back and forth.

"Good heavens," she said. "How absolutely delicious."

He cut a slice for himself. Gods, this *was* a good cake. Rich, bittersweet, even more decadent when eaten with his hands. He didn't even pretend to be polite. After all, he was in the wilderness with a dragon.

Cinderella licked the frosting from her mouth with her forked tongue. She stared at the rest of the cake, floating in the air, with such longing that Sikandar grinned.

"More?" he asked.

"Please."

He finished his first slice and served her another.

"To be perfectly honest," she said, "I'm not sure a chocolate cake qualifies for breakfast."

"Not even an entire chocolate cake?"

"Especially not an entire chocolate cake. Very improper."

He started on a second slice. "I'm not sure I care. Being improper has its benefits."

"Oh?" She glanced sideways at him. "How improper?"

He couldn't help smiling at her curiosity. "Nothing too exciting. When I was studying at the University of Naranjal, before I was expelled, I was more of a bookworm."

"How did you go from bookworm to…?"

"Murderer?" He took another bite of cake and thought while chewing. "By birthright, I suppose. But I'm by far the least exciting of the Zerian brothers."

"Why were you expelled?"

He grimaced. "Because my family banished me and stopped paying tuition. Surprisingly, the rumors about me being a murderer weren't a problem. Everyone at the University of Naranjal expected as much from a Zerian."

"Are your brothers also sorcerers?"

"None of them were born with magic. Not like me."

"That's rather exciting." Her eyes sparkled.

Why was she looking at him like that? Like she might admire him or find him intriguing?

"Is it?" he said.

"You can teleport and make cakes float in the air."

He laughed. "Such valuable life skills."

"You're a charmer, Sikandar."

Heat burned his ears. She didn't need to flirt with him to guarantee his loyalty—one of his sister's most common tactics.

He decided to confront her directly. "Why such flattery?"

"Because you're a sorcerer who's also enchanting." She smirked. "Forgive me for the puns."

So, she was just teasing him. "Enchanting?" he repeated dryly.

"Bewitching? Spellbinding?"

"I can't forgive you for the puns if you won't stop."

"Sorry!"

She didn't sound very sorry.

Late in the afternoon, when the snow lay ankle-deep, they arrived at Agatha's Academy of Magic.

"It doesn't look anything like the advertisement," she said.

He arched his eyebrows. "You expect honesty in advertising?"

"I expected it to look more polished."

The Academy was anything but polished, with crooked towers and blood-red grapevines smothering the bricks. Mossy gargoyles glowered at them from the roof.

He brushed snowflakes from his shawl. "We could stand outside, admiring the architecture—"

"Which is a bit rough around the edges."

"—or we could go inside and not freeze to death."

Cinderella's sigh escaped in a plume of white. "Will they allow a dragon and a sorcerer?"

"Aren't they sorceresses?"

"Witches, technically. And, of course, they study magic only to become more marriageable. A proper young woman would never dream of a *career* in magic."

He scratched the back of his neck. "Sorcerers are improper?"

"You aren't a young lady seeking a husband, so it's all right for you to profit from the arcane arts."

"Profit?" He glanced around as if looking for coins. "I haven't made any money yet."

She coughed. "I'm afraid I'm penniless."

"Don't worry, I'm not expecting a windfall for breaking the curse. Just the jewel."

"Of course."

He rubbed his fingers together. "Shall we? Before we succumb to frostbite?"

"It's not *that* cold."

"You have a fire in your belly."

Cinderella sniffed. "Would you like me to ignite you?"

"No, thank you."

Sikandar marched up the steps of the Academy, knocked snow from his boots, and dragged open one of the oak doors. It swung out with a groan. "Ladies first."

She rolled her eyes. "I'm not a lady."

"Doubtful." He smirked. "You spend an awful lot of time acting ladylike."

She hid her smile behind her claws. "I consider that a compliment."

Together, they entered the Academy. The entrance hall soared to lofty rafters. A gaggle of uniformed schoolgirls froze by a staircase. One of them dropped her armload of books, which spilled across the polished marble.

"Pardon the interruption," Cinderella said. "But we're seeking help to break a curse?"

Agatha Black, the headmistress of the Academy of Magic, seemed unperturbed by a dragon, even one that scarcely fit in her office. Cinderella's wingtips brushed tall bookshelves crammed with leather-bound tomes. The air smelled of honey-sweet beeswax, though the candles remained unlit while snowy light poured through the windows.

Agatha steepled her fingers on her desk. "This is highly irregular. Here at the Academy, we prefer to avoid vulgarities such as curses and other dark arts."

Sikandar noted the woman's restraint with magic. She wore minimal glamours, just a touch around her storm-gray eyes and ebony hair. Her elegant dress wouldn't have been out of place within Knightsend Castle. Her office's library simmered with potential trapped within enchanted books.

"Can you help us nevertheless?" he asked.

Agatha looked not to him, but to Cinderella. "I have never seen a young lady become a dragon." Her lips twitched. "At least, not literally. This enchantment is a first."

Sikandar wrinkled his nose. "How much do you know about curses?"

Agatha inspected him as if finding him lacking. "How exactly are you acquainted with Miss Cinderella Darlington? I don't believe you ever told me your name."

"Sikandar Zerian of Azurum."

The headmistress's nostrils flared. "Zerian. I see. And what are your qualifications?"

Was this an interview? "I studied at the University of Naranjal for three years."

"Pardon?"

"The University of Naranjal," he repeated.

"I've never heard of it."

"It's over a thousand years old. Older than this place, I'm sure."

"How enlightening." Agatha pursed her lips. "I had imagined the tribes of Azurum passed down their folk magic in their tents in the desert."

Folk magic? Tents in the desert? His shoulders stiffened. For heaven's sake, he wasn't even sure why he expected the headmistress to be less ignorant. This was, after all, a backwoods school he had never heard of in Azurum.

"Sikandar suggested we come here." Cinderella tucked her tail around her claws. The dragon managed to appear both prim and proper. "Please, Headmistress, we would be forever grateful for any assistance you can offer."

Agatha nodded. "We may be able to identify the curse."

"Thank you ever so much!"

She smiled benevolently. "First, it's time for high tea. You must be both starved and chilled to the bone."

Though Sikandar *was* cold, he curled his lip. "High tea?"

"How gracious of you," Cinderella said, excessively polite. "We would be delighted to join you for tea."

"You," he said. "Not me."

They both stared at him, making him feel like a barbarian.

He tried softening his tone. "We aren't here for teatime."

"Sikandar," Cinderella said, "we traveled all this way, and it's practically a blizzard outside."

"Have your tea. I will be in the library." He tossed a cool look at Agatha. "I'm assuming you have one?"

"Yes." The headmistress had a brittle smile. "We can manage quite well without you."

"Good to know."

"You may join us in the Great Hall should you tire of literary distractions."

"I'm here to learn about the curse. Hopefully, I will."

"Hopefully," Agatha said.

"Thank you." As if she been paying him equal respect.

If dragons could pout, Cinderella would have been. "Sikandar, please, stay for tea."

"Let him go, sweetheart." Agatha laughed. "He clearly prefers the company of books."

"True," he muttered on the way out.

The library redeemed Agatha's Academy of Magic.

A fabulous library, the kind most often seen within dreams. Shelves towered to the ceiling, bowing under the weight of uncountable books. Sikandar tilted back his head to take in the highest bookshelves. Despite their irritating headmistress, this school might help him after all.

He found the section on curses and hexes and began scanning the shelves. Beeswax, old paper, and secrets perfumed the air. Outside the diamond-paned windows, the snowfall thickened. A glimmer of amethyst caught his eye.

The jinni smiled at him through the window.

Swearing, he jumped back from the glass. Between one blink and the next, she vanished. He shuddered and rubbed the goosebumps on his arms. Lack of sleep helped her invade his mind. Even with the Cerulean Sea between them both, he couldn't deny the unbreakable bond between the jinni and himself—her master.

While he delved into the books, his thoughts kept drifting to a single impossible possibility. He hated even wondering it. He refused to say it out loud.

With his third wish, could he break the dragon curse?

NINE

CINDERELLA

Cinderella had expected the witches at the Academy of Magic to wear ragged black rather than tidy gray uniforms. And she certainly hadn't expected high tea to be such a spectacle.

A grand fireplace crackled and warmed the chilly stones of the Great Hall. Witches perched on benches by a vast oak table. High tea itself dazzled the eye: lavender cupcakes decorated with quivering butterflies, tiny cucumber sandwiches without crusts, tarts overwhelmed by fruits, and scones accompanied by clotted cream, strawberry jam, and lemon curd.

"As if you read my mind!" Cinderella said.

Agatha smiled. "Please, join us."

Was there room at the table for a dragon? The headmistress waved her hand at a spot on the floor. Rather than delicate porcelain and silverware, Cinderella had been given an inelegant brass bowl, as if she were an oversized dog.

"For tea," Agatha said. "Considering your proportions."

Cinderella lowered her gaze. "Thank you." At least it wasn't a trough.

She lay down by the bowl with as much dignity as she could muster. When she smiled, the nearest witch shuddered at her fangs. Why had Sikandar refused her invitation? She would have felt less out of place with him by her side.

Cinderella dipped her head and sipped the witches' tea. Heat nearly scalded her tongue—perhaps it would have, if she weren't a dragon. It didn't taste like black or green or even jasmine tea. Nothing like the spices in Sikandar's chai. Rather, it had a mossy quality, and a bit of bitterness, as if it had been plucked from a forest floor. Quite strange.

Agatha watched her drink. "Are you fond of the flavor?"

"Quite," Cinderella lied.

A witch helped herself to a butterfly cupcake. She plucked off the wings and discarded them on a saucer. Merely an enchantment, though it did turn the stomach.

"Tell me," Agatha said, "who were you before the curse?"

Cinderella blinked, taken aback. "An ordinary girl, of course."

Agatha inspected her with glittering eyes, as if she found this answer improbable. "You had no inkling of the curse?"

"None."

"Your mother or father didn't think to warn you?"

She frowned. "Both of them passed away."

"An orphan," said the headmistress. "Of course."

"What do orphans and curses have to do with each other?"

"Tragedy tends to beget tragedy."

Cinderella drank more of her tea to avoid having this conversation, which was frankly rude. She hadn't slept well after hunting in the forest last night. Fatigue weighted her bones with lead. By the time she drained her bowl, her eyelids drooped.

Clumsy, she knocked over her bowl. It clattered across the floor.

"My apologies," she mumbled.

Thank goodness dragons couldn't blush. The bowl glinted just out of reach. She groped for it, her claws clinking against the brass. It rolled farther away.

The world tilted. Cinderella slumped onto the stones.

Darkness seeped into her eyes like spilled ink. Blinking did nothing to clear her vision. What was wrong? Was this the curse? She sucked in a ragged gasp, fighting for air, until she lost her hold on consciousness entirely.

She returned to the night her father died.

He lay on his deathbed. Candlelight flickered over his gaunt, sallow cheeks. She knelt beside his pillow, all of her tears already spent.

"Ginevra." His breath rattled in his chest. "My little juniper."

"Father," she said, since there was nothing else to say.

Wasting sickness had taken his laugh and the sparkle from his eyes. She hardly recognized him.

"Your mother's diary," he said. "Find it."

"She kept a diary?"

He fumbled for her hand and pressed an ornate golden key into her palm. "Read it. You must."

Shadows devoured her father.

She knelt in the garden by her juniper bush. Wind rustled her gown of mourning black. She picked dusty blue berries from the juniper's snakeskin leaves.

When she was a girl, she strung the berries on necklaces. This would be her last chance to do the same, since her stepmother hated the juniper bush. An ugly, wicked plant, with berries of poison good only for gin, the devil's drink.

The garden disappeared, and she lingered by the fireplace.

Spicy-sweet perfume infused the smoke. As she watched, her namesake burned to ash.

Cinderella woke in a cage.

Her head throbbed with every heartbeat. She lifted her head gingerly and looked around.

This wasn't the Great Hall, but a dungeon beneath the school. Dank mold slicked the stone walls. Witchlight flickered in lanterns, a pale glowworm green.

"Hello?" Cinderella coughed, her throat raw.

The witches. The tea. It had tasted so bitter…

How long had she been unconscious? Minutes? Hours?

She struggled to her feet. Her scales rustled against the iron, and her tail slipped through the bars.

"Sikandar?" she called. "Sikandar! Where are you?"

The library. Unless the witches had captured him, too.

Footsteps descended stairs to the dungeon. The shape of a man separated from the darkness.

"Sikandar?" she called. She gasped when he stepped into the light. "Your Majesty!"

King Archibald Charming.

The ruler of Viridia strode into the dungeon as if entering a throne room, his face armored by bland arrogance. Perhaps he had seen a thousand dragons in his life, and she was the least interesting by far. He hadn't bothered with guards.

"Speak," King Archibald said.

The King of Viridia wanted you dead.

God, was she going to be sentenced to death?

Cinderella bowed her head. "Your Majesty," she said, "please accept my most sincere apologies for your castle. I never intended to remodel the ballroom."

"You think I give a damn about some architecture?"

She spoke breathlessly, as if clever words would prove how civilized she was, despite her scales and claws. "Well, Your Majesty, I understand it must have been rather expensive, more than a little plasterwork and—"

"Silence!" His voice boomed in the dungeon. "Confess, dragon, why you came to Knightsend."

"Prince Benedict invited me to the ball."

"How long have you been telling my son lies?"

Her jaw dropped. "What lies?"

"You deceived him. Disguised yourself."

"I didn't know! I didn't know a curse would turn me into a dragon at the stroke of midnight."

He flared his nostrils as if he wanted to breathe fire himself. "Benedict told me your name. Your true name. Don't lie to me, Ginevra Darlington."

"You want the truth? I wanted to save Umberwood Manor."

"Your mother's sacrifice was already repaid."

She gripped the cage in her claws. "What sacrifice? What did she do for Queen Eira?"

King Archibald bared his teeth. "Too much and not enough."

Before she could ask what he meant, the king abandoned her in the dungeon and returned to the witches who had betrayed her. Only then did she allow herself to cry. Sobs wracked her body. Steaming-hot tears puddled by her claws.

"Cinderella!" A whisper in the dark. "Cinderella?"

She blinked fast. "Who is it?"

"An evil sorcerer from Azurum."

"Oh, thank goodness!"

He crept from the shadows. "I was in the library."

"Of course." Her smile trembled.

"The king arrived with enough fanfare that it distracted me from researching the curse. Then I overheard two witches muttering about the dangers of knocking out someone with both magic and chloroform." He wrinkled his nose. "I don't think this is a very good school, their calculations were completely off. The witches kept glancing in my general direction suspiciously, so I escaped their attention and found you."

"Do they know where you are?"

"I hope not." He looked at the stairs. "We need to get the hell out of here, before the king's men take you. They brought a wagon, big enough to hold this cage."

"They aren't going to kill me?"

"Not now, at least."

She let out a shuddering sigh. "Which could be worse. More inventive forms of death."

He lifted the padlock on the cage. "Gods, I could have spent more time learning lockpicking magic."

"Never had aspirations of being a sneakthief?"

"Not once." He dropped the padlock. "Melt it."

"Excuse me?"

"You can breathe fire. Melt the lock."

"I don't know if I can."

"Try."

She held her breath. Fire ignited within her chest. When she breathed flames onto the lock, the iron glowed from cherry red to orange.

"Hotter," he said.

A little lightheaded, she filled her lungs with air again. Flames rushed from her jaws. The iron shifted from orange to white-hot, though it still wasn't melting.

"Stop!"

His fingers sketched an intricate pattern. When he waved at the lock, a flurry of snow blew onto the iron. The cold magic shattered the metal, shards chiming on the floor. He yanked open the cage door with a screech.

"You're welcome," he said.

She rushed to freedom and stumbled over her own claws. He caught her by the shoulder, then jerked back. Wincing, he shook his hand. His fingertips looked red.

"You're too hot to touch," he said.

"Sorry!"

"No time to be embarrassed."

Together, they crept upstairs from the dungeon.

"You first," she whispered. "You're a bit more inconspicuous."

He peeked through the door at the top of the stairs. "Let's go."

The hallway beyond the door was equally as charming as the dungeon, festooned with mildew and cobwebs.

Cinderella fought a mad urge to laugh. "They didn't advertise this part of the Academy in the brochure."

"Didn't they?" he deadpanned.

She followed him to another staircase. This one led to a corridor decorated with paintings of unicorns and sea serpents. A schoolgirl let out an ear-splitting shriek.

Sikandar muttered a swear. "Run!"

They sprinted away from the witch. Sikandar dodged around the corner, but Cinderella took the turn too fast and slid into the wall. Pain throbbed in her left wing. Panting, she scrambled after him, straight into the entrance hall of the Academy of Magic. Sikandar hauled open one of the doors and held it for her until she ducked through.

The king's men stood guard in the falling snow.

"Dragon!"

Cinderella didn't wait for the king's men to mount their horses. She sprang from the steps of the Academy and bounded across the lawn, churning snow and mud beneath her claws. The mountains gleamed like teeth in the twilight.

Behind her, horses whinnied. She risked a backward glance.

The king's men slapped the reins and kicked their steeds, but the horses balked in the snow, the whites of their eyes gleaming. They feared her, the dragon.

Sikandar caught up as she hesitated. "Keep running!"

She bolted into the wilderness. Pines blocked the sky. Goose-feather snowflakes drifted between the pines and pillowed in the shadows. They struggled through the deepening snow until they had lost their pursuers.

Cinderella's heart pounded so hard it made her woozy. Sikandar slumped against a log and struggled to catch his breath. Their ragged gasps disturbed the solemn forest. The lights of Grimleigh winked in the valley below.

"Are they gone?" she said.

He exhaled in a cloud. "Not forever."

"God." The icy air burned her lungs. "How long was I unconscious in that cage?"

"Two hours? At most?"

"You were in the library for two hours? You could have helped!"

"Excuse me, but I *was* helping you. Unlike those witches." He said the last word like an insult.

"Have you ever woken in a cage? Alone and frightened?"

His frown wavered as if he was struggling to remain angry. "You never should have trusted them."

"They seemed so nice."

He curled his lip. "Until they drugged your tea. Besides, the headmistress was anything but nice to me."

"She was rather rude."

"You could have disagreed with her," he said bitterly.

"I'm not like her."

"If you say nothing, does it matter?"

His words struck her like arrows. "I suppose it doesn't. Please accept my apology. Sikandar, you have been so kind and sweet to me, even though I'm a dragon."

He ducked his head. "Sweet? No."

Was it her imagination, or was he blushing the slightest bit?

"What else would you call it?"

He shook his head. "I accept your apology."

She sighed. "We should have never gone to Agatha's Academy of Magic. We gained nothing but danger."

"Ah, but I'm delighted to tell you that you're wrong."

Sikandar unbuckled his pack and hauled out a massive book bound in crimson leather.

"What is that?" she said. "A book from their library?"

"*Aetheria's Compendium of Transfiguration.*" Snow fell upon the open pages, white on white. "With a potion to transform someone cursed back to their true form."

TEN

SIKANDAR

Evening faded from violet to indigo. Snow drifted down around them and cast a spell of silence upon the forest. Sikandar's fireflies danced around *Aetheria's Compendium of Transfiguration*. The book was unfortunately vague.

"I'm not sure how long the potion will last," he warned.

"I don't care!" Cinderella shook the snow from her wings. "Even one second would be worth it."

Doubtful, especially since he had to brew the potion first.

He thumbed through the thousand pages of the *Compendium*. The edges had become fuzzy from years of readers. "The critical ingredient is an extremely rare mushroom. *Amanita mirabilis*, the Miraculous Deathcap, which feeds only upon underground magic in caves of crystals."

"Miraculous Deathcap?" She shuddered. "Surely that must be a poisonous mushroom."

"Oh, it is," he said cheerfully.

"Sikandar!" she wailed.

"But not in the hands of any halfway decent sorcerer."

"I should hope you're halfway decent." She tilted her head. "Where do we find a cave of crystals?"

"Aren't there any in Viridia?"

"Yes, but they aren't the kind of place a proper lady would go. I never had a reason to visit."

He rummaged in his pack, his fingers clumsy from the cold. "Let me check my map."

The mountains looked like a jagged zigzag, lacking any symbols to mark the location of caves. Viridians weren't that advanced with cartography, were they?

He kneaded his forehead. "We could buy a better map."

"Wait." Cinderella tapped the map with one claw. "Scaldwell."

"What's in Scaldwell?"

"Hot springs. Invalids bathe there and breathe the vapors."

"Neither one of us is an invalid."

She scoffed at him. "I may not be trained in the art of sorcery, but I'm not entirely ignorant of geology. Don't caves of crystals require volcanic activity? If we go to Scaldwell, we may very well find one near the hot springs."

"Of course." Why hadn't he thought of that? And hot springs sounded much better than this endless snow. "Even if we find a cave of crystals in Scaldwell, and we find the Miraculous Deathcap, we can't brew the potion."

The dragon's wings wilted. "Why not?"

"We're missing ingredients. Void saffron, which costs a fortune, along with ember coriander and kraken ink."

"Kraken ink? I don't suppose you know how to fish?"

He raised his eyebrows. "Any decent alchemist should sell these ingredients. In Azurum, at least."

"Scaldwell isn't too far away."

"Would they have an alchemist?"

"They treat invalids there, remember?"

"Good point."

He cupped his hands to his mouth and blew on them to warm his icy fingers. His wool shawl hadn't been woven with Viridian temperatures in mind.

"Please don't freeze to death," Cinderella said.

His laugh clouded the air with white. "Thank you for asking politely. It's too damn cold."

"We can't sleep here, can we?"

He shook his head. "Maybe you can, but I would be useless to you by morning."

"Well, that won't do. We should fly somewhere warmer."

"Fly?"

"I assume these wings aren't decorative." She stretched her wings overhead, then let out a hiss of pain and folded her left wing. "Bruised myself a little."

"When?"

"Escaping the Academy. I crashed into the wall."

"Are you all right?"

He touched her hurt wing, her skin soft under his fingertips. She stifled a whimper.

"Sorry." He retreated a step. "I didn't mean—"

"I know."

He looked away, flustered. "Please, go ahead."

She retreated from him and unfurled her full wingspan, which was undeniably magnificent. When she flapped her wings, falling snow whirled in eddies of air.

"I feel silly," she said.

"You're a dragon." He couldn't look away. "You're meant to fly."

She rolled her eyes. "It's not as though I learned how to fly as a hatchling. I never hatched."

He smirked. "Yet you breathe fire like a natural."

"True," she said, modestly.

She beat her wings harder, tossing snow with every downstroke, wind buffeting his clothes.

A growl rumbled from her throat. "We aren't high enough."

"What did you have in mind? A cliff?"

"A cliff might work."

He followed her uphill. "Don't jump into the void."

The pines looked gnarled and windswept at this elevation. When they reached a rocky slope, where no more than junipers grew, she braced herself with her claws in the rubble. Icy wind whistled past them and blew most of the snow sideways before it could touch the ground.

"Cross your fingers," Cinderella said.

"But—"

She bounded along the slope, her talons scrabbling against rock, until the wind caught her like a kite and lifted her into the air. Her shriek echoed off the mountains.

"Sikandar!" She clawed at nothingness. "How do I land?"

He ran in her shadow. "Close your wings!"

She plummeted and tumbled across gravel and slush.

"Cinderella!"

He was at her side in an instant. Laughing, she righted herself and shook out her wings.

"I flew." She sounded giddy. "I flew!"

"You did," he said, his hands shaking. "Please be careful."

Recklessly, she flung herself into the air again. She carved out a path in the twilight sky. He ducked as she soared overhead. In the shadow of the dragon, he fought the urge to run, his pulse hammering in his throat.

Terrifying. Gorgeous.

He wanted to be there with her.

She tilted her wings and sliced through the air, then caught the wind and rode it higher.

"Cinderella!" He cupped his hands to his mouth. "Come back!"

She dove back to him. After she landed, she held her wings wide, ready to leap into flight again. Snowflakes sizzled where they fell upon her indigo scales. She stared at him with a feral intensity, like the eyes of a hawk.

He held out his hand. "Cinderella." He spoke her name in a husky whisper.

She blinked as if waking from a dream. "That was…"

"Wonderful?"

"More than wonderful. Exhilarating." Her claws closed around his wrist, startling him. "Fly with me."

"How?"

Her grip tightened, a light press of talons against his skin. "I…"

"What?"

"Ride me." She blurted it out. "It's the only sensible option."

"Is it?" he stammered.

"We won't leave footprints if we fly. The king's men will find it harder to track us in the air."

He raked his hands through his hair. "Are you sure?"

"Yes." She lay at his feet. "Climb onto my back. Carefully!"

He fussed with the sleeves of his shirt, like that would help him, then placed his hand on her shoulder and swung his leg over her back.

"This is nothing like riding a horse," he muttered. "Or a camel."

"Did you just compare me to a camel?"

"No! That wasn't what I meant."

She glanced sideways at him. "Hold on."

"To what?"

"My horns?"

He leaned over her neck and wrapped his fingers around them. They swept from her brow, shimmering crystal, before curving into graceful points. If she wanted to, she could gore a man to death, though she seemed much too polite.

"Don't let go," Cinderella said.

Sikandar's thighs tensed. She leapt from the earth, scattering rocks and snow, and carved her way into the sky. As she beat her wings, her powerful muscles flexed beneath him. The ground rushed away below them.

He clung to her horns, dizzy with vertigo. "I can't look."

"But it's beautiful!"

When he opened his eyes, the forest bristled far below them, a pelt of silver pines. Mountains loomed in the twilight, a breathtaking sweep of snow and rock.

"It is beautiful," he murmured. "Almost as beautiful as you."

His words were lost in the wind.

They flew until the lights of Grimleigh dwindled in the distance, then landed in a valley for the night. Snow hadn't yet fallen here. Frost glittered under the stars.

Cinderella curled under a tree. Sikandar sat nearby without touching her, until she sheltered him under her wing. Slowly, he leaned against her shoulder.

"Better," she said.

Tension eased from his muscles. He tilted back his head and rested it against her scales.

She was, after all, warmer than him.

"Something strange happened at the Academy," she said.

"Stranger than being drugged and locked in a cage?"

"Well, yes, in fact. When King Archibald came to question me, he mentioned my mother's sacrifice. I had never heard anyone speak of it that way before."

Sikandar shook his head. "What did she sacrifice?"

"I haven't the slightest clue. But that must have been the great service she did for Queen Eira. When the king spoke of it, he seemed bitter. Angry, even. He told me my mother's sacrifice had already been repaid."

"Umberwood Manor."

"Yes, but why? I tried to ask the king what she had done for the queen. He bared his teeth at me, like a wild animal, and said, 'Too much and not enough.'"

"We need to find out what she did."

"I know."

He gazed beyond the curve of her wing at the night beyond. She sighed, her chest rising under his head. He breathed in her scent of burnt toast and jasmine tea.

Strange, how he found a dragon comforting.

"Back in the cage," she said, "I dreamed of my father's death."

His heart ached for the pain in her voice. "Those kinds of dreams can be difficult."

She was silent for a moment. "I remembered what my father said to me on his deathbed. He gave me the key to my mother's diary, which he told me I must read."

"What did her diary say?"

"I don't know. I never found it."

"Do you still have the key?"

"Yes, hidden in my bedroom."

Sikandar rubbed his chin, the rough stubble reminding him that he hadn't shaved in days. "When you fled from Knightsend, you left behind a crystal claw."

She hid her broken claw, self-consciously. "And?"

"I cast a spell on it to find you."

She licked her lips. "Could the key lead you to the diary?"

"Precisely."

Her shoulder tensed beneath him. "Sikandar, we just found the book on transfiguration, but I need to know what's in my mother's diary. I need to fly to Umberwood."

"After daybreak."

"But—you agree?"

"I will help you however I can."

She relaxed, her wing lowering over him. "Thank you."

"Are we falling asleep like this?" He folded his hands together, since they were inexplicably sweaty. Jitters danced in his stomach.

"Are you planning on freezing to death?"

"Not tonight."

"This would, of course, ruin my reputation. We're unmarried. I'm not even wearing clothes."

"How scandalous."

She laughed. "Good night, Sikandar."

"Good night."

Morning. In the pale blue sky of dawn, they flew to Umberwood Manor. Cold wind stung Sikandar's eyes. He wrapped his wool shawl tight around his face.

Cinderella landed in an old apple orchard that smelled of cider. He slid from her back on shaky legs. She snapped up an apple, crunching it between her fangs, but he wasn't hungry. His stomach writhed like a nest of serpents.

"Wait for me in the orchard," he said.

She huffed. "I would love to singe my stepsisters."

"Better for you to hide, and for me to pretend I'm a royal sorcerer sent by Prince Charming."

"Why would he do that?"

"To find his future bride. He fell madly in love with her at the ball, but she fled at midnight, frightened away by the dragon. He ordered sorcerers to scour the kingdom."

She tilted her head, studying him. "You're good at lying."

"As a Zerian, I should take that as a compliment." He flashed a smile, since he was joking. "Where should I look for the key?"

"In my bedroom, under my mattress."

"Where is your bedroom?"

"Top of the stairs, in the attic. The shabbiest room in the house, you can't miss it." She paused. "Pretend you need the bathroom. It's at the bottom of the stairs."

"Good idea. And I should dress for the part."

He rummaged through his pack and found his coat of midnight blue silk. When he cleared his throat, Cinderella turned her back on him. She didn't try peeking this time.

He tugged his jacket straight. "How do I look?"

She turned around. Her gaze traveled the length of his body. "Even more handsome."

Handsome? That was unexpected. He coughed and fidgeted with the sleeves of his jacket. "Like a mysterious sorcerer?"

"That, too."

"Perfect." He ignored the heat in his ears. "Wait for me?"

"I will."

He started walking down the path, but she shook her head. "The other way."

"Thank you."

Umberwood Manor guarded a lawn silvered by frost. The old house looked like it had been built from cobblestones, held together by a lot of ivy. He wasn't an expert on Viridian architecture. Stone monsters snarled at him from the gutters, and many windows watched him like eyes. He hesitated at the door, which was grander than expected, crafted from oak and iron. He squared his shoulders before knocking.

From inside, he heard the muffled sound of running footsteps.

The door groaned open, and a young lady peered at him. Tall, willowy, and brunette.

Her velvet dress looked expensive, but a servant hadn't answered the door for her. Sikandar knew how the truly wealthy lived. This was but a pale imitation.

Her gaze traveled along his skin and his brocade silk. "Yes?"

"Good morning. Is this the Darlington residence?"

"It is. And you are?"

"Sikandar Zerian." Better to pepper lies with truth. "A sorcerer from the royal family of Viridia."

"Miss Eulalia Darlington." One of Cinderella's stepsisters. "Can I help you?"

"At the ball, Prince Charming fell in love with a young lady." She leaned closer as he spoke. "Sadly, the budding romance was interrupted by the dragon."

"And he sent a sorcerer?"

"More than one, throughout the kingdom of Viridia. To pinpoint eligible maidens with magic. With any luck, one of you will marry the crown prince."

Eulalia's fingertips flitted to her neck. "I see."

"Mr. Zerian!" Delicata jostled her sister out of the doorway.

He smiled politely. "A pleasure to see you again, Miss Delicata."

"You know him?" Eulalia said.

"From the ball." Delicata lowered her voice to a conspiring whisper. "Wasn't the dragon horrid?"

"Very," he said.

"I thought I might swoon!"

"I'm sorry to hear that," he said, having all too recently been unconscious himself.

Eulalia sniffed. "I had my smelling salts at the ready."

"Might I come inside?" he said. "I don't mean to intrude."

Delicata whipped open the door. "Our mother is out at the moment. Please, come into the parlor."

He followed the sisters into Umberwood Manor. They brought him to a room packed with furniture of dark wood and carpeted by rugs imported from Azurum.

"Make yourself comfortable," Eulalia said. "We were just about to have breakfast. Delicata, fetch the teapot, and some of the crumpets. Marmalade also, the fancy kind."

Delicata pursed her lips. "Yes, sister."

Sikandar sank onto a plush loveseat. "Thank you."

"You're most welcome." Eulalia sat primly on a chair. "Tell me more about Prince Benedict's future bride."

"She's undeniably beautiful. Everyone commented upon that."

Just as he expected, Eulalia stroked her hair from her face, preening at the perceived compliment.

"What kind of magic?" she said.

"Pardon?"

"What kind of magic will you use to find the prince's bride?"

"Divination, of course."

Balancing a silver tray of tea and crumpets, Delicata returned to the parlor. She set the tray down on a low table, her cheeks pink, and brushed a lock of hair from her face.

"Sugar? Cream?" she said to Sikandar.

"Neither."

Delicata poured him some black tea. Discreetly, he dipped his finger into the cup. Just shy of scalding, but not enchanted in any way. He sipped the tea, glancing around the parlor. He didn't see any magical artifacts, just cabinets displaying porcelain figurines of little angels. Something about their flat painted eyes made his stomach uneasy.

"Mr. Zerian." Eulalia crossed her ankles. "Surely Prince Benedict remembers what this girl looks like. Or perhaps her name. Why scour the kingdom to find her?"

"It's a vast kingdom. Magic was required." He drained the rest of his tea and put down the cup with a decisive clink. "If you will excuse me, which way is the bathroom?"

"By the stairs," Eulalia said, "the first door on your right."

As he left, Delicata murmured, "Isn't he good-looking?"

"Yes, but I don't trust him."

He opened the bathroom door and shut it again without entering, loud enough to be heard from the parlor. Inspired, he cast a spell to lock it from the inside. That would buy him more time if they went looking for him.

Careful not to creak the stairs, he ascended to the top floor of Umberwood Manor.

Cinderella hadn't been lying. Her bedroom in the attic had to be the shabbiest room in the house. Clean of dust and cobwebs, but decorated with broken furniture and threadbare rugs. Her bed had a pitifully thin mattress. He rummaged under it until his fingers closed around a cool metal object.

A golden key.

He knelt on the rug and half-closed his eyes. The hairs on his arms prickled as he cast the spell. Magic heated his blood. At least diaries had no emotions of their own.

Where are you?

He focused on the scent of paper, the feel of slightly wet ink smudging under fingers.

The spell pulsed with the blood in his veins. Growing stronger.

He followed it downstairs to a library. It wasn't as grand as the library at Agatha's Academy of Magic, with crooked and gap-toothed shelves, as if books had been sold off piecemeal. The scent of musty paper hung heavy in the air.

Sikandar didn't read a single title, nor any of the words in the books open upon the desk. He trailed his fingertips along the tomes.

There. *This* book.

Magic seeped from the spine like frost melting on his skin. It looked unremarkable, a slim volume bound in shabby brown cloth. It took him a second to decipher the ornate Viridian lettering along the spine. *A Natural History of Parasites.* When he tried to open the book, the pages felt glued together.

Glamoured.

Under his fingers, brown cloth faded into blue leather. He peeled the glamour away. A golden lock sealed the pages. When he fitted the key into the lock, it clicked.

That was all he needed to know.

He slipped the diary and key inside his coat. Cold magic lingered near his chest.

"Are you lost?" Delicata's voice startled him from the doorway.

"Yes, and distracted. I'm a bit of a bookworm."

She shut the door to the library. "Mr. Zerian," she murmured. "Sikandar. I need your help."

This was unexpected. "How can I help you?"

She had a feverish glint in her eyes. "I don't want to marry Prince Benedict Charming. I don't care how many sorcerers he sent to find his new bride."

"I can remove your name from consideration."

She clutched his wrist. "Aren't you from Azurum?"

"Yes."

"I'm suffocating in this ugly old house." Her fingers tightened around his wrist. "I don't care what my mother wishes. Save me from this life that isn't my own."

He loosened her fingers. "Miss Darlington… Delicata…"

"Take me with you."

She backed him against a bookshelf and kissed him. Stunned, he froze with her lips against his. He caught her shoulder and pushed her back, trying to be gentle.

"Delicata." He sounded hoarse. "No."

"Please," she said, the desperation raw in her voice.

"Goodbye."

He strode out of the library and nearly crashed into a stranger.

Lady Darlington.

It could only be Cinderella's stepmother. Ornate glamours clung to her. Her hair shimmered between purple and silver, and her eyes gleamed an inhuman violet.

Her nostrils flared as if she smelled rot. "Who are you?"

"Mother!" Delicata ran out. Words tumbled from her mouth. "Mr. Sikandar Zerian just arrived. He's a sorcerer sent by Prince Benedict to find his future bride."

Lady Darlington went white. "A sorcerer?"

"Yes, and—"

Her mother slapped her across the face. "You utter fool. Letting a strange boy into the house!"

Eulalia slunk from the parlor. "I had my suspicions."

"And a *magic* boy?"

Delicata's cheeks turned lobster red. "But—"

"Silence!"

Sikandar sidestepped Lady Darlington. "My apologies, ladies, I didn't mean to cause any alarm."

She turned on him. "What do you—?"

"Good afternoon to you!" He caught the doorknob on his way out and shut the door in her face.

He fled from Umberwood Manor into the forest.

ELEVEN

CINDERELLA

Once upon a time, Umberwood Manor had been a home.

While Cinderella's mother and father were still alive, none of the rooms at Umberwood were locked away or shrouded under dust cloths. No windows were shuttered every day. Instead, sunlight poured through air that was not mildewed. In this house, there was space to breathe.

Now, returning to Umberwood choked her throat.

She lurked in the woods alone, so near and yet so far away from ever returning.

Sikandar bolted through the trees.

"What happened?" she said.

"Ran into your stepmother." Panting, he shook his head. "Ran *away* from your stepmother."

"I'm thrilled you have mastered prepositions," she said dryly.

"Also… your stepsister kissed me."

"What?" Cinderella shrieked the word. "Which one?"

"Delicata."

"Kissed you?"

"That's what I just said."

"God!"

What was this twisting in her gut? Jealousy? Her stepsister had kissed Sikandar first, before Cinderella even had the chance. Dragons couldn't kiss.

She had never even kissed anyone before.

"What did you do?" she asked, dreading the answer.

He frowned. "Escaped her clutches."

"Was… was she your first kiss?"

"No." His frown deepened. "Why do you ask?"

"Because then I would have to murder Delicata and bury her in a shallow grave?"

His eyebrows shot skyward. "That seems extreme."

"I'm rather envious."

He rubbed the back of his neck. "Of kissing me?"

"Never mind! I said nothing. Banish the thought from your memories, please."

"Consider it banished," he said, but he still looked confused.

She clasped her taloned hand to her chest. "Did you find the diary?"

"I did, in the library."

"Really?"

"It had been glamoured into *A Natural History of Parasites*. The pages wouldn't even open."

"May I see it?"

He took a small blue book from his jacket. "The key fit the lock. I haven't opened it yet."

She leaned over his shoulder, which was easy enough, since she was taller. When he opened the diary, nothing exploded or burst from the pages. The words had been inked with flourishes that reminded her of curling vines.

Her mother's handwriting.

And on the very first page: *The Diary of Vivendel.*

Sikandar hesitated. "Would you like to read it yourself?"

"I'm not sure I can turn the pages with these claws. Look, I see a ribbon halfway through."

Blue and tattered. He flipped to that page.

January 31st

Queen Eira asked me again, but I refused. I suspect that I may not refuse Her Majesty a third time.

-V

February 2nd

Her Majesty confessed to me that she is expecting a baby, and fears it is already too late. She cannot risk the future heir of Viridia. I must think of the good of the kingdom. I must not be selfish and think only of my own dreams.

Why, then, am I gripped by guilt and indecision?

-V

Cinderella grimaced at the words. "Is she talking about Prince Benedict? Or another baby?"

"I don't know," Sikandar said.

She kept reading.

February 4th

Queen Eira has promised me a reward for my sacrifice. No longer will I have to work as a lady-in-waiting. I will have a title and manor of my own.

Her Majesty does not know this, but I am not certain that I will ever be a mother. As a girl, I survived a terrible pox. The doctor told me I may very well be barren. There is no way to know for certain. I might go for years without a miracle.

If I tell Her Majesty, there will be no question in the matter. The curse will be mine.

-V

Cinderella gasped. "The curse!"

"Should I turn the page?" Sikandar said.

"Please."

February 13th

It is done.

-V

February 15th

I am still in great agony, but the pain lessens with every day.

Her Majesty tells me I have saved Viridia. She dotes upon me as though she were my lady-in-waiting.

Yesterday, His Majesty the King issued a proclamation to announce the upcoming birth of their first child. The kingdom rejoices. The people know nothing of the monstrous curse intended for the heir to the throne.

I alone carry this secret, and pray I will never carry a child.

-V

It felt like ice slid down her spine. "Oh god," she whispered.

She sank onto the fallen leaves, all of the strength abandoning her legs. Her heartbeat whooshed in her ears.

"Cinderella?" Sikandar closed the diary. "Are you all right?"

"My Fairy Godmother told me. She came back to me one night, in the wilderness, and told me I must have been born with the curse. I didn't want to believe her."

"Your Fairy Godmother returned?"

Blackness shrank the edges of her vision. "I feel faint."

"Breathe."

She braced her head in her claws. She focused on filling her lungs until the darkness faded.

"Prince Benedict was meant to be cursed," she said. "Not me."

Sikandar's fingertips touched the back of her neck. "We can still break the curse."

"God, and Umberwood—" She choked on the word.

Her childhood home had been payment for her mother's sacrifice. Nothing more than a bribe.

"When is your birthday?" he asked.

"My birthday?" She lifted her gaze. "Not for another month."

He ran his thumb over his lips, which was distracting enough for her to forget her next question.

"I wonder," he said, "why the curse struck at midnight. At the ball, when everyone was watching."

"It seems awfully convenient."

"Your Fairy Godmother's enchantment may have loosened the threads of the curse."

"Is that… a good thing?"

Sikandar lifted one of his shoulders in a lopsided shrug. "I can't be certain yet. I need to read more about the curse." He flipped backwards through the diary.

"Who cursed Queen Eira? And why?"

He said nothing, squinting at the pages.

Blood rushed through her veins and left her burning with heat. Prince Benedict was galloping around Viridia with his sword, promising to slay the dragon he should have become that night at the ball. He was the true beast.

And she had all but begged him to save Umberwood.

What an utter fool she had been!

"I'm going straight to the castle." She flared her wings. "I'm going to burn it to the ground."

Sikandar's gaze snapped away from the diary. "Excuse me?"

She curled her lips. "Prince Benedict lied to my face. He flirted with me and danced with me when he *knew*."

"Cinderella."

She snarled. "God, I want to destroy his smug smile."

"Cinderella, wait." He pocketed the diary in his jacket. "Prince Benedict is an idiot."

"I know!"

"Which means he may be oblivious. Why would they tell their heir about the curse?"

"Why wouldn't they?"

"Why would he invite you to the ball if he knew?"

"To mock me?" She dug her claws into the dirt. "To kill me in front of everyone?"

He shook his head. "Doubtful. He doesn't seem like the type to plan. We, however, can."

"What are you proposing?"

"Fly to Scaldwell with me. Find the cave of crystals. Once I brew the potion, you can be a girl again. We can return to Knightsend and pretend the curse is broken."

"Why pretend?"

He arched his eyebrows. "You can talk to the royal family instead of burning down the castle. Find out who cursed Queen Eira, and why. Find the truth."

"Isn't it in my mother's diary?"

His eyebrows dropped into a frown. "Unless the king and queen lied to your mother."

She gritted her fangs. "Umberwood was never enough."

"This curse was never meant for you. But we can still break it."

Tears blurred her eyes before spilling down her cheeks. They sizzled on the fallen leaves.

"Sikandar." It hurt to force the words past her aching throat. "I've lost so much already."

He rested his hand on her shoulder, waiting for her permission, until she leaned into his touch. When she bowed her head, he hooked his hands behind her serpentine neck and tugged her into an embrace. He rested his cheek against hers.

"I know what it's like to lose everything," he said.

"How do you keep going?"

"Losing your past can't stop you from finding your future."

She pulled back, just enough to meet his gaze, and god, how she wished she was a girl. She could at least ask him if he wanted to be kissed. Now, she had nothing.

"I'm sorry," she said. "I'm crying all over your silk jacket."

He shrugged. "Enchanted against rain. Though dragon's tears might be a little hotter than rain."

"I ruined your handkerchief before, didn't I?"

"Probably."

She laughed a broken laugh. "Thank you."

TWELVE

SIKANDAR

Scaldwell slumbered under moonlight and snow. They flew over the resort town's hotels and bathhouses without stopping. Cinderella winged her way higher in the sky. Gripping her horns, Sikandar leaned toward the ground, his eyes narrowed against the wind and snowfall.

Far below, magic hummed in the bones of the earth.

"There!" he shouted.

Steam cloaked a meadow. When the breeze shifted, the moon's reflection glittered in pools of aquamarine. Judging by the terrain, these hot springs were inaccessible to tourists, perhaps even secret from most travelers.

Good thing they had flown here.

Cinderella dipped one wing, losing altitude, and drifted in a slow spiral. They landed on a boulder at the edge of a pool. Brimstone scented the steam rising from the water. When she knelt, he slipped from her back and staggered, his legs numb both from riding and the cruel wind.

"Careful!" She caught him by the elbow. "Don't fall in."

Crouching, he dipped his fingertip into the pool. "It's not that hot. We could bathe in it if we wanted."

"Perhaps after we find the cave of crystals?"

"Of course." He bit back a smile. "Then we could open our own inn here, and charge a premium."

"Not an inn. A bed and breakfast."

"Of course." He rubbed the goosebumps on his arms. "We must be close to the crystals."

"How can you tell?"

"Magic."

"What does it feel like?"

Snow creaked underfoot as he walked toward the trees. "Hard to describe. Depends on the magic, but for all kinds, there's always a sensation of raw energy."

"And the cave of crystals?"

"Underground magic is distinctive. Nothing else reverberates in your bones the same way."

She blew out an excited little breath. "Let's hurry."

He flexed his fingers, which were starting to feel like icicles in the glacial cold. Why hadn't he brought gloves? He glanced back longingly at the hot springs. If this was fall in Viridia, he grimaced at the thought of winter.

They trudged through the forest. Boulders slumbered around them under blankets of snow. At the bottom of a cliff, the magic tightened a knot in his gut.

"Here," he whispered.

He pressed his hand against the rock wall. Beneath the slick shell of ice, raw power hummed. He broke away, his head whirling like he stood on the brink of a cliff.

"Sikandar?" she said.

He rubbed his forehead. "Look for an entrance."

"I hope we don't have to dig." She glanced at her talons. "I would rather not break another claw."

Sikandar followed along the cliff. Icicles dripped from a gash in the stone. Beyond, in the darkness, an emerald light glowed inside the heart of the mountains.

They shared a glance.

He dodged between the icicles. The dragon shattered the ice as she followed him. A cloud of steam drifted from the cave like an exhalation before vanishing.

"Amazing," he murmured, and a laugh escaped him.

Green crystals encrusted every surface of the cave, glowing from within. Waterfalls and rivulets tumbled between their dazzling facets before falling into mist-shrouded pools below. Shivers rushed over his skin. Magic sang through the minerals here, and an answer hummed deep in his bones.

"I see it!" Cinderella said. "The Miraculous Deathcap."

"Where?"

She pointed with one claw.

"*Amanita mirabilis*," he said.

A clump of slick mushrooms sprouted from a crystal. They were pale blue, dotted with white, and larger than he had expected. He wrapped his shawl around his fingers before plucking all the deathcaps. Better not to be poisoned.

Water rushed in the silence between them.

"Time to go," he said.

They left the cave of crystals. Steam cloaked the hot springs.

She stayed close to him. "What next?"

He double-checked *Aetheria's Compendium of Transfiguration*, though the words lurked in the shadows.

"Void saffron, ember coriander, and kraken ink." He took a bottle from his pack and corked the Miraculous Deathcaps inside. "But it's too late for the alchemist."

"Can't we simply help ourselves to the ingredients?"

He gave her a look. "I'm a sorcerer, not a sneakthief."

"Heavens no, we wouldn't *rob* the alchemist." She laughed nervously. "We would leave payment, of course."

"Of course," he repeated. "Just breaking and entering?"

"Well… yes."

He sighed. "I should go alone."

"But—"

"Dragons aren't exactly unobtrusive."

"At least let me fly you down to Scaldwell?"

"Just don't let them see you."

She knelt in the snow, folded her wings tight, and waited for him to climb on. He braced himself with a hand on her neck and swung his leg over her back.

This was all still so strange.

"Ready?" she said.

He clutched her horns. "Yes."

She took off in a whirl of snow and mist. The aquamarine pools dwindled below. When the lights of Scaldwell glimmered among the trees, she landed at the edge of town.

"Sikandar." She hesitated. "I…"

He slid from her back. "What is it?"

"Be careful," she murmured.

"I will."

Gods, it was too late to back out now. The indigo dragon leapt into flight and disappeared against the night sky. His exhalation fogged the air.

Time to rob an alchemist.

The sign of a golden serpent marked the alchemist's shop. Sikandar cupped his hands against a window, to block out the glare of moonlight, and peered inside. Jars and boxes of ingredients cluttered the shelves.

Why had he agreed to do this?

He jiggled the doorknob. Locked, though unguarded by magic. He glanced around the deserted street before casting a spell to persuade the locking mechanism to relax. This sorcery drained a little of his power and summoned a yawn.

Quickly, Sikandar slipped into the alchemist's shop.

He closed the door with a soft click, then wrinkled his nose at the scents fighting for supremacy: whiffs of aromas like black pepper, gunpowder, frankincense, and rotting lemons. Fatigue tugged at him, urging him to sit down. He ignored the temptation and tiptoed deeper into the shop.

"Void saffron," he whispered, "ember coriander, kraken ink."

In the back of the shop, the glass doors of a cabinet gleamed. Inside, a vial contained the unmistakable black stamens of the void saffron's bloom. The cabinet door rattled instead of sliding open. Again, he cast a spell to unlock it.

Damn it, he hadn't eaten enough today.

There wasn't time for self-pity, so he took the void saffron and hunted for the rest of the ingredients. He found the ember coriander, its feathery leaves glowing a soft red, and the kraken ink, a thick liquid darker than the night.

After stashing the bottles in his pack, he counted out ten silver coins. Who knew if that covered the prices in Viridia, but it was better than stealing.

He left the coins in a tidy stack on the counter, near a ledger.

"You're welcome," he muttered.

The door crashed open. "Halt! King's guard!"

A rush of streetlight blinded Sikandar. He froze, his legs locked, his hand near the coins.

One of the king's guard edged into the shop, aiming a pistol. "Drop your weapons."

"I don't have any, sir." Cold sweat dotted Sikandar's face. While he talked, he sketched a spell in the air. "Please, put down the gun. I paid for the ingredients. See?"

The guard's finger twitched on the trigger.

Time slowed to a crawl.

Sikandar traced the last stroke of the spell the instant an explosion rattled the windows. The bone-ache of teleportation hit his skeleton, and he jerked into the void.

He fell into a snowy forest.

His ears were ringing from the bang at the alchemist's shop. Heat pierced his left arm like a searing poker. When he touched his bicep, his hand came away red with blood. Teleportation didn't do that, even when it went wrong.

He had been shot.

The bullet must have hit his arm while he was teleporting away. It burned more than hurt, along with the unnerving warmth of his own blood soaking his shirt.

Where the hell was he? He had meant to teleport back to the cave of crystals, but clearly getting shot had skewed his spell. He swore.

He began running across the snow, his feet quick with lingering fear. A glance back showed blood following him like a dotted line. Steam drifted through the trees, a cloud of silver sliced by moonbeams. The hot springs.

"Cinderella!"

When the dragon soared over the trees, a rush of relief swept through him and left him weak.

She landed at his side. "Sikandar! Oh my god, is that blood?"

"King's guard shot me."

"I can't bear to look at blood. It makes me faint!"

"Don't faint. Please. We can't both be unconscious."

His knees betrayed him. He sagged against a tree. No matter how hard he gripped his arm, it wouldn't stop burning. Blackness constricted his vision.

Time to lie down in the snow and sleep.

"Sikandar!" She caught his wrist. "Don't close your eyes."

"Tired," he muttered.

"I need you to help me."

"Can't brew a potion like this."

"No, I need you to walk. This way."

He forced his eyes open. She wrapped her wing around him and urged him onward. He leaned on the dragon, his hand flat on her scales, and relied upon her strength.

Together, they struggled to the pools of aquamarine.

He dropped his pack and followed it down. She tucked it under his head, like a pillow, and covered him with his shawl. Damn, he was getting blood on the wool, wasn't he?

"Lie down!" Cinderella said.

"I am." He wasn't trying to fight. "Gods, it's cold."

She bounded to a fallen branch and snapped it into pieces between her claws. After stacking pine cones for kindling, she ignited the wood.

"Careful," he said. "Don't burn down the forest."

"I know how to build a fire." Nevertheless, she contained the flames within a circle of stones.

"Do you know how to cook?"

"Yes. Why?"

He forced a laugh. "Never teleport on an empty stomach."

"You teleported here? After being shot?" She fussed over his shawl. "Sikandar, be more careful!"

"Either that or get arrested. Or get killed first. Really have made a mess of things, haven't I?"

She pressed her lips together. "You're still bleeding."

"More blood than I expected." Talking about it logically kept terror from snapping at his heels.

"Take off your shirt."

He thought about making a joke, but he couldn't think of one. Grimacing, he braced himself on his good arm before tugging the shirt over his head. The bloody cotton clung to the bullet wound before he peeled it away.

She tore cloth from his ruined shirt. "Hold still."

Showing admirable precision, she bandaged his arm with her talons. She tugged the cotton tight, to slow the bleeding, and finished it with a knot.

Why didn't it hurt like he thought it should?

"Wait here," she said, "and don't die!"

"I'll try my best not to disappoint."

Beating her wings, she launched herself into the air.

Blood seeped through the bandage on his arm. He lay under the shawl again. His eyelids fluttered shut. Snowflakes fell upon his face. He drifted in a twilight between sleeping and waking, magic no more than a faint echo in his bones.

Cinderella landed with a rabbit in her jaws.

"You caught that?" he said, his eyes wide open now.

"You need food." She dropped her prey at his feet. "I suppose you can't eat it raw."

"I'd rather not."

After skinning and gutting the rabbit, she spit-roasted the meat. His teeth chattered despite the fire, the heat no more than a distant sensation on his skin.

"Ah." He clenched his jaw. "It's starting to hurt."

A dull, sickening ache that throbbed with every heartbeat.

"Sikandar! Stay awake."

He focused on the aroma of cooking rabbit. It wasn't enough to spark his appetite, but he knew he had to eat after exhausting his magic on teleportation.

What a terrible sorcerer he was.

"Eat," she said.

She held out a roasted leg of rabbit. He accepted it one-handed. After the first bite, even the mere taste of the meat revived him enough to keep eating.

"More," she commanded.

He did as the dragon said, until nothing but bones remained.

"Thank you," he said. "I'm feeling better."

That was the truth, despite the pain lodged in his arm and the strange numbness in his left hand. When he clenched a handful of snow, it slid between his fingers. Sorcery could heal him. He could do it himself, once he was strong.

His throat unclenched enough for him to breathe.

THIRTEEN

CINDERELLA

Cinderella didn't want to let Sikandar out of her sight.

An ashen hue replaced the warmth in his brown skin. Before she bandaged him, he had been losing enough blood that she feared he would fall asleep and never wake up. Tears blurred her eyes, and she blinked fast to hide them.

"Are you still hungry?" she asked.

"A little." His voice sounded rusty. "You don't have to bring down an entire deer for me."

"Was that a joke?"

He raised his eyebrows. "For you, I try."

"I'm not sure I want to leave you alone."

"Do I look that bad?"

She didn't confirm his suspicions. "How about some chai? Tea does wonders for the constitution."

"Thank you."

He was still using the pack as a pillow, so she gingerly unbuckled it. He leaned away, cradling his injured arm against his chest. The bullet had exited through the back of his arm, so at least she didn't have find it and dig it from his flesh. The very idea made her woozy.

She found a bottle full of glowing red leaves. "What's this?"

"Ember coriander."

"You found it?"

"Along with void saffron and kraken ink." He managed a weak smile. "Don't worry, I paid for them."

"And the king's guards still shot you?"

His smile faded. "What did you expect? I'm not Viridian."

She didn't know what to say except, "I'm sorry."

After finding the copper kettle and tin of chai in his pack, she glanced at the hot springs, then thought better of it and packed the kettle with snow to melt over the fire.

"The king's guards will be looking for me," he said.

"But you teleported away."

"They know I'm a sorcerer. We shouldn't stay here."

Words boiled over inside her. "We're not running away while you're hurt. Sikandar, you could have died."

His mouth hardened. "I was stupid and got caught."

"You are not stupid."

"I will be if we don't escape."

Her temper flared. "We're staying here!"

He flinched before he looked away. Why was she shouting at him when she cared?

God, she cared about him. More than she would ever admit.

"The snow melted," he muttered. "You can add the chai."

Afraid her voice would betray her, she swallowed back everything she wanted to say. She added tea and spices to the kettle. The scent reminded her of him, she realized.

She was realizing a lot of things tonight.

"Maybe you're right," she said. "Maybe we should go to Scaldwell and find a place to sleep."

"The king's guards would find me first."

"Not if we're clever."

"Clever?" He glowered. "If anyone sees a wounded brown boy from Azurum, it's all over."

"You can't be the *only* brown boy in Scaldwell."

He scoffed. "Besides, you would be the only blue dragon."

"Why not a glamour?" If she could have snapped her fingers, she would have. "Disguise yourself as someone else, just long enough to book a room."

He stroked the stubble on his chin, which was quite distracting. "I studied glamours, but I wasn't good at them. Doubtful that I could glamour an entire dragon."

"Don't glamour me. Brew the potion instead."

His sigh clouded the cold. "I can't fault your logic."

"So, it's a yes?"

Jaw clenched, he unpacked a shirt and put it on, avoiding his wound. "I need your help."

"Anything."

"Bring me *Aetheria's Compendium of Transfiguration*, and open it to the recipe, please."

She fetched the book. "I don't understand half of these words."

"Luckily, I do."

"Sarcasm doesn't suit you."

He had the nerve to frown at her, as if this was all her fault. Wasn't it? He had taken a bullet while trying to help her break the curse.

He scooped snow into a tin pot and balanced it on a flat stone by the fire. She kept glancing at him, then glancing away, not wanting him to catch her caring.

Steam hissed from the kettle. "That's the tea," she said.

He glanced at it. "Could you?"

"Of course."

She poured steaming chai into the copper cup for him. His fingertips met her claws, and she retreated from his touch. He sipped the tea before wincing.

"Too hot?" she said.

"But thank you for brewing it."

"You're most welcome." She winced. Formality increased the distance between them.

"It's a shame it's not proper chai, with sugar and milk, but of course this isn't Azurum."

Would she never see him again after he returned to Azurum?

The aquamarine pools glittered like a duchess's best jewelry. Her reflection wavered but did not change. When she sank into the water, it rippled over her scales like warm silk. Above her, pinpricks of starlight pierced the royal blue sky. She sighed.

By the fire, Sikandar muttered what sounded like a swear, judging by the tone.

"What happened?" she said.

"Singed my finger while adding the ember coriander."

"Are you all right?"

He nodded, his expression shadowed. Brewing the potion in a battered tin pot, over a campfire, with only one arm, wasn't the most ideal of circumstances.

She sank lower in the pool, until only her head was above the surface. Like a sea monster in the middle of an unknown sea. The constellations blurred together above, maidens and scorpions and heroes armed with swords.

"Cinderella?"

His voice startled her. "Yes?"

"Wake up."

She jumped out of the pool. Water pattered from her scales onto the rocks. "I wasn't asleep."

"You were snoring."

While he had been brewing the potion in the bitter cold. She wanted to evaporate into mist. "Please accept my apologies. I had meant to keep an eye on you."

"Why?"

"To make sure you are feeling all right."

He coughed suspiciously, as if trying not to laugh. "Thank you, but I'm fine." His eyes glinted in the firelight. "You were only asleep for fifteen minutes, at most."

"Oh."

"Enough time for me to finish brewing the potion."

She perked up. "Now?"

"Yes."

"Really?"

"Yes! Come see for yourself."

She skittered over to him. Quicksilver liquid shimmered inside the tin pot.

"Save it," she said. "We need to fly closer to Scaldwell."

Sikandar poured the potion into three glass bottles. He corked the remaining Miraculous Deathcap in another bottle, then stashed the ingredients in his pack.

"Ready?" she said.

He dipped his head. "Keep low and out of sight. Land on the outskirts of Scaldwell." After struggling to pick up his pack, he clutched his wounded arm.

"Let me carry that for you."

"Thank you."

"Are you sure you can hold on?"

He hesitated. "Yes."

She lay down in the snow and let him climb onto her back. He gripped one of her horns.

"Ready." Pain sharpened his voice. "Easy."

Cinderella swept her wings and leapt into the night. She soared just over the trees. Needles bristled under her claws, near enough that snow scattered in her wake.

She prayed he wouldn't faint and plummet to his death.

Beyond the forest, the lights of Scaldwell twinkled in the night. She glided down in an empty field. When she landed, he slid from her back and staggered against her.

"Sikandar!"

He shook his head. "Dizzy."

She resisted the urge to check his bandage. He dropped to his knees, but it was to unbuckle his pack.

He poured the potion into the copper cup. "Drink."

"What if it doesn't work?"

"Then I can brag about nothing but a thrilling gunshot scar."

"I suppose you *are* feeling better," she muttered, "if you want to joke about your wound."

The potion sloshed in the cup, as thin as wine. She brought it to her lips before knocking it back.

The first taste: lingering chai.

The second: midnight bitterness and a sour-sweet flavor like jam stewed from damson plums.

"Well?" he said.

"That's peculiar." She kept swallowing, the potion refusing to leave her tongue. "I don't think—"

Magic crashed over her in a wave and dragged her underwater.

Pain crushed her in its fist. Her skeleton twisted, bones grinding into new shapes. She clenched her teeth to keep herself from crying out. They ached as they shrank from fangs to a dull human bite. She lost the armor of her scales and the daggers of her claws. Her wings withered away.

The magic receded and left her washed up.

"Cinderella?"

Shivering, on her hands and knees, she opened her eyes. Snow burned against her raw pink skin, as if her dragon scales had been scraped clean. She flexed her fingers.

"I'm a girl again," she whispered.

Why didn't she feel relieved? Just numb.

Sikandar cleared his throat. "You might want this."

He held out his shawl to her, waiting. Oh god, she was naked. He averted his gaze, but how much had he seen already? She snatched the shawl from him and clutched it to herself. Standing too fast, she stumbled. He caught her by the wrist.

She gasped at the jolt of his skin against hers, no armor of scales between them.

One touch, unlike any other she had ever felt before. Heat flooded her body and left her shivering. Her lips parted before she licked them. When he released her wrist, the warm imprint of his fingers faded in the cold night air.

She stole a glance into his eyes. "You're taller than me."

He brought his knuckles to his mouth. "You don't have blue eyes."

"They're hazel, aren't they?"

"But you were a blue dragon."

"I was wearing a blue dress at the ball." She bounced on her heels and resisted the urge to spin. "You broke the curse."

He shrugged. "For now."

She threw her arms around him. "Thank you!"

The sorcerer froze like she had attacked him.

She leapt back. A blush scorched her face. He stared at her without blinking, his lips parted and his eyebrows sky-high.

"Your arm," she stammered. "I'm sorry! Did I hurt you?"

"Not much."

"I'm so sorry." The shawl slipped a little. She tugged it up and hid her smile behind her hair.

He shoved his hands into his pockets. "I have spare clothing for you. It might be too big, but it's better than nothing."

"Thank you." She wanted to hug him again but didn't dare.

Like a gentleman, he turned around while she dressed, his hands folded behind his back. His clothes were only a little too long for her. Barefoot, she wiggled her toes, which were starting to go numb in the cold.

"I don't suppose you have another pair of shoes?" she said.

"Not in your size." He hesitated. "Are you decent?"

"Now I am."

When he turned back, he twisted his mouth. "I wonder how long the potion will last."

Her smile wilted. "I'm more worried about you and that gunshot wound."

"I'll live." His shoulders straightened. "Time for the glamour."

She had never seen a glamour cast before. Her stepsisters and stepmother bought bottled enchantments or went into town for beautification appointments.

"No mirror," he muttered, "and only one good hand."

His fingers sketched invisible symbols in the air, which rippled like heat rising higher. He closed his eyes and walked through the shimmer. His black hair faded to blond, and his skin turned a shade paler than even Cinderella's.

When he opened his eyes, they were forget-me-not blue.

"How do I look?" Sikandar said, his voice unchanged.

"Like a parody of a Viridian boy."

"Why are you grimacing?"

She shuddered. "Your eyes remind me of Prince Benedict's."

"Do they?" Like he hadn't even noticed.

"Can we hurry? Before my toes freeze?"

He offered his hand, as if escorting her out of this snowy field and onto the dance floor. She hesitated, since he looked like a stranger, before taking it.

Together, they walked into the sleepy town of Scaldwell.

"Oh!" Her excited gasp puffed in the air. "Look!"

He tensed, his fingers tightening around hers. "What?"

"A bed and breakfast."

Snow blanketed the steep roof of a charming wooden chalet. Moonlight glinted on a hanging sign, which had been carved and gilded with the classic Viridian symbol for a bed and breakfast: a dormouse curled in a teacup.

"Can we stay there?" she said. "Please?"

"I can't refuse, can I?" A smile shadowed his mouth. "That seems like a dangerous proposition."

She tugged him closer. "I see a light inside. It's not too late."

When they entered the chalet's tiny lobby, warmth poured over them from a crackling fire. A white-haired old man bent over a desk, jotting down notes in a ledger.

"Good evening," said the innkeeper. "Welcome to Hotel Edelweiss."

It seemed rather grand to call this sweet little chalet a hotel. Lord, this place was charming.

"Good evening, sir," Sikandar said, in a very Viridian accent.

"Call me Chester. Looking for lodging?"

"Yes, a room for the night," Sikandar said.

"Very good. Your names?"

"Simon Darlington and my wife, Ginevra."

Wife? Heat scalded Cinderella's cheeks, but she didn't dare correct him. She faked a smile.

"Newlyweds?" said Chester.

"Yes, sir."

"Congratulations, Mr. and Mrs. Darlington. Would you like our honeymoon suite? It has a tub in the bathroom with water from the hot springs. Quite lovely."

"Please."

After Sikandar paid, Chester beckoned them deeper into the chalet. The innkeeper didn't seem to notice her bare feet, or their lack of wedding rings. He unlocked the door to the honeymoon suite and waved them inside.

"Breakfast is at seven o'clock sharp," Chester said.

Humming, he lit the fairy lamps and fed wood to the banked fire. The room prepared to his satisfaction, he handed Sikandar the keys and smiled in a jolly way.

"Have a good night!" Chester waved as he left.

Cinderella locked the door behind him. "Newlyweds?"

Sikandar shrugged and tossed the keys onto a nightstand. "You could have been my fiancée, but that seems riskier in Viridia. Too scandalous to share a room together."

"I could have been your sister!" she spluttered.

"Wouldn't two beds cost more than one?"

She scoffed. "I'm sure the honeymoon suite is the costliest one in Hotel Edelweiss." She folded her arms across her chest. "And now we *do* have to share a bed."

He shrugged. "I can sleep on the floor."

"You can't!"

"What kind of gentleman would take the bed?"

"A *wounded* one."

He dropped his pack on a chair and tossed his shawl over the back. "Don't worry about me."

"But you're hurt. I care about you."

"Why?" He went into the bathroom but left the door open. "We both know why I'm breaking the curse." The sink's tap squeaked, followed by the rush of water.

She did remember his promise, but so much had changed.

Hadn't it?

He left the bathroom, water clinging to his face. He had broken the glamour. She couldn't look away from the curve of his lips or his impossibly long eyelashes. Everything unspoken buzzed inside her ribs like a bottle of fireflies.

"What happens at Knightsend?" she said.

"We hope the potion holds."

That wasn't what she meant. "You don't understand."

"You're right." His eyebrows arrowed in a frown. "I don't."

FOURTEEN

SIKANDAR

Why was she looking at him like that? Like she wanted him to say something, do something? Firelight glittered in her hazel eyes, an echo of the dragon within her.

He couldn't think straight. He strode across the room to put more distance between them. When he leaned against the wall, pain stabbed his wounded arm.

"Sikandar?" she said. "Are you all right?"

He clutched his bicep. "Forgot for a moment."

"Lie down." Concern sharpened her voice. "Please. I insist that you take the bed tonight."

After glancing at the quilt, he shook his head. "I'm dirty."

"Isn't there a tub in the bathroom? With water from the hot springs? You're paying for the honeymoon suite, so you might as well take advantage of it."

"Right."

Clenching his jaw against the pain, he stripped off his shirt. She looked away, even though he had been shirtless before, but of course it had never felt like this before. Tension thickened the silence between them. Before she could speak, he grabbed his pack and retreated to the bathroom.

His heart wouldn't stop pounding.

He couldn't stop thinking about the heat in Cinderella's eyes. Like she wanted more from him.

After locking the door, he took off the rest of his clothes and knelt by the tub. When he twisted the tap, steaming water poured out. It smelled faintly of brimstone.

He climbed into the tub and ducked underwater.

His pulse rushed in his ears. He closed his eyes and held his breath until his lungs burned.

Sikandar.

The jinni whispered in his ears.

Come to me.

He burst from the water with a gasp. Shaking his hair from his eyes, he gripped the edges of the tub. Steam clouded the air. He waited for it to darken, to solidify into the shape of the jinni. But he remained alone.

Cinderella didn't know.

She didn't know *him.*

He worked the soap into lather and tried to scour the lingering guilt from his skin. Clean, he toweled himself off and dressed in a pair of cotton trousers. His wounded arm slowed him down. Damn, he had gotten the bandage wet.

In the bedroom, Cinderella gazed through the window.

"Better?" she said.

Her voice still belonged to a blue dragon. Hard to believe she was a girl, if only for now.

"Yes." He avoided looking at her. "The bathroom is all yours."

"Thank you."

While she took a bath, he removed the bandage and inspected the wound in the mirror. It had stopped bleeding, but his skin looked red and angry.

Sickened, he forced himself to look away from his reflection.

Worse, when he tried to clench his left hand, his fingers still felt weak and useless.

Gods.

Sikandar sank onto the bed and stared at the flickering glow of the fairy light on the nightstand. A simple enchantment, trapped in cut glass. He focused on the magical flame until it burned brighter, then let it die down.

He was a Zerian. An evil sorcerer. A murderer.

He was wrong to hope for love.

Cinderella returned, wringing her hair in a towel, her cheeks still pink from the bath. He imagined her in the water for an infinitesimal fraction of a second, before he banished the thought of her naked from his mind.

He had, of course, already seen her naked when she transformed.

"Are you all right?" she said.

"Yes," he lied.

"Oh, your bandage! You need a new one."

She tore another strip of cloth from his ruined shirt and wrapped it around his arm, her fingers gentle, her face even gentler. He looked away.

"Sikandar," she said.

"Yes?"

"I know you have to return to Azurum." She exhaled. "Just let me have this one night?"

His shoulders stiffened. "What are you asking?"

"There's only one bed. We could, perhaps, sleep together." She blushed so red her freckles vanished. "Only in the most innocent sense! I'm not asking for more."

"I wasn't imagining more until you mentioned innocence."

"Sikandar!" She tied off the bandage. "You know what I mean."

He struggled not to smile. "You might have to elaborate."

"I would like to lie next to you tonight." She was still blushing. "On the same bed."

"Go ahead," he said, amazed he sounded casual.

He braced himself on his unhurt arm and moved closer to the edge, to give her space. She fluffed a pillow with exaggerated care before she lay beside him.

He had never been in bed with a girl before, even like this, and his heart hammered against his ribcage. He breathed in, breathed out. Just to cool his blood.

"Tomorrow," he said, "we should return to Knightsend."

"Already?"

"I suspect the potion won't last beyond morning."

"What a shame. After I promised you would love the breakfast at a bed and breakfast." She exaggerated a pout. "How much of the potion did you brew?"

He thought of the quicksilver liquid, bottled in his pack. "Enough for two more doses."

She sighed. "I suppose we shouldn't waste it on breakfast."

"Better breakfast than Knightsend Castle."

"What do you mean?"

"Find out how long the potion lasts before confronting the royal family of Viridia. I doubt any of them would react favorably to you turning back into dragon."

"True. They won't believe you've broken the curse."

"After you drink the second dose, they will." He forced out a bitter laugh. "By the time that wears off, I will be long gone with the Jewel of Oblivion."

The sheets rustled as she clenched them. "Abandoning me?"

It sounded so cruel. "I didn't mean it like that."

"I'm not sure what else you could mean."

"I can't stay at Knightsend. That would ruin any chance you have of finding the truth."

She let out a shuddering sigh. "I don't want to do this alone."

"But you must."

"And you must return to Azurum?"

Her words hollowed out his chest. "Yes."

"Alone?"

"I don't—what? Are you asking to come with me?"

She rolled to face him. "A dragon in Azurum might be as useful as a sorcerer in Viridia."

"Not very?" he said, wryly.

"Flying and breathing fire have their perks." She bit back a smile. "But Sikandar, after all you have done for me, I would like to help you in return."

Why? Honor? Pity?

"I did this for the Jewel of Oblivion," he said.

"At first?"

"At first," he agreed. "I…"

"Go on."

"I can't promise anything, but my third wish might be enough to break the curse forever."

She leaned closer to him. "The jinni?"

"Yes." He ignored the twist in his guts. "Though I lost the lamp in the deserts of Azurum."

Intentionally, though he didn't mention that secret shame.

She looked into his eyes. "You would do that for me?"

Yes, without hesitation. But he couldn't confess that to her yet.

Instead, he said, "The potion won't be enough. Unless you want to keep drinking it forever."

"If we found the lamp, couldn't I make the wish myself?"

"Sadly, no." He grimaced. "The jinni will remain chained to me until I make all three wishes. Otherwise, my family would have taken the lamp from me."

"They sound delightful." She raised her eyebrows. "But you have suggested yet another way that you might help me, when I would like to return the favor."

He gazed into the shadows. "You owe me nothing."

"I beg to differ."

"I want to make my last wish and be rid of the jinni forever. She plagues my thoughts."

"Why wouldn't you use the wish for yourself?"

He clenched his jaw. "It would be wasted."

"Why not wish for the Jewel of Oblivion?"

"I can't. Not without finding the lamp first, which requires me to return to Azurum." He raked his fingers through his hair. "And I can't return while I'm banished. Setting foot on Azuri soil would equal imprisonment or death."

"So, the jewel will let you go home?"

"Yes."

"Sikandar." She tucked her hair behind her ears, an endearing gesture. "Let me know how I can help you, if you want my help. You don't need to return to Azurum alone."

He swallowed hard. "Understood."

She jumped out of bed, snuffed the fairy lights, and climbed under the sheets. He held still, so he wouldn't touch her by accident, and remembered to keep breathing.

"Good night, Sikandar."

"Good night."

What if he asked her for a kiss? Would she say yes?

Gods, he didn't have the guts.

When he returned to Azurum, he couldn't hide his past life. He couldn't pretend to be anyone but a Zerian. She wanted a Sikandar who was nothing more than a mirage.

Sikandar wished his dreams were his own. Whenever he tried to sleep, memories choked his thoughts, like an overgrown thicket of thorns in his skull.

He couldn't forget the night of his sister's wedding.

Jawahir married King Ali of Azurum without a word, her face hard, while her new husband grinned like he had won a prize. Her last husband, Murad, had been a handsome, small-minded man. When Murad died from the bite of a well-placed viper, she mourned him for only a month.

A paragon of the Zerian family.

In the palace courtyard, moths bumped drunkenly against lanterns, knocking powder from their wings. Jasmine and honeysuckle fought with spices in the lingering heat of a summer evening. Red wine burbled over a white marble fountain. From the wrong angle, it looked like blood.

The bride and groom sat on silk cushions by the fountain. They smiled and greeted their guests.

Jawahir shimmered as a bride should. Bangles gilded her arms. Emeralds and sapphires had been woven in her braid, the jewels echoing the meaning of her name.

Over the whirl of the wedding, Sikandar met his sister's gaze.

Jawahir stared back with glittering black eyes, shadowed by kohl, and he didn't recognize the emotion. Sharper than steel, more brittle than glass. Jawahir attacked life like a tiger did prey. Sometimes, he felt like that prey.

A shiver crawled down Sikandar's spine. He looked away, pretending to be interested in a pretty oud player. When the musician winked at him, warmth crept in his cheeks. He distracted himself with saffron rice pilaf studded with currants and pistachios, slow-cooked lamb stew, and endless *naan* hot from the oven, shimmering with melted butter.

Jawahir ate nothing. King Ali drank enough wine to drown in.

Did the wish dry the king's mouth with a secret, undefinable sense of dread? Did he know, deep in his gut, that he had never fallen in love with his bride?

Stomach churning, Sikandar walked to a copper samovar of tea. A servant offered him honey-drizzled pastries—a dozen layers of flaky dough stuffed with ground walnuts. He waved her away before pouring himself a cup of what turned out to be pink milk tea, a chai the color of roses.

The jinni's lamp chilled his heartbeat.

He slipped his hand inside his jacket. His fingertips touched brass cold with slumbering magic.

"Sikandar!"

He grimaced at the sound of Zafar's voice. "What is it?"

"Doesn't Jawahir look angry?"

Zafar, his eldest brother, pursed his lips with faux concern. The same lips that girls gossiped about kissing. Zafar was too handsome for his own good. He had his silk coat tailored to flatter his lean polo player's muscles.

"I don't know why," Sikandar said. "She's marrying a king."

Zafar poured himself a cup of chai before sipping it pensively. "He's not even an old, fat king."

"He's certainly drunk."

The middle brother, Taj, drifted over to the samovar. He balanced a pastry on a plate of hammered brass, as delicately as if it were a relic. He had curly hair and a wide-eyed look that often got him into—and out of—trouble.

"Have you seen more of these pastries?" Taj said.

Zafar rolled his eyes. "Really? You're thinking about food, with so many beautiful girls around?"

Taj shrugged. "Good food." He bit the pastry.

Zafar clapped him on the shoulder. "Wish me luck. I'm off to talk to that oud player."

"Good luck," Sikandar muttered.

His brothers knew about the jinni. Even while he held his breath, waiting for the second wish to crumble into dust, they celebrated their good fortune.

As night verged on dawn, Sikandar escaped his family.

He abandoned the palace and teleported deep into the desert. Sand undulated to the horizon, dunes glittering in the moonlight. The lamp rested leaden in his pocket.

Two wishes would never be enough for them.

He dropped to his knees and dug at the sand with his hands. It kept spilling back into the hole until he swore and cast a freezing spell. He tossed the lamp inside.

When he broke the spell, the desert devoured the lamp.

FIFTEEN

CINDERELLA

Cinderella woke before Sikandar. His eyelashes shadowed his cheeks. She couldn't stop gazing at his beautiful mouth. What would his lips feel like under hers?

Heat scalded her face. Rather than let him catch her staring, she slipped out of bed and escaped to the bathroom. When she returned, he was yawning.

"Breakfast?" she said brightly.

He frowned, his hair rumpled from the pillow. "The potion?"

"Hasn't run out yet."

"Wait." He rubbed the sleep from his eyes. "Let me put on the glamour before we go."

A necessary illusion, even though she found his disguise much less appealing than reality. Her stomach fluttered when she remembered their ruse from last night.

She was pretending to be his newlywed wife.

Sikandar grabbed his pack and shawl, she noted, no doubt ready for a quick exit.

Hotel Edelweiss served breakfast as a buffet: poached eggs on toast, bacon, sticky buns, hothouse strawberries, and crumpets with butter, lemon curd, and blackcurrant jam. A merry fireplace crackled in the dining room while snowflakes drifted down outside. Coffee and toast scented the air.

Cinderella clasped her hands as if in prayer. "Finally!"

Her mouth watered as she helped herself to a few rashers of bacon and a sugar-glazed sticky bun that smelled delightfully of cinnamon. Sikandar chose a lone crumpet, with a pat of butter, then followed her to a corner table.

"Morning!" A steel-haired old woman wheeled over a trolley. "You're the first ones down to breakfast."

"We could hardly wait." Sikandar glanced at Cinderella.

"My name is Golda," said the old woman. "Tea or coffee?"

"Tea," they said together, purely by accident.

"Perfect." Golda smiled. "You must be the newlyweds in the honeymoon suite."

Cinderella's cheeks heated. "We are," she stammered.

"Chester and I have been married for an eternity." Golda winked at them both.

Sikandar reached across the table and clasped Cinderella's hand. He smiled in a devastatingly handsome way, as if he were spellbound by his new bride.

Gracious, she couldn't swoon over breakfast.

Golda poured them each a cup of tea, then left the pot along with cream and sugar. "Enjoy!"

"We will, thank you," Sikandar said, as Golda left the room.

Cinderella smoothed her napkin in her lap. "You're too good at pretending," she muttered.

"It's not hard to pretend."

"No need for flattery."

He managed to look angelic. "I would never lie to you."

Her ears hot, she spooned sugar into her tea. This was only a ruse. Wasn't it?

He buttered his crumpet meticulously. She focused on breakfast, trying not to wolf it down. Dragon it down? She stifled a laugh as she bit into the sticky bun.

"*Mmm.*" She tilted her head skyward. "Heavenly."

"Am I missing out?" Sikandar said.

He had half of a crumpet left, so she nodded. "Would you bring me some of the strawberries while you're at the buffet? And a slice of toast with poached egg?"

"My pleasure."

They were alone in the dining room, so she licked sticky bun icing from her fingers. Sikandar caught her doing it and raised his eyebrows, but didn't protest. He set down another plate with strawberries and egg on toast.

"Thank you," she said.

She poked the poached egg with her fork and let the golden yolk seep into the toast.

"You were right," Sikandar said.

Crunching into the toast, she raised her eyebrows. "Hmm?"

"About bed and breakfasts. I see the appeal."

She polished off the egg and toast. When she picked up a strawberry, her nails stabbed the red fruit.

Not nails.

Claws.

They slid from her fingertips like those of a cat. Unlike a cat's claws, they lengthened into wicked crystal talons. She snatched a napkin to hide her hands.

"Your eyes." Sikandar spoke in an urgent murmur. "They have gone from hazel to gold."

"Potion?" she whispered.

"No. Not yet." He clasped her hand and tugged her to her feet. "We have to go. Quickly."

They fled from the Hotel Edelweiss.

Plunged into the cold, she hugged herself. God, she was still barefoot in the snow. Her teeth began to chatter. He tossed his shawl around her shoulders.

Burning prickled her arms. Blue scales cracked her skin.

"This way," Sikandar said.

He placed his hand on her back, a gesture that felt protective, and guided her ahead. They hurried through the streets of Scaldwell, avoiding passersby.

A cramp bent her double. She staggered against him.

He held her until the pain faded. "Keep going."

"I can't," she gasped.

"You can. See? There's the forest."

Her hair tumbled in her face. "I'm sorry."

"You don't need to apologize."

His words granted her the strength to keep going. She followed him into the snowy trees, where at last she could let the dragon out. She hugged herself, her hands pressed against her arms, losing the softness of her skin to armor.

"Turn around," she said.

He did as she asked, and she stripped her borrowed clothes from her body. Shuddering, she fell to her hands and knees, fighting the inevitable transformation.

Had she lost her one chance to kiss him?

If only she had been braver.

Her hands clenched fistfuls of snow as her spine arched. Wings burst from her shoulder blades. She groaned through clenched fangs and closed her eyes. The curse unfurled through her body like a poisonous flower in bloom.

She opened her eyes. A dragon again.

"It's over," she said. "Back to hideous beast."

Sikandar's exhalation clouded the air. "You're beautiful."

"I don't believe you." She flattened her wings against her spine. "Besides, it doesn't matter if you think I'm beautiful or not. I'm the one who has to be a dragon."

"Why would I lie to you?"

"So I won't roast you like a marshmallow?"

A sad smile bent his mouth. "That feels like so long ago."

"It does."

"And now it's time to say goodbye."

Darkness fell as they flew from Scaldwell to Knockingham. Few lights winked in the velvet blackness beneath them. On the outskirts of the city, Cinderella landed and drank the second dose of the potion. This time, she craved the midnight bitterness and the hard rush of transformation.

Shivering, she dressed quickly in the cold night. Sikandar waited with his back turned.

"Ready," she said, though she wasn't sure she would ever be.

He met her gaze. His face looked gray in the shadows. He hadn't complained the whole flight here, but he still cradled his wounded arm against his chest.

"Remember," he said, "we both need to tell the same story."

"I know."

"Otherwise, this will all be for nothing."

She hugged herself tight. "I'm no good at lying."

"Tell fragments of the truth. You're a girl again, aren't you?"

She twisted her mouth. "Momentarily."

"Let's go."

Knockingham slumbered behind an old wall, built for bygone days, though the city still closed its gates after nightfall. They stopped at the gatehouse.

One of the guards slouched behind a barred window, lanternlight flickering over his face. "State your name and business." He sounded supremely bored.

"Sikandar Zerian of Azurum. I'm here on royal business."

The guard yawned. "Sure you are."

Another guard clattered down from the ramparts and lifted a lantern to their faces. "That's the sorcerer, you idiot. Captain of the guard told us to keep a lookout."

The first guard straightened with a jerk. "If he's the sorcerer, where's the dragon?"

Cinderella stepped into the light. "Here."

"You?"

"I'm the girl who turned into a dragon at the stroke of midnight. He broke the curse."

Both guards shared a glance.

"His Majesty will deal with you," said the second guard.

The gate rattled open.

The guards marched them through the streets. On the cliff, Knightsend loomed over the city like a gargoyle in its aerie. They climbed the road to the castle.

Candles guttered as wind gusted inside the castle's entrance hall. The guards escorted them into a gloomy library that smelled of sleek leather and cigars.

King Archibald sat behind a desk designed to be imposing. Bejeweled rings glinted on his meaty knuckles, which he rapped against the desk's polished wood.

"Bring them here," he said.

A guard shoved Sikandar between his shoulder blades. He stumbled into a perfunctory bow. Before anyone could touch Cinderella, she dipped into a curtsy.

"Your Majesty," she said.

"As promised, I broke the curse," Sikandar said. "Cinderella is no longer a dragon."

"I'm not bloody well blind," King Archibald grumbled.

"As payment, you promised me the Jewel of Oblivion."

"Queen Eira did. But they tell me you burglarized an alchemist's shop in Scaldwell."

"They failed to notice the money I left on the counter." Sikandar shrugged. "Your Majesty."

"Impertinence won't do you any favors, boy."

Sikandar clenched his jaw, one of the muscles ticking.

"Your Majesty." Cinderella kept her gaze downcast. "It was my idea to take ingredients from the alchemist's shop and leave coins on the counter. We never meant to rob anyone of anything, and Sikandar was only trying to help me."

King Archibald grimaced. "To hell with the alchemist."

"Your Majesty?"

"Theft is the least of my worries. What do you want?"

"Once again, the Jewel of Oblivion," Sikandar said.

"Not you," said King Archibald. "*Her.*"

Sweat dampened under her arms. "I… I had hoped to speak with Prince Benedict Charming."

"Why?"

Fragments of the truth. She could do that. "When he invited me to the ball, I thought it a dream come true. The curse turned my dream into a nightmare."

"And you into a nightmarish beast."

She met His Majesty's gaze. "I'm not a beast! Not now. I'm a girl, with a girl's feelings."

"What are these *feelings*?"

"I want a second chance at happily ever after."

The king's chair creaked beneath his bulk as he leaned back. "With my son?"

She knew what she must say. "Yes."

The word left a sour taste in her mouth.

The king waved imperiously. "Summon my son at once. I grow weary of this whole debacle."

"Yes, Your Majesty." One of the guards hurried out.

As she waited for Prince Benedict, her stomach clenched. Shame? Anticipation? She wasn't sure. She glanced at Sikandar, but he was avoiding her gaze.

"Your Majesty," Sikandar said. "The dragon is gone."

The king stared him down for a long moment, as if the sorcerer might change his mind. "And you will be paid." He snapped his fingers at the remaining guard. "Bring the sorcerer to the treasury. Give him the Jewel of Oblivion."

"Thank you, Your Majesty."

Sikandar strode to the door, but halted on the threshold. When he glanced back at Cinderella, she shivered. God, she couldn't fathom the depths in his dark eyes. If she embraced him goodbye, would he hold her tight, the rest of them be damned?

Would he kiss her?

"*Amanita mirabilis*," he said.

And then he left her without another word.

King Archibald spoke. "What the devil did he say?"

"I haven't the slightest clue," she lied.

But he had reminded her of the temporary nature of her humanity.

The sorcerer was gone.

Tears blurred her eyes. She blinked fast to hide them, but couldn't hold them back any longer when Prince Benedict arrived. She stifled ugly sobs against her knuckles.

Benedict stared at her in dismay. "Cinderella?"

"I'm sorry." She hid her face in her hands. "May I—may I have a handkerchief?"

Silently, the prince offered her one made of fine linen.

She dabbed at her eyes before she surrendered niceties and blew her running nose. Dressed in borrowed clothes, her hair dirty, she was surely hideous.

The king growled out a sigh. "Benedict, the curse is broken. She's yours now."

Yours. A chill shivered down her spine. What did that mean?

"Take her out of here. Find her a bedroom."

"Yes, Father."

Benedict offered his arm to her. When she rested her hand on the crook of his elbow, his muscles tensed beneath her touch, but he managed to smile at her.

"Cheer up," he said. "No need to cry."

She swallowed back a sob. Did he know the dragon curse had been meant for him?

Benedict navigated the shadowed corridors of Knightsend. Servants bowed or curtseyed as they passed, but she could feel their stares drilling into her back.

They stopped at an oak door.

"Here you are," Benedict said. "The Rose Room."

With a slight smirk and a flourish of his hand, he flung open the door. She pressed her fingers to her lips. Illuminated by candlelight, a bedchamber glistened in pink silk and crystal, like a rose bejeweled with dew. Her bare feet sank into the plush rug when she stepped inside. It was impossible to resist wriggling her toes in the luxury underfoot.

A princess belonged here.

She folded the handkerchief into smaller and smaller squares, hiding the tearstains on the prince's monogram. When she offered it to him, he shook his head.

"Keep it," he said.

"Thank you."

Benedict kept blinking whenever he looked at her. "Why did you come back?"

"I couldn't stop thinking of that night at the ball."

Which was completely true. She pressed her lips together and pretended to be demure.

He inspected her face as if the dragon still lingered. "The curse is truly broken?"

"Yes," she lied, but her blood turned to ice in her veins.

The potion.

Sikandar had taken the last dose with him, along with the rest of the Miraculous Deathcaps.

"What is it?" Benedict said. "You're as white as snow."

"The sorcerer. He has something of mine."

Benedict's nostrils flared. "He stole it?" He reached for his waist as if expecting a sword.

"No." She stopped him with a hand on his chest. "He's not a thief! He must have forgotten. But I have to find him."

"Where did he go?"

"The treasury."

"Follow me."

They spiraled down a tower staircase, footsteps echoing off stone, and ducked through a door. Mildew tainted the grandeur of a wood-carved hallway. At the end of the hallway, brass monsters snarled on a door that had to be the treasury. Two guards protected the riches within.

"Where's the sorcerer?" Benedict said.

"Gone, Your Highness," said the guard. "Escorted him out of the castle moments ago."

Cold rushed over her skin. "Excuse me."

She dashed down the hallway and whirled up the spiral staircase, around and around. Dizzy, she retraced her steps to the entrance hall. She shoved through the groaning doors of the castle and stumbled into the night.

She ran down the drive, the stones cold under her bare feet.

"Sikandar!"

He waited for her on the road. "Cinderella?"

Hope shone in his eyes, bright in the moonlight, and stopped her in her tracks. She clutched the stitch in her ribs, unable to speak, not sure what to say.

"*Amanita mirabilis*," he repeated. "You forgot the potion."

"Oh." The word escaped her as a puff of air.

He had meant to remind her.

Sikandar rummaged in his pack. "Keep this safe. It's the last dose." He held out a bottle, the quicksilver potion shimmering within.

Her hands trembling, she looked for a place to hide the bottle in her borrowed clothes. She glanced back at the castle, praying the darkness hid them.

Praying Prince Benedict hadn't cared enough to follow.

"You have pockets in the trousers," Sikandar said. "There."

"Thank you."

He hesitated. "I should go. Before anyone sees us."

"Will you take the Jewel of Oblivion and return to Azurum? Will I never see you again?"

He averted his gaze. "I don't know."

A knot in her chest tugged tighter and tighter, her longing turned into agony.

"Good night," he said, as if this wasn't also goodbye.

"Sikandar, wait. Please. Just—"

"Cinderella." Pain roughened his voice. He looked away.

"May I kiss you?"

"Gods." He turned back, his face half in shadow. "Yes."

They collided in a crooked kiss. She touched her hand to his cheek and nudged him straight. He tasted sweet, like chai. He exhaled against her lips before kissing her back deeply, his fingers tangled in her long hair. Trembling, she clung to his neck with one hand. Her other hand rested against his cheekbone, the rasp of stubble so thrilling and strange.

They broke apart.

His mouth looked so soft and vulnerable. She pressed her hand above her heart, which hammered against the cage of her ribs. The world contracted to a pinpoint.

"Say something," she whispered.

SIXTEEN

SIKANDAR

She looked at him so expectantly, but all words had fled his mind. The kiss left him thunderstruck, his skin still tingling with lightning. He touched her silky hair, the color of apricots in the moonlight, and tucked it behind her ear.

Finally, his brain caught up with his body.

"Cinderella..." He sounded hoarse, so he cleared his throat. "You know it's too late."

A shuddering sigh escaped her. "It's never too late."

"I can't stay."

"Wait for me," she said. "Let me come with you."

"I can't give you what you deserve."

"Why?"

"I'm Sikandar Zerian of Azurum."

"That's exactly who I wanted to kiss." Her eyes glimmered. "I've never been allowed to want anything before. I've never even kissed another boy before you."

"I was your first kiss?"

"Yes."

"I'm flattered," he said, and he meant it. "But I can't be your happily ever after."

"I refuse to believe that." She touched her fingertips to his cheek, tentative at first, and then with more certainty. "Kiss me again," she murmured.

How could he say no?

This time when he kissed her, she leaned against the length of his body, and the shape of her fit him like a puzzle piece. An involuntary groan escaped him. She hooked both hands behind his neck and dragged him even closer.

It hurt too much to pretend.

He retreated from her embrace. "Goodbye, Cinderella." His voice snagged on her name. "I have a long road ahead of me before I'm home."

Abandoning Knightsend, Sikandar walked to Knockingham and wandered the streets. Pea-soup fog clung to the city and dulled the sharp edges of bricks and iron. He found an inn, the Marmalade Cat, and paid for a room.

He locked the door, tossed his pack on the bed, and slumped beside it on the floor. Bracing his elbows on his knees, he pressed his hands to his gritty eyes.

He ignored the ache where his heart had once been.

When Cinderella burst from the castle, her hair streaming behind her in the night, for one stupid moment he had been tempted to ask her to run away with him. But he couldn't do that to her. Couldn't drag her into his own failures. Especially not after the right kiss at the wrong time.

He unpacked the reason he had come to Viridia.

The Jewel of Oblivion.

Cradled in his hand, as big as a goose egg, the gemstone glittered the deep, dark purple of twilight. The jewel's power slumbered next to his skin.

It wasn't time for them to forget. Not yet.

He hadn't yet worked out how much magic this would cost him, especially while wounded. He stripped off his shirt and inspected the bandage. Blood seeped through the cotton, enough to make him woozy. Better to leave it alone, so it would stop bleeding. He supposed he needed stitches. When he clenched his left hand, he could barely make a fist.

What damage had been done?

Part of him wanted to just sell the damn Jewel of Oblivion and pay for a healer. But he needed the jewel. He dropped onto the bed.

Mercifully, he slipped into a dreamless sleep. He woke around dawn, when the fog glowed gray with tentative light. Downstairs, nobody else had risen yet.

Sikandar chose an unobtrusive corner table in the Marmalade Cat. He ordered coffee, toast, and sausages from the bleary-eyed barmaid. She didn't look much older than Cinderella, though her hair was red instead of blonde.

"Thank you," he said, when she delivered his food.

"Welcome," she muttered.

As he ate, his knife lay unused by his plate, since his left hand remained untrustworthy.

An orange tabby leapt onto a chair and chirped, her tail a question mark. When Sikandar held out his hand, the cat bumped her head against his knuckles. Was the cat the inn's namesake, or had they taken in a lucky stray afterward? Either way, the feline looked sleek and happy.

He fed the cat a sausage, which she gobbled down before eyeing the rest of his breakfast.

"Cat," he said, "don't get fat."

The barmaid smiled at him before her gaze slid away. She wiped down a nearby table.

"Excuse me," he said. "May I ask for a recommendation?"

"Not at all." She tucked her hair behind her ears. "Best dessert we have is the apple crumb cake."

"Sorry, not food."

"Oh?"

"I need a healer and the next ship bound for Azurum."

"You mean a doctor?" She gripped the rag. "What for?"

"To heal a wound."

"You got hurt? Where?"

He hesitated. Why was she looking at him like that, with her lips bent into a pout? Did she pity him? Of course, if he told her that the king's guards had shot him while he was robbing an alchemist's shop, chances were good that she would throw him out of the Marmalade Cat.

"You're bleeding," said the barmaid.

Damn it, she was right. He had been stupid enough to wear a gray shirt, and red stained his sleeve.

He put down his fork. "I should go." Before anyone else saw.

"Wait. My little brother is studying to be a surgeon. Practicing on dead bodies and all that."

Cadavers? He wrinkled his nose. "That's kind of you, but—"

"Johnny's good. Gets top marks from all his teachers."

As if sensing his distress, the marmalade cat twined between his ankles before flopping at his feet.

"I don't have a lot of money," Sikandar said.

"That's fine." The barmaid wiped her hands on her apron. "You'd be better practice than a stiff."

He was glad he was sitting down. "All right."

"Business is slow, so my friend in the kitchen can cover for me. Are you well enough to walk?"

"How far?"

She clucked her tongue. "Never mind that. I can fetch my brother. Why don't you lie down upstairs?"

"Thank you," he said.

"What's your name?"

"Sikandar Zerian."

"I'm Molly." She whipped off her apron. "Back in a jiff."

Sikandar didn't trust himself to stand yet, so he ate the rest of his food—minus the last sausage, which was the marmalade cat's tax. Done, he took the stairs one step at a time. The tabby purred and rubbed against him.

"Cat," he said, "if you trip me, we might both die."

The tabby ignored his warning and darted into his room before he could close the door. The barmaid—Molly—had given him sound advice about lying down. He wasn't a fool, so he did just that. Blood bloomed wider on his sleeve.

"Gods," he muttered. "I hate Viridia."

Somehow, the marmalade cat ended up on his chest. She kneaded him in the ribs, her claws needling him through his shirt, and weighed considerably more than he had expected. Probably all that begging for sausages.

"Remind me not to feed you again," he said.

The cat purred. He could have sworn the brat was smiling. Trapped, he sighed and closed his eyes.

A knock on the door jolted him awake.

Bracing himself on his elbow, he struggled to get out of bed. The movement triggered a sickening wave of pain in his arm. Mercifully, the cat jumped off of him.

"Who is it?" he called.

"Molly. And Johnny."

He unlocked the door. The red-headed barmaid was overshadowed by her dark-haired brother, who was both tall and big. He had the physique of someone who sawed through bones and yanked out teeth.

"Look at Ginger." Molly nodded at the cat. "She trusts him."

"What happened?" Johnny said.

Sikandar stepped aside. "Got shot."

No point in hiding the wound. He stripped his shirt over his head and cradled his arm.

Johnny rolled up his sleeves. "Molly, fetch me some hot water."

"I can't play nurse for long," she said, on her way out the door.

"When did this happen?" Johnny said.

"Few nights ago." Better to be vague.

Johnny cocked his head. "Gambling debt? Angry husband?"

"No and no." Sikandar's laugh sounded hollow. "I have never been gambling or been with a girl."

Johnny snorted. "This must have been exciting for you, then."

"Thrilling."

"I'm about to take off the bandage. Sit down."

Sikandar obeyed, since he didn't want to pass out around a stranger, or worse, a surgeon-in-training. Johnny unknotted the bandage and peeled it free where it stuck wetly to the skin. Sikandar hoped he wouldn't be sick.

"How did this happen?" Johnny said. "Really?"

Did he want to know, or was he making conversation to distract Sikandar from the pain?

"If you know the truth, will you stop treating me?"

"Hell no," Johnny said, "I took an oath."

"I robbed an alchemist's shop."

"Robbery!" Molly said, returning with a teapot.

Sikandar made the mistake of looking at the wound. It was a lot bloodier than he remembered.

"Anything else?" she said.

"No." Woozy, Sikandar shook his head. "Not after the king's guards shot me."

"I wasn't talking to you." Molly looked to her brother. "You need anything else from me?"

"Liquor," Johnny said. "Hundred proof."

"Right away."

Johnny poured hot water onto a towel and wiped the wound clean. The towel turned pink.

"Surgeon-in-training?" Sikandar said.

"Right."

"How long until you graduate?"

"Who knows."

Johnny opened a briefcase on the bed. It contained needles and thread, like a sewing kit. Perhaps rag dolls and people weren't all that different to stitch up.

Molly brought a bottle of whiskey. "The cheap stuff."

The alcohol wasn't meant to clean the wound, since Johnny poured a shot of liquor. "Drink."

"I don't drink alcohol," Sikandar said.

Johnny squinted. "What? Why not?"

"Some sort of religious thing?" Molly said.

"No." Sikandar shrugged. "I'm not very religious."

Truthfully, it was because he had seen what happened when his mother and father drank. Their laughter became shouting matches late into the night. In the morning, the servants often scrubbed vomit from the rugs. Nobody outside of the Zerian family knew about this shame.

"Then what?" Molly said.

"We don't have any chloroform to knock you out." Johnny offered the shot again. "Drink the whiskey."

"Just stitch me up," Sikandar said.

"Suit yourself."

Johnny abandoned the whiskey and focused on suturing. Razor pain cut through the sick throb of the gunshot wound. Molly lingered, unperturbed by blood or needles.

"Nearly done," Johnny said.

"What about my hand?" Sikandar said.

"What about it?"

He curled his fingers. "I can't make a fist."

"Bullet must have hit a nerve. Might heal, might not."

The marmalade cat peeked into Sikandar's pack before batting something across the floor.

The Jewel of Oblivion glinted in the light.

"What's that?" Johnny's gaze snapped to the gem.

"You said you didn't have a lot of money!" Molly swooped on his pack. She crumpled his embroidered silk coat in her hands. "What are you, some sort of prince?"

Sikandar faked a smile, his mouth dry. "If only."

"Then who are you?" she demanded.

"A sorcerer from Azurum."

"A sorcerer!" Johnny paled. "Why didn't you heal yourself?"

"I'm too hurt. Magic isn't free. The more you summon, the more it demands from you."

The siblings looked at each other, as if gauging him as a threat.

"You're a sorcerer from Azurum," Molly repeated. "And you're on the run from the king's guards."

"No," Sikandar said. "King Archibald let me go."

"The king?" Molly's jaw dropped. "Don't you dare lie to us."

"I'm telling you the truth. Ask His Majesty."

"He would never speak to two commoners like us."

"That isn't surprising. King Archibald does appear to be a pompous jackass."

Johnny yelped a laugh. "That's what the rumors say."

The Jewel of Oblivion remained on the floor. Unforgotten. Everyone kept glancing at it.

"I can't pay you much," Sikandar said. "Otherwise, I can't afford a ticket on the first ship to Azurum."

"What about that jewel?" Molly said.

"I need it."

She folded her arms. "What's so special about it?"

"Magic." He paused. "Dangerous magic."

"We helped you out of the goodness of our hearts."

Sikandar snorted. "You helped me because Johnny was tired of practicing on cadavers."

Molly lifted her shoulders. "True."

"Listen," Sikandar said. "I may be wounded, but I'm still a sorcerer. I know how to work magic. Have either of you always dreamed of an enchantment?"

Perhaps Molly and Johnny lacked imagination. They couldn't decide on an enchantment, arguing over never-ending cauldrons of stew and other impossible requests.

Finally, Sikandar said, "Why not a coin that jumps in your hand when you snap your fingers?"

Molly and Johnny shared a grin.

"Yes!" Johnny said.

"A golden coin," Molly added.

Crucially, it wasn't difficult to cast the enchantment. While Molly and Johnny took turns stealing the coin from each other, he snuck out the door.

The cost of magic left Sikandar bone-tired but alive. He walked away from the Marmalade Cat with the Jewel of Oblivion and enough money to buy a ticket to Azurum. He was tempted to pay for another night at the inn, but he wasn't sure he trusted Molly and Johnny. He didn't want to become just another cadaver for surgeons-in-training.

It wasn't hard to find the docks in Knockingham.

Seagulls whirled overhead, slicing through the wind, and squabbled over fish guts in the streets. Sikandar wrinkled his nose at the briny stink. A forest of ship's masts bristled over the rooftops of the city. He scanned the rigging.

The blue-and-gold flag of Azurum flew on a sleek clipper.

Malik, who captained the clipper, was a brown man weathered from years of sun and saltwater. They had sold tea and spices imported from Azurum, and were loading Viridian wine and wheels of cheese. Their destination: Zarkona, a city on the southwestern coast of Azurum.

Sikandar's heart leapt at the name.

"Take me to Zarkona." It was a relief to speak Azuri, his first language. "Take me home."

"For a price," said Captain Malik.

"Of course."

Sikandar emptied his pockets of money in exchange for a cabin below deck. It was simple, just a single berth and a dingy porthole. He cleaned the glass with his sleeve, which let in a little more sunlight, and squinted at the gray ocean. They would leave in a day, after they finished loading their cargo.

Three days at sea.

He hadn't seen his family since they had banished him. Two months felt like an eternity.

Would his brothers welcome him home? His sister?

They had grown up together, in a house on the outskirts of Zarkona, where they climbed the fig tree in the courtyard to steal sticky-sweet fruits. Jawahir was older than him, and so perpetually one step ahead, until he outgrew her in height and education. Their parents had never considered her eligible for school. Nothing beyond private lessons in etiquette and music, to make her more pleasing to a future husband.

And of course, Sikandar had thrown his future away.

Admission to the University of Naranjal. A promising career as a sorcerer. Gone.

Even if they forgot who he had been, he doubted they would love who he had become.

SEVENTEEN

CINDERELLA

The night Sikandar left, Cinderella returned to the Rose Room.

She flung herself onto the bed and sunk into the featherdown mattress. A silk canopy shimmered above.

Benedict, the curse is broken. She's yours now.

Was she a possession of the crown prince? Would he expect her to demonstrate her gratitude?

A knock on the door made her jump.

When she answered it, a maid brought her a choice of nightgowns, all of them adorned with ribbons and lace. Cinderella chose the simplest, but declined the maid's offer to dress her, instead sending the poor girl to bed.

Cinderella hid the bottle of potion in the nightstand, locked the drawer, and tucked the key under her pillow. The nightgown slipped over her skin like a whisper.

When she snuffed the lamp and rested her head on the pillow, the scent of spices touched her nose.

Chai.

She had nearly forgotten the borrowed clothes lying crumpled over the sheets, where she had tossed them. She held the shirt to her nose before breathing deep.

Sikandar.

Her mouth started to tremble. What had she done?

She had let him go, when she might never see him again. When such pain darkened his eyes at the memories of his family. But he had kissed her and walked away.

She couldn't help him. Could she?

In the gray light of dawn, Cinderella was woken by a maid sweeping ashes from the fireplace. Not the maid from last night, but a thinner woman with dark hair.

"Please," Cinderella said, "there's no need."

The maid spoke meekly. "It will soon grow cold, milady."

"I can tend to the fire."

"Milady?" The maid stared at her. "Begging your pardon, but I'm nearly done."

Cinderella glanced at her hands, still chapped and calloused from years of chores at Umberwood. Princesses didn't dirty themselves with work, did they?

"Thank you," Cinderella said. "When is breakfast?"

The maid stacked kindling in the fireplace. "I can have it brought up to your room."

So, the royal family didn't dine together in the morning.

She bit the inside of her cheek. She hadn't seen Prince Benedict since last night, and she wasn't even sure he knew more about the dragon curse. King Archibald seemed just as clueless, though perhaps that was a clever ruse.

Queen Eira knew about the curse. Knew her mother.

"Would you like a bath before breakfast, milady?"

That had to be a subtle way of saying she reeked. Cinderella let out a nervous laugh. "Please."

"Wonderful, milady. I can have the bath ready in a jiffy."

The bedchamber had its own bathroom, with indoor plumbing and a clawfoot tub in gleaming porcelain. Soon, steam wafted from water sprinkled with dried rose petals.

"Ring me if you need anything," said the maid.

She curtseyed before sweeping out of the bedchamber, no doubt off to tackle her endless chores.

Cinderella locked herself in the bathroom.

After undressing, she climbed into the tub. Heat caressed her skin and sank into her bones. She lathered a bar of soap into bubbles, scented with lemon and almond. The perfume relaxed the knots of tension in her muscles.

When she washed her leg, she froze.

Blue scales.

Seven of them glittered along her shinbone. She scrubbed at them until her skin was red and raw, but the dragon scales remained. Evidence of her monstrosity. She pried her fingernails under the edge of a scale but froze when pain stabbed her flesh. She didn't want to hurt herself.

She slid lower in the tub until everything but her face was underwater. Her heartbeat whooshed in her ears, a muffled sound that tempted her to sleep. But she couldn't linger, waiting for the dragon to escape.

Leaping from the tub, she splashed water onto the tiles. Trembling, she fumbled with the bathroom lock, her claws gouging varnish from the door. When the lock clicked open, she ran into the bedchamber. She flung the pillow from the bed, found the key, and unlocked the nightstand.

Quicksilver potion glimmered in the glass bottle.

She grabbed the last dose and fled into the bathroom. Knocking back the potion, she swallowed midnight bitterness, chased by the sour-sweet flavor of plums.

Agony gripped her skeleton and forced her bones to obey.

The bottle fell from her hand and cracked on the tiles. She dropped to her knees, clutching her stomach, before she retched. Nothing came up, thankfully, since she hadn't eaten a bite. Slowly, the curse ebbed from her body.

Her eyes watering, she held out her hands.

No sign of claws. She peeked at her shins, unblemished by scales. Droplets of potion shimmered on the tiles. Crawling across the bathroom floor, she touched each drop and licked her fingertips. Desperation sickened her.

Each dose of potion had lasted no more than twelve hours. She had until nightfall to find out the truth about the dragon curse. After that, it would be too late.

God, she had no chances left.

And the only one who could help her was going to Azurum.

A knock rapped on the bathroom door.

"I—I'm not decent!" she called.

"Milady?" The maid sounded uncertain. "May I help you dress?"

"Yes!" Cinderella clung to the tub and dragged herself upright. "One moment, please."

She hid herself behind a towel and opened the door.

The maid looked at her blankly. "Her Majesty the Queen requests your presence."

She clutched the towel tighter against herself. "When?"

"Now."

"Did she say why?"

"No, milady."

Refusal would, of course, be impossible.

Queen Eira waited in a tower adorned with tapestries. Her emerald-green gown billowed around her chair by the window. Her silvery hair had been braided and pinned to her head like a crown, though she wasn't wearing one.

Cinderella dipped into a deep curtsey. "Your Majesty."

Curiously, she hadn't seen the queen at the ball. Her Majesty had a reputation for secrecy.

"You must be Cinderella." Queen Eira inclined her head. "Or shall I say, Ginevra Darlington?"

"Yes, Your Majesty."

"Sit."

Glancing around, Cinderella found another chair. She clasped her hands in her lap to stop them from shaking. The queen stared at her with her pale gray eyes.

Silence poured into the space between them.

"I knew your mother," said the queen. "Vivendel."

Cinderella fidgeted in the chair, her tailbone uncomfortable. "Before she went to Umberwood." She was afraid to say too much.

"Why are you here?" Queen Eira asked.

Cinderella swallowed hard, her mouth parched. She hadn't drunk anything since waking up this morning. "For a second chance at happily ever after."

"Spare me your stories," said the queen, her tone that of frosty boredom. "Why return to Knightsend after such a disastrous debut at the ball?"

Cinderella twisted her fingers together. "If only I had spoken to you that night."

"What do you want from me? No one ever comes to a queen wanting nothing."

"Breakfast and a cup of tea?" A nervous laugh escaped her.

The queen pursed her lips. "I want the truth."

"Then we want the same thing." She straightened her spine. "My mother told me that she had been gifted Umberwood Manor in exchange for a great service. I didn't understand what she had sacrificed until I found her diary."

The curse will be mine.

Queen Eira's face betrayed nothing. "You already know."

"She took the curse meant for you and your firstborn child. Meant for the crown prince."

"Indeed she did."

Cinderella bit the inside of her cheek, focusing on the pain, and asked simply, "Why?"

"Vivendel understood the necessity of sacrifice." Queen Eira arched one eyebrow. "The Crown gifted her a small fortune and Umberwood Manor in return."

Cinderella met her gaze. "Who cursed you? Why?"

Her Majesty let out a long sigh and gazed out of the window. Sunlight glinted on the waterfall as it plunged over the cliff. She did not look away as she spoke.

"An enemy of Viridia."

Cinderella waited until the silence grew unbearable. "Who?"

"Does it matter?"

"To me, it matters very much. I was born with a curse that didn't belong to me."

Queen Eira turned from the window. "Your mother's fault."

"Pardon me?"

"She chose to marry and have a child."

Cinderella bit back her unkind words. "What did you do to deserve the curse?"

"I refused a powerful man who wanted me."

It was all too easy to believe her. Cinderella reached halfway for the queen before stopping herself. She would have touched the back of Her Majesty's hand, but she suspected that such a gesture would be both unwanted and forbidden.

"The curse could not be broken." Queen Eira's eyes sharpened to steel. "I summoned every witch and wizard in the land, but they could save me only by transferring the curse to another woman. Your mother agreed."

As if her mother could have disobeyed the Queen of Viridia.

Her Majesty tilted her head, her face an icy mask. "Why haven't you returned to Umberwood?"

"Umberwood was never enough."

"What is the cost of your discretion?"

"My… discretion?"

"Your mother's diary should have been burned to ashes."

Sweat slicked Cinderella's hands. She hadn't come here to blackmail the queen, and yet the queen was willing to bribe her into silence about the past.

"I don't know," Cinderella said, which was the truth.

"How did that sorcerer boy break the curse?"

Fragments of the truth. "He brewed a potion."

The queen stared at her without blinking. "Go."

"Thank you, Your Majesty." As if she had given her anything other than a dismissal.

"Return to me when you can name your price."

Cinderella cringed when she walked past the ballroom, where masons and carpenters were rebuilding the window and balcony she had destroyed as a dragon. Endlessly, the waterfall roared over the cliff and dulled her thoughts.

She didn't belong here.

The curse lurked beneath her skin, ready to burst into scales and fangs and claws. If only Sikandar were here to help her uncover the truth. He would probably go to the castle library and read massive books on sorcery, ones she couldn't even begin to understand.

Dizzy, she leaned against the cold stone wall of the castle.

She hadn't eaten or drunk anything today, and it had taken a toll upon her strength. She wanted nothing more than to sink onto a cushioned sofa and have tea.

She retreated to the Rose Room. Breakfast was not, in fact, waiting for her already. Famished, she rang the bell for a servant. Her maid from last night arrived.

"Yes, milady?"

"Could you have breakfast brought up?"

"Begging your pardon, but it's late for breakfast." The maid clasped her hands in front of her apron. "The cooks have already started on lunch for the castle."

"It doesn't have to be fancy. Bread and cheese?"

The maid's eyebrows rose, as if no royalty in the castle would ever allow such common food to cross their lips. "Bread and cheese. Yes, milady. Will that be all?"

"And tea, please."

"Of course."

The maid curtseyed out of the room.

A little shaky, Cinderella lowered herself into a chair. She gnawed on her thumbnail until it was ragged and sore. Earlier, she had been utterly outclassed by Queen Eira, who had thrown her no more than crumbs of the truth.

The maid knocked before entering with a tray. "Where shall I put this, milady?"

"Here." Cinderella patted a table. "And please, there's no need to call me *milady*." It hadn't been so long since she had worked as a servant in Umberwood.

The maid blinked a few times. "What else should I call you?"

"My name?"

"Pardon me, but that would be too presumptuous."

Cinderella sighed. "Never mind."

"Yes, milady."

"Wait." Cinderella tore open a roll of soft white bread. "Before you go, is there a library?"

"Yes, of course. Would you like me to fetch you a book?"

"That won't be necessary. Could you give me directions?"

Evening darkened the sky to the purple of a bruise. Inside the castle library, candlelight glimmered on the gilded spines of books. There must have been thousands that crowded the shelves, from marble floors to vaulted ceilings. The whole library smelled of beeswax, old paper, and secrets.

Cinderella pinched the bridge of her nose. The beginnings of a headache throbbed in her skull. She had flipped through dozens of books.

And for what?

She was no closer to the truth about the curse.

"One more book," she whispered.

A Modern History of the Viridian Monarchy. A monstrous tome, bound in black leather. She dragged it out and lugged it over to a table. The pages were slippery with gilt.

"Queen Eira," she whispered, cracking it open.

Words swam together into meaningless ink.

Why would the royal family write down their shameful secret? Who else knew of the curse?

"Cinderella!" Benedict's voice rang out under the high ceiling. He strolled across the polished marble with a crooked smile. "Why have you been hiding here?"

She thumped the book shut as if she had been caught reading something indecent. "I'm not hiding."

"And yet you're acting so secretive."

"I'm not!"

The longer he looked at her, the wider his smile grew.

Heat crept over her cheeks. "Why are you staring at me?"

"Because you're blushing."

"I wasn't blushing until you started staring at me."

He laughed. For heaven's sake, was he flirting with her? After she had turned into a dragon in his ballroom, and he had chased her with his sword drawn?

Questions burned in her ribs like embers.

She wanted to ask him about the curse, and the man who cursed his mother, but she wasn't sure how. Or if he knew more about his family's dark secrets.

"Why are you here?" Benedict asked.

Exactly the same question his mother had asked.

She bit the inside of her cheek. "I'm looking for a book."

"Not the library." He waved away her comment. "Knightsend."

"Oh. I…"

"Father tells me you want another chance."

"Yes?" she said, wishing she could stop blushing.

He smirked. "I'm not surprised."

She peered through her eyelashes, pretending innocence. "You're not worried about the curse?"

"Why should I be?"

Had he been sheltered from the truth?

"The curse is broken," he said. "And you're here with me. What more could a prince ask for?"

Benedict kept smirking at her, one of his eyebrows raised. He acted like he had been told he was smart and charming all his life, and never had to prove it.

"But Benedict—"

"Shh."

As he stepped closer, she backed against a bookshelf. His eyes were as blue as hottest flame.

"I know what you want," he murmured.

Trapped by the bookshelf, she froze. He was the crown prince, and she was in his castle.

"You do?" she asked.

"Let me show you."

Benedict kissed her with supreme confidence. He stifled her murmur of protest with his mouth. He fitted her against his body, one of his hands behind her neck, the other at her waist. Her shoulders tensed, her fists at her sides.

He leaned away. "How was your first kiss?"

As if she hadn't already kissed Sikandar.

"Surprising," she lied.

"Let me educate you."

He kissed her again, harder, his tongue skimming her lips. What should she do? He didn't seem to care that she wasn't kissing him back. Of course, he expected her to be a blushing virgin, with no experience or desires of her own. If she touched him, he might think her too forward.

This was nothing like kissing Sikandar.

She didn't want to kiss Benedict. She didn't even like him.

Trying to be gentle, she pushed him away.

"Aren't I who you want?" He looked at her with genuine confusion and disappointment.

"I don't know," she repeated, when the answer was no.

"Relax." Benedict kissed her on the forehead, sweetly, but his hands twisted in her skirts. "Trust me," he murmured. "Let me take care of you."

But she didn't trust him. He didn't even know the truth.

"Benedict," she said. "What did your mother and father tell you about the dragon curse?"

"Not much." His jaw hardened. "Curses don't happen to good people."

Her jaw dropped. "How can you say that?"

"That's not what I meant."

"You think I deserved to be transformed into a dragon?"

"No. It's something my father told me. You asked!"

She forced out a laugh. "Doesn't your father know?"

A crease deepened between Benedict's eyebrows. "Know what? Why are you being like this?"

Heat rose inside her like magma. She clenched her trembling fists, wondering how fast she would be locked in the dungeon if she punched a prince. God, but wouldn't it be so *satisfying* to knock that stupid look off his royal face?

"You had no clue," she said. "All your life, you enjoyed luxury and privilege, never knowing you escaped any consequences. Never knowing it was meant to be you."

"Me?"

"You should have been the one to turn into a dragon at the stroke of midnight. Not me."

Benedict shook his head. "You're not making any sense."

"Ask the queen." She bared her teeth. "The curse was meant for her firstborn child. The heir to the throne. *You*. But she pawned off the curse on my mother."

He stared at her with wide, blank eyes. "No."

"It's the truth!"

"I don't believe you."

A guttural growl rumbled from her throat. He backed away. Blood rushed under her skin, followed by a stinging like nettles.

The curse.

"Oh god," she whispered. "No."

Benedict backed away. "What's wrong?"

"I have to go."

"Now?"

"I'm sorry—it's—feminine troubles," she stammered.

"Pardon?"

She clutched his shoulders and steered him out of her way. Claws scythed from her fingers. When she bolted for the door, a cramp stabbed through her guts.

"Cinderella!"

Pain brought her to her knees. "Stay away!"

"What the hell is wrong with you?"

Her back arched, wings bursting from her shoulder blades, shredding her gown. She clawed at the marble floor as if she could drag herself back into her true body. Her skeleton wouldn't obey, her bones rebelling against her will.

But it was too late.

Her skin splintered into blue scales. A tail snaked from her spine. The soft shape of her body vanished, replaced by hard angles. The curse left her shaking on the marble.

A dragon once more.

Benedict's mouth twisted into a sneer. "You lied to me."

"I'm sorry," she said. "I should have told you, I—"

"You disgust me."

As if he hadn't kissed her moments before.

Rather than wait for him to summon the guards, she whirled for the nearest window.

This time, when she shattered the glass, she knew how to fly.

EIGHTEEN

SIKANDAR

Sikandar couldn't return home until all had been forgotten.

Then, perhaps, he could be forgiven.

He cradled the Jewel of Oblivion in his hands and rubbed his thumb over the gemstone's twilight facets. Slumbering magic nipped at his skin like cold fire.

The longer he held it, the more jasmine scented the air.

Night-blooming flowers that starred the darkness outside his bedroom window back home.

Sikandar dropped to the floor of his cabin, where he sat cross-legged with the jewel in his lap. Sweat from his palms fogged the gem's facets. He hoped he had enough magic for this. And he wouldn't fall unconscious.

If he didn't wake up, then none of this would matter anyway.

Closing his eyes, he fought the urge to drop the jewel and crawl into his bunk.

"Forget," he whispered.

Power flared to life in his bones. And the jewel answered him. The world melted away around him as he returned to one night, the night he had killed a king.

Beneath a violet sky, the sun fading fast, a caravanserai shimmered like a mirage in the desert. Sikandar's white mare pricked her ears before breaking into a trot. Her hooves slipped as they cut across the flank of a dune. He patted her neck, glad she could have water and alfalfa soon.

"Sikandar!"

He twisted in the saddle. Taj waved at him from the top of a dune. His brother's spirited black gelding pawed at the sand, impatient to reach the caravanserai.

Sikandar cupped his hands to his mouth. "Yes?"

"Slow down!" Taj called. "Jawahir is falling behind."

The white mare pinned her ears, annoyed by all this shouting. Sikandar sighed. After the marriage, Ali had gifted Jawahir with an abominably slow magic carpet.

Grumbling camels plodded over the dunes, ridden by the royal guard. Behind them, Jawahir's magic carpet floated at the pace of a brisk walk. Jawahir reclined on pillows, serene, and shaded her eyes from the low slant of the sun. The wind ruffled her robes. Sikandar's little nephew, Kamran, popped out from under a pillow and waved vigorously.

Sikandar grinned. Kamran was two and thought the desert was amazing. They got to drink out of canteens, eat handfuls of dried dates, and watch ornery camels spit at the royal guard. Kamran wouldn't stop talking about staying at the caravanserai in the middle of nowhere, or seeing his father, King Ali, after a week apart.

Sikandar's grin vanished.

Kamran was the only good thing to come from Jawahir's marriage to King Ali, though Kamran loved his father with the innocence of a child. His mother had hidden her bruises from him. He wouldn't understand why King Ali needed to die.

Tonight.

"Ready?" Taj asked.

He knew nothing of Sikandar's plan to kill the king. The fewer who knew, the better.

"Ready," Sikandar said.

Taj kicked his gelding's ribs. Sikandar urged his mare into a gallop and thundered past. They skidded to a halt outside the arched entrance of the caravanserai.

The courtyard of the desert inn had been built around an oasis, the water shadowed by the fronds of date palms. On the first floor, in the alcoves overlooking the courtyard, merchants unburdened their camels for the night. Music drifted from the tavern on the second floor. Sikandar cocked his head. Flutes and an oud. A lively tune at odds with the knot in his stomach.

He took his time unsaddling his mare, bringing her to water, and feeding her a few dates as a treat. In his mind, he traced the intricate structure of a deadly curse.

His fingers twitched, remembering the shape of magic.

"Aren't you hungry?" Taj leaned against the sandstone bricks of the stable doorway.

"A little," lied Sikandar, his stomach churning.

"The king will be here soon."

Sikandar stroked the mare's nose. "I know."

"Let's eat."

Together, they climbed upstairs to the tavern, where years of cooking infused the air. They tore apart buttery naan and shared an eggplant stew that was spicy even for Sikandar, who liked heat. Maybe guilt was burning up his stomach.

A royal guard advanced. "Sikandar Zerian?"

Sikandar's shoulders stiffened, though he had been expecting this summons. "Yes?"

"The Queen Consort wishes to speak to you."

Taj snorted. "You mean our sister?"

The guard stared blankly at his sarcasm.

Sikandar pushed his chair from the table. "I'm ready."

The guard led him to the eastern corner of the caravanserai. Brass lanterns illuminated the corridor. Two more guards flanked the door to a bedchamber.

Sikandar paid less attention to them than the exact location. He would need to return later tonight.

Ushered into the room, he found Jawahir alone.

"Leave us," she told the guards.

Jawahir locked the door behind them, quietly, before she sank onto the bed and clutched a silk pillow to her chest. She gazed out the window at the courtyard.

"Tonight?" Sikandar said.

"Tonight." Jawahir wouldn't look at him. "He drinks himself senseless most nights, but I will spike his wine with a sleeping draught. He won't wake."

Sikandar swallowed, his mouth desert-dry. "When?"

"Midnight, most likely."

"Most likely? Jawahir, I don't want to teleport into here while he's still awake."

She turned to him with hollow eyes. "Trust me."

He had no choice.

When Sikandar teleported back, at midnight, King Ali sprawled across the bed. His breath reeked of wine. He looked dead already, except for the snoring.

Jawahir knelt by the bed. "Wait," she whispered.

She struggled to twist a ring of protection from her husband's bloated finger. Ostentatious, gold and amethyst, with magic to keep him safe from evil sorcery.

"Don't worry," Jawahir said. "I will add it back once he's dead."

"Appreciated."

Sikandar slipped a dagger from his sleeve.

Obviously, he couldn't stab the king's heart. This needed to look like a natural death, one untraceable to the Zerian family. And he knew what the king deserved.

Sikandar's hands trembled as he lifted the dagger. He refused to look at Jawahir while he cut open the tip of his own finger.

This curse demanded blood.

He sketched the intricate lines of the spell on Ali's face. Red streaked the king's skin.

"Hurt my sister again," he murmured, "and you will die."

The curse flared bright red before vanishing.

"Is it done?" Jawahir said.

Sikandar touched his finger to his lips. "Yes." He glanced at the door, thinking of the guards.

Jawahir dipped her head. "Go."

Sikandar teleported into his own room. Alone. Safe.

His knees buckled and he sagged against the wall. Before tonight, he had never cursed anyone to die. Certainly not the King of Azurum. He rubbed his temples with the heels of his hands. Gods, if the royal guards caught him…

Jawahir would protect him. She was the best liar he had ever met.

Exhausted from the cost of magic, he stumbled into bed. He stared into the darkness until sleep conquered him.

He was woken by voices in the courtyard.

Jawahir, pleading with her husband, asking him to come back to bed. Ali, refusing her request, his words thick with wine and disdain for his wife.

The jinni's wish had forced him to marry her, but had his heart been too withered for love?

Sikandar gripped the edge of his window as he watched them.

Ali pissed into the oasis as the royal guards looked on. He told Jawahir he had sobered up enough to find himself something else to drink. Someone else for his bed.

"No," Jawahir said.

Ali staggered closer. "What did you say?"

"Enough."

"I am your king."

"And I am your queen. Treat me like one."

He laughed, an ugly sound, and struck her across the mouth.

Their guards didn't even flinch. How many times had they seen this before?

From the window, Sikandar gripped the stones. He forced himself not to defend her.

The curse would save her.

Ali clutched his ribs. With a strangled grunt, he dropped to the sand. The guards rushed to their fallen king.

"Help him!" Jawahir cried, already sobbing.

She had always been the best at deceit.

King Ali did not die.

He rested in bed at the caravanserai, and his healers announced he had weakened his heart from overindulgence. He would need to stop drinking and womanizing. No one else knew of the curse. Not even their brother, Taj.

When Jawahir summoned Sikandar to the royal bedchamber, they watched the king sleep. Outside the windows, night still clung to the sky, the dark purple of a bruise.

Alone together, neither one of them spoke for a long time.

Jawahir's eyes glittered darkly. "He isn't dead."

"I know," Sikandar whispered. "I'm sorry."

"What did you do wrong?"

He hated curses. Nasty, intricate magic that tangled and cut like thorns. "Gods, I made a mistake."

"What mistake?" She spat the words.

"I said he would die. I didn't say when."

"Now." Jawahir turned on him, clutching him by the shoulders. "End it now."

"I can't."

"You can." She touched her fingertips to her split lip. "You let him hurt me."

"I hoped he wouldn't."

"You knew he would! You should have just killed him."

Sikandar swore. She was right.

"Wait here," he said. "Make sure no guards enter."

His hands clammy, he gripped the wrist of the sleeping king. Teleportation vomited them both into the desert, where dawn stained the horizon red.

Ali slumped against him, dragging him to his knees.

Gods, he had to do this before he woke.

Sikandar sketched a spell in the air, one not meant for death, but most spells could be fatal in the hands of a sorcerer. He held the cold, blue magic in his fingers.

"I'm sorry," he whispered.

He drove the magic into the king's chest and froze his heart. Ice splintered through his veins. Ali's heartbeat thudded one last time under Sikandar's hand.

He waited in the desert, holding the dead man in his arms.

The ice melted soon enough, leaving no trace of sorcery, but he couldn't return. Not while his traitorous body betrayed him by shaking uncontrollably. He swallowed down acid until he lost the fight, then hunched over the sand and vomited.

"Gods save me," he whispered, a chant under his breath. "Gods save me."

He had no choice but to kill him. To save his sister.

Then why did he want to jump into quicksand and let it swallow him whole?

He waited until he could force his body to obey, then teleported back with the king.

Gasping, Sikandar lurched into reality. He slumped on the floor of the cabin, the Jewel of Oblivion rolling across the wood. Every bone in his body ached.

Acid burned his throat as he crawled to his knees.

Hunched over a chamber pot, he vomited what little he had eaten. He coughed until nothing came up. Shaking, he filled a glass with water, swigged a mouthful, and spat.

Forgetting the king's death wasn't enough. He needed to unravel more threads of memory.

Only he would remember, after he was done.

Sikandar clutched the Jewel of Oblivion in his clammy hands. He closed his eyes again.

Back in Zarkona, back home, his parents screamed at him.

"Jawahir told us everything."

"Did you try to defy us? Did you try to save him?"

"Your sister was humiliated."

"You are a disgrace to the Zerian name."

"Thank the gods we are merciful. You deserve so much worse than banishment."

Their faces crumbled into ashes.

He hadn't been there when Jawahir had confessed to them, but the Jewel of Oblivion let him hunt down their memories. He left nothing but a shadowy emptiness in their minds, and rumors of drunkard king who died of a bad heart.

No one would know he was a murderer.

No one but himself.

NINETEEN

CINDERELLA

Umberwood was never enough.

Never.

Cinderella soared from Knightsend Castle, so bright with rage that she swallowed back fire.

Her mother had died before telling her the truth about the curse, had never seen her fall to the floor, her body twisted into that of a dragon.

Her mother's sacrifice had been for nothing.

A stolen title. A fortune, squandered. And a manor house Cinderella would never call home again. Had her stepmother already started the auction in her absence?

She flew high over Viridia as the countryside slumbered. It would have been beautiful, if she hadn't been hollowed out inside. An empty space where her heart once was.

They had taken everything from her and left her a monster.

Fog cloaked Umberwood Manor, all the windows dark, except for candlelight that leaked from Lady Darlington's bedroom. She was still awake. Still here.

Cinderella folded her wings and plummeted like an arrow. The ground rushed up to meet her. When she snapped open her wings and landed in the garden, the shock of it rattled her teeth. Her claws dug into the wet, rich earth.

Here were the tidy herbs she had tended.

Here were the meager boundaries of her happiness.

Tears fell, glittering, into the lawn. She left scorched grass in her wake. At the front door, she dragged her claws across the wood, wondering which of her stepsisters might scream, wondering if they were still asleep.

Did all of them know about the dragon curse?

Cinderella lashed out with her claws and smashed one of the biggest windows. Shards tinkled on the hardwood floor she had swept so meticulously for years. She folded her wings and slithered through the window. Broken glass crunched underfoot, but her armor of scales protected her. Her horns scraped the ceiling until she ducked her head.

Muffled footsteps thumped overhead.

Eulalia and Delicata ran downstairs in nightgowns, Eulalia clutching a candlestick like a weapon.

Delicata screamed, her hand at her mouth. "Mother!"

A growl rumbled from Cinderella's throat. "Where is she?"

"My god." Eulalia's jaw dropped. "Cinderella?"

Delicata clung to her sister's elbow. "We saw you at the ball. We saw you... *turn.*"

When Cinderella bared her teeth, they shuddered at her fangs. "Umberwood is mine."

"But you're a dragon," Eulalia said, like an idiot.

"Get. Out."

They kept standing there with their mouths agape.

"Mother!" Delicata shouted again, as if she could save them from the monster in their house.

Cinderella's stepmother descended the stairs. Lady Darlington clutched a silk robe to her chest. Her face looked like a white mask, flawless and blank.

Cinderella's knees went watery. She shrank low against the hardwood as if she could make herself small enough to disappear. Even now, even when she returned as a dragon, she hated how her body betrayed her around her stepmother.

Like she was still no more than a helpless little girl.

Cinderella forced herself not to run away. "You knew?"

Lady Darlington thinned her lips. "Be more specific."

"You knew I was cursed to become a dragon?"

"Yes." Lady Darlington tugged her robe tighter. "Your father told me before he died. Begged me to keep his secret. He confessed his daughter was an abomination."

Even Eulalia and Delicata let out little gasps, as if this was scandalous yet delicious gossip.

"My father would never say that," Cinderella whispered.

"And yet, he did."

Such shame gripped her belly that she wanted to retch. She wanted to peel the scales and spikes from her skin, to prove to them she wasn't a hideous monster. To prove to them that she was worthy of respect.

But she remembered Sikandar's words, his voice an echo in her ears: *You're beautiful.*

"There's nothing left for you here," Lady Darlington said.

"Umberwood is mine." Cinderella's claws gouged ruts in the hardwood.

Lady Darlington laughed, a sound as brittle as ice breaking. "Preposterous."

"Quiet!" Cinderella had no wish to hear, once again, how her father had left her a pittance for an inheritance. "Tell me. The Fairy Godmother. Was she hired by you?"

Lady Darlington puckered her lips as if she had tasted something rotten. "Hardly. Your father foolishly thought a Fairy Godmother might help you secure a husband when you came of age. Why he wasted his money, I haven't the slightest clue. He knew the curse could not be broken."

Cinderella dug her claws into the floorboards, the wood creaking as she gouged it. "Even the Fairy Godmother told me to flee into the wilderness."

"Prudent advice."

Eulalia, still clutching the candlestick, glanced at her mother. "Why haven't we been given a Fairy Godmother?"

"Don't be greedy," Lady Darlington snapped. "Besides, take one look at Cinderella. She's hopelessly unmarriageable. Unemployable even as a servant."

When Cinderella flared her wings, she shadowed her stepfamily. "You never paid me."

"Pardon?"

"You treated me as a servant in my own home for years, and you never paid me."

"No," Lady Darlington said. "Room and board were provided."

Cinderella snarled. "You heartless, evil witch."

"Watch your language," Lady Darlington said, as if she still had the power to chastise her.

"Umberwood is mine," Cinderella said again, "and you will never take it from me."

She studied the mildewed wood and dusty grandeur of Umberwood, a place once dear to her heart, a childhood haven, but one haunted by too many painful memories. Her hopes and dreams had been ruined beyond repair.

"Never," Cinderella repeated.

Delicata whimpered and backed away, perhaps the only one among them smart enough to be afraid.

Cinderella held her breath for one second. Two. Three.

She let it out as fire.

Flames rushed from her jaws. They devoured curtains, the cloth tattering as it smoldered, and crawled along the wallpaper. Her stepsisters ran from Umberwood in their nightgowns, but her stepmother stood defiant in the flames.

Cinderella stared her down. "Get out of my house."

She exhaled a blast of fire that crawled along the rug and left cinders in its wake.

Lady Darlington fled.

Fire devouring Umberwood around her, Cinderella lost herself in the beauty of destruction. She walked through the flaming halls and turned all her memories into ashes. She climbed the stairs to her bedroom in the attic.

It would never be her home again.

All the tension rushed from her muscles. She sagged against her bed and bowed her head against her pillow. How many dreams and nightmares had she been caged inside, night after night? How long had she been waiting to escape?

And to think, she had imagined living in Umberwood forever.

Some hopes were shackles.

Smoke billowed above until it became hard for even a dragon to breathe. When windows shattered under the scorching heat, wind whirled inside and fanned the flames. Coughing, she ran out. The stairs burned, crumbling beneath her footsteps, but she had wings. She soared over the flames and rammed the front door; the wood splintered off the hinges.

Cinderella burst into the night and rose from the ashes.

Below, her stepfamily huddled in the garden as they watched Umberwood burn. They couldn't profit from her mother's sacrifice any longer. No one could.

She abandoned her past and winged higher into the sky.

TWENTY

SIKANDAR

Screams woke Sikandar.

He grabbed his pack, which was heavy with the Jewel of Oblivion, and bolted above deck.

The moon dominated the sky, the inky purple of midnight, and its light glittered in the harbor. People were running through the streets of Knockingham, and it took him a second to understand what they were shouting.

"Dragon!"

He gripped the railing of the ship. "Cinderella."

The dragon soared over the city, her scales gleaming indigo. She tilted a wing and circled over the docks.

"Cinderella!"

He waved his arms over his head. Then he remembered he was, in fact, a sorcerer.

If only he weren't so tired.

He chose a simple spell, common at weddings and children's parties. With his left arm wounded, he focused on sketching the required symbol with his right hand.

He tossed a ball of green light into the air.

It burst, brighter than a firework, into a thousand shimmering shards. The green magic glinted off the dragon's scales. Sailors cursed and dropped to the deck.

Cinderella plummeted toward the ship.

He inhaled through his teeth. "Wait! Don't—"

She raked forward her talons. At the last moment, her wings snapped open, killing her speed. When she landed on the ship, it lurched and creaked wildly under her weight. Ropes groaned as they strained against the dock.

"Sikandar!" Tears shone in her fire-bright eyes. "I found you."

He swallowed hard, finding himself speechless.

How had he missed her so much?

Lamplight glinted off the gunmetal aimed in their direction. The crew brandished pistols at them.

Captain Malik arrived on deck. "Sorcerer!"

"Sikandar," he corrected. "We've met."

"Why did you summon this dragon?"

He hesitated. "I can see why you would think that."

"Pardon me, sir," Cinderella said, "but he didn't. I was looking for him."

"Get off my ship," Captain Malik ordered.

Cinderella met Sikandar's gaze. "Come with me."

Glancing at the guns, he nodded. "So long as we don't make any sudden movements."

With his hands raised, Sikandar strode across the deck. Sailors flinched away like he might set them on fire. Slowly, he climbed onto the dragon's back.

Captain Malik aimed at Sikandar's heart. "Go. Now."

Cinderella pumped her wings hard, and the downdraft shook the rigging of the ship. Sikandar ducked against her neck, praying the captain didn't have a delicate trigger finger. The dragon skimmed the water, struggling to gain altitude, until she caught a gust of wind and rode it skyward.

They flew high over Knockingham. The lights of the city glittered below, scattered diamonds on black velvet. Knightsend Castle loomed over it all.

"Where do we go?" Cinderella cried, over the wind.

"Away from here," he replied.

She flew to a tiny island just off the coast of Viridia, nothing more than an overgrown rock with room for a gnarled pine tree above the cliffs. Waves broke on the island and misted them with saltwater. Sikandar dismounted on unsteady legs, since the distance to the surf gave him vertigo.

Her eyes glimmered in the moonlight. "Why were you leaving?"

Had she forgotten he intended to return to Azurum?

"What do you remember?" he said.

"I remember that you wanted to go home to Azurum, but I can't remember why." She hesitated. "It's the strangest sensation. Like a word on the tip of my tongue."

What else had she forgotten? Their first kiss?

He exhaled, hard. "The Jewel of Oblivion."

She stared into the distance. "You needed to make everyone forget. Why?"

He was a murderer. And she didn't know.

"I was banished," he said. "But I can go home now."

"I was so worried you had already left."

He ignored the way his heart did a little leap. "What happened? Back at Knightsend?"

"I confronted Queen Eira about the curse."

"And?"

"She believed the curse was unbreakable. I don't know if she believed anything I said."

"Did she summon the king's guards?"

"No, but I had to pretend the curse was broken, so it was easy for her to evade my questions."

Sikandar tilted his head. "What did she say?"

"She had been cursed by a powerful man who wanted her, so I assume she must have refused an evil sorcerer." She glanced at him. "No offense."

"None taken," he said.

"Queen Eira admitted my mother took the curse meant for the royal heir. But she also blamed my mother for marrying and having a child, even though my mother believed herself to be barren. Was the queen being cruel or ignorant?"

He shook his head. "I'm not sure it matters."

"She offered to buy my silence," Cinderella continued, "but no price seemed high enough. When I said nothing, she dismissed me from her presence."

"And the potion ran out?"

"Not yet. I was in the library, reading about the royal family, when Benedict found me. He definitely believed the curse had been broken. He… he kissed me."

Anger jolted his muscles. "He did?"

She shuddered, clamping her wings against her spine. "And it was an awful kiss. He didn't seem to care that I didn't want it. If the curse hadn't turned me back into a dragon, I don't know what would have happened next."

"Gods." He breathed deeply to cool down. "Should we turn around and murder him?"

"No!"

"I'm not joking."

"Sikandar, no."

"Are you sure?"

She flicked her tail. "If we kill the Crown Prince of Viridia, we will never escape to Azurum."

"We?"

Her sigh clouded the air. "I can't go back home."

"You could ask Queen Eira for Umberwood."

"No, I couldn't."

"Isn't that what you always wanted?"

"It would be an impossible request." Her golden eyes glittered. "I burned Umberwood to the ground."

His head snapped in her direction. "Your childhood home?"

"Yes."

"But why?"

"It wasn't home any longer. Not after I knew the truth about the dragon curse."

"You said Umberwood was your rightful inheritance."

"I once believed it belonged to me. But now I believe it should belong to no one."

"Not even you?"

She stared into the waves. "When I saw my past turning to ashes, I felt the weight of years disappearing into smoke." She met his gaze. "And now I'm free."

"Cinderella." He lowered himself onto the rocks gingerly, putting no weight on his wounded arm. "Aren't you afraid you will regret your decision?"

"My heart tells me it was the right choice."

He didn't want to ask what else her heart told her, afraid the answer would hurt him too much.

"Gods," he said. "I wish I had such certainty."

"Sikandar, let me come with you. Please."

He blinked fast, unable to name the ache in his chest. It had to be sea spray stinging his eyes.

And then it hit him.

"Of course." He focused on the fragmented moonlight glittering on the water. "You remember the third wish. That's why you want to come with me to Azurum."

"Yes," she said, frowning.

She wanted his help. Their relationship was transactional, just as it had been with his family.

He didn't want to know why she had kissed him. Perhaps that had been nothing more than a desperate attempt to make him stay, because he was useful.

"Sikandar, I…"

"Yes?"

She wouldn't look at him. "I wanted to thank you."

He grimaced. "Don't thank me until I find the jinni's lamp."

"Isn't it lost? Buried in the desert?"

"Yes, but the jinni wants me to unearth it."

"I trust you."

Gods, she wasn't joking. If only she knew who he was. "Cinderella, this will likely end in disappointment. I don't want to lie to you. Or give you false hope."

"I understand."

But so many words remained unspoken in her eyes.

She didn't even remember he was a murderer. Couldn't even remember, thanks to the Jewel of Oblivion. When would she start to wonder about his past?

Fear paced inside his chest like a caged tiger.

"In truth," he said, "you don't need to be there. For the wish."

"I can't in good conscience let you go alone. At least let me fly with you to Azurum. After all, I ruined your ticket home the moment I landed on that ship."

His stomach lurched. "Good thing they didn't shoot us."

"Admittedly, I don't know the way to Azurum."

"I have a map."

He slung his pack from his shoulders, wincing at the pain in his arm, and flattened the crumpled map. He could read by moonlight, without the need for summoning fireflies. She traced the coast of Viridia with her claw.

"We must be on Fishbones Island," she said.

"Agreed." He slid his finger across the Cerulean Sea. "And there's Azurum."

"I thought it would be farther away."

He glanced back at her. "I'm not *that* exotic," he deadpanned.

She ducked her head, and he suspected she would have been blushing if she were still a girl.

"How long is the journey?" she asked.

"By ship? Three days."

"And by dragon flight?"

"Maybe a day, maybe two."

His arm still throbbed with pain, and he hoped he hadn't pulled any of the stitches. He surreptitiously peeked under the bandage, but she caught him looking.

"Are you all right?" she said.

"Back in Knockingham, I had someone stitch up my arm."

"Who?"

He grimaced. "You don't want to know."

"Actually, I do."

"A barmaid's brother studying to be a surgeon."

"Sikandar!" Her eyes flashed. "That sounds quite unsafe to me. Let me look."

"Carefully. You have claws."

"I can still be gentle, can't I?"

When she reached for his wrist, her touch was as fleeting as a moth. Delicately, she picked at the knot on the bandage. When it came loose, she smiled.

"Claws helped," she said.

"Fair point."

"But I'm worried the wound might be infected now."

A wave of nausea rippled through him. The skin around the stitches looked red and angry.

"I hate that you might be right," he said.

"Thank goodness I found you."

"There's no need." Clumsily, he tried to cover his wound. "I can take care of myself."

"Stop trying to bandage yourself, you're doing it wrong."

He clenched his jaw. "Am I?"

"Let me change the bandage."

"It doesn't matter."

"Of course it does! It matters because I don't want you to do something foolish and die. If you leave that filthy rag on, the infection will only get worse."

Smoke drifted from her nostrils. He edged away.

"Don't," he said.

She growled. "You're impossible."

"Oh, *I'm* impossible?"

"Yes!"

"You don't need to baby me."

"I'm not. Is it so hard for you to ask for help?"

Yes, it was, but he would rather deny her the satisfaction of an answer.

Glowering, he reached into his pack for his ruined shirt. He tried to tear the cotton with his teeth, but he lacked the fangs of a dragon. Swearing none too subtly, he tossed the shirt away and pretended to inspect his stitches.

"Sikandar." She waited for him to look. "Tell me the truth."

He cocked his head. "About?"

"Was it wrong of me to kiss you?"

TWENTY-ONE

CINDERELLA

Shadows darkened his eyes. "It was the wrong time."

Wrong? She wanted to shrivel into a husk and be blown away by the wind. He was refusing to look at her now, as if the memory of kissing her was too shameful. God, had she been utterly and completely wrong about him?

"I know it was impulsive of me." Her words trembled.

"Cinderella."

"I'm nothing more than a curse to break. A puzzle to solve."

"I don't think of you that way."

She swallowed with some difficulty. "Maybe I don't understand why you're still helping me." A fragile hope made her words brittle around the edges.

Why wouldn't he confess his true feelings?

"I promised to break the curse," he said.

She growled out a sigh. "Again, you tell me that."

He remained frustratingly resistant. Without waiting for him to come to his senses, she took his ruined shirt from him and tore a strip of cloth with her claws.

"Hold still," she said, and he let her bandage his wound.

"I don't understand what you want from me."

"Nothing. I want *you*."

He let out a sigh. "Forgive me if I find that hard to believe."

"Why would you say that?"

"Because no one has ever wanted me without wanting something from me." His shoulders slumped under the weight of his confession. "My family least of all."

"They are wrong about you," she said fiercely.

"You haven't even met them."

"I know. But my stepfamily never wanted me, beyond what I did for them as a servant."

"Is that why you burned Umberwood to the ground?"

"It's why I refuse to let my past define me any longer. And why I choose my own future."

He bowed his head. "It isn't that simple."

"Do you want to go home?"

"I miss Azurum," he said, but he halted, as if any more words would be too painful to say.

It hurt to even look at him like this. She wished she wasn't hard and armored by scales. She wished he could see how much she cared.

"Why don't you want me to come with you?" she said.

"I never said that."

"You were about to return to Azurum without me! How would I ever find you again?"

"A mistake." His jaw clenched. "I was wrong to abandon you."

"Is that what you wanted?"

He shook his head. "I should have told you to meet me."

"I don't want to stand between you and your family."

"My family can wait." His words sharpened. "They will summon me to the palace soon enough. I would rather spend my last wish on you."

"You would?"

"Yes." He locked stares with her. "In a heartbeat."

"And I would fly across the sea for you."

"Then we understand each other."

But he sat apart from her, his shoulders rigid with tension, as if she might fight him. When he glanced into her eyes, his own glittered with unspoken words. She wanted desperately to embrace him, but she resisted the urge.

Worse, she didn't dare tell him the truth.

She was falling for him, so hard and fast it scared her.

They flew across the Cerulean Sea.

They navigated by the stars, since Sikandar said every decent sorcerer had to be educated on astronomy. When dawn painted the sky lavender, the next island broke the horizon. Her wings ached as she pushed harder.

She rode the wind hard, soared over the beach, and landed in the dunes. The sand here was whiter than sugar, the shadows purple in the early morning light.

"Let me check the map." Sikandar slid from her back and staggered. "Gods, my legs are stiff."

"My *wings* are stiff."

He swayed, then crumpled to his knees.

"Sikandar!"

"Tired," he muttered.

She touched his forehead. Even through her scales, heat radiated from his skin.

"You have a fever," she said.

"Just need to rest."

He dropped his pack on the sand and rested on it like a pillow. Sweat dampened his face.

"We can't stop," she said. "We have to go to Azurum."

"The map."

She unrolled it on the sand. "Where are we?"

"Sugar Island." Sighing, he closed his eyes.

She slid her claw along the paper. "Look. Sugar Island is the last island before Azurum, if we skip all these tiny ones in between. We're almost there!"

"Can I stay here?"

"Sikandar!" She glared at him. "I'm not leaving you on this desolate island, despite how pleasantly named it may be. There's no sugar here, or any food, for that matter."

"Actually, sugarcane merchants named the island."

"Oh, who cares!"

A smile shadowed his face. "Anyone with a sweet tooth."

"Don't argue with me. We're flying to Azurum, where we will find a doctor to help you."

"A doctor?" He wrinkled his nose. "I want a healer."

"What's the difference?"

"Healers know sorcery, at least in Azurum."

As Sikandar struggled upright, she braced his elbow to help him stand. Crouching, she waited for him to climb onto her back once more. He slung on his pack and leaned against her shoulder. His hair shadowed his eyes.

"It's too far," he said.

"No, it isn't. I can make it to Azurum."

"How do you know?" Despair thickened his voice.

"Because I trust my own strength. I survived years of backbreaking servitude. Every cruelty my stepfamily could fling at me. All you have to do is hold on."

He laughed hollowly. "That's the part I'm worried about."

"Time to go." She nudged him with her wing. "Get on."

"You're very persistent."

Despite his protests, he settled between her shoulder blades. His hand curled around her horn again.

"Do you still have the Jewel of Oblivion?" she said.

"Of course." He paused. "Why wouldn't I?"

"We left the ship rather abruptly."

"You're talking just to distract me, aren't you?"

"Perhaps."

She beat her wings, her muscles aching, and lifted off from the dunes. Sugar Island dwindled beneath them. He clung to her back with the last of his strength. The sun leaned over the horizon, bringing with it a heat that reminded her of summer.

After an eternity over endless waves, a slice of land cut the sky.

"Sikandar!" She shouted over the wind. "Is that Azurum?"

"Yes."

His fingers grasped at her horn, slipping, and she beat her wings even harder. Beneath her shadow, the water lightened from deep blue to shallow turquoise. The land ahead promised lush emerald forests along a ribbon of pale sand. Wind gusted from the coast of Azurum and blew her slideways. She tilted her wing down and circled toward the shore.

Sikandar slid from her back and plummeted into the sea.

A scream tore from her throat.

When he hit the Cerulean Sea, she wasn't even sure he was awake. She folded her wings and dove after him, headfirst, piercing the water like a javelin.

He sank into the depths, darkness swallowing him whole.

Kicking deeper, she caught his wrist in her claws and surged toward the light. She surfaced, gasping, and struggled to keep them both above water.

His eyes were closed, his body heavy. A wave bunched beneath them, pushing them toward shore, before it curled in the shallows and shoved their heads underwater again.

Spluttering, she spat water. When the next wave came, she swam hard and clawed her way onto a beach of dazzling white sand. Surf broke on the rocks around them. The retreating wave tried to yank them back into the sea. She crawled higher and dragged the unconscious sorcerer with her. Every muscle in her body protested the effort.

"Sikandar!"

Another scream threatened to burst free. Was he breathing?

He crumpled on the sand, as limp as seaweed, his black hair clinging to his face. When she rolled him over and thumped him on the back, he started coughing up mouthfuls of seawater. He sucked in a ragged gulp of air and squinted at her, droplets glittering on his dark eyelashes.

"Cinderella?"

"You nearly drowned." Her voice shook. "Are you all right?"

He licked the salt from his lips. "Thirsty."

Shouts punctuated the waves.

Men on horses galloped down the beach. Six of them, armored in leather. As they advanced, sunlight glinted off their scimitars and the dull gunmetal of rifles.

Sikandar forced out a word. "Guards."

TWENTY-TWO

SIKANDAR

When Sikandar lived in Zarkona, he left his bedroom window open at night. During the winter, breezes billowed inside and cooled his skin. During the summer, the scent of jasmine infused the hot and heavy air.

Always, the crashing of the Cerulean Sea shushed him to sleep.

This time, when he jolted awake, the waves sounded too loud. Where was he? Outside the lattice window, the moon shone like a slice of melon. His sweaty clothes clung to his skin. He kicked off the sheets—he needed to cool down.

A silver-haired man shuffled into the room, dressed in the white robes of a healer.

Of course. The hospital in Zarkona.

"Where did she go?" Sikandar rasped. His throat felt like he had swallowed broken glass.

The healer rested his hand on his shoulder. "Who?"

"Cinderella." He struggled to speak. "The dragon."

"Sleeping in the courtyard."

He exhaled. "Good."

"Surrounded by guards."

His stomach curdled. "I remember now."

"So, you're Sikandar Zerian?" said the healer.

"Yes." There wasn't any point in denying it.

The Jewel of Oblivion had saved him. Otherwise, he would be rotting in the dungeon already.

His family would not have hesitated.

"My name is Farid," said the healer.

"Farid," Sikandar repeated. "I'm grateful for your aid."

The healer dipped his head. The hospitals in Azurum treated people of any faith or reputation.

"You have magic in your blood." It wasn't a question.

"How—?"

"I could feel it while I was healing you."

"I studied at the University of Naranjal." Sikandar swallowed, his mouth parched. "Water?"

Farid poured some into a glass. "Drink."

Sikandar rolled onto his elbow and sipped the water. "How long have I been asleep?"

"All day and most of the night." Farid tilted his head. "We entranced you before healing you."

Sikandar twisted his arm. The wound was gone, his skin the shiny pink of a new scar. He clenched the fingers on his left hand, most of his strength returned.

"Did anyone ask about me?" He drank more water.

"No."

He struggled to swallow the mouthful of water. Some idiotic part of him, a remnant of himself as a little boy, hoped his mother would visit him in the hospital. That she still cared, since he was still her son but, of course, he hadn't been on his deathbed. That made him unimportant. He could imagine her sneering in the palace.

"Your fever hasn't broken," Farid said. "Rest."

Under armed guard. Until his family decided to summon him to the palace and question him.

"Yes." Sikandar sagged onto the cot. "Thank you."

Farid pressed his fingers to Sikandar's wrist to check his pulse, or perhaps read the magic in his veins. Either way, he seemed satisfied with his recovery.

He wanted Cinderella. To talk to her, if nothing else.

"Can you bring the dragon to me?" he said.

"Possibly."

Farid left without another word.

Alone, Sikandar stared at the moon. Waiting.

"Sikandar?" Cinderella lingered just outside his door, her eyes glowing golden in the shadows.

Sitting up made his skull pound. He clutched his head.

"Are you all right?" she said.

"Just a headache." Wincing, he pinched the bridge of his nose.

Her claws clicked across the tiles. "The sickness went deeper, into your blood. You've been fighting the infection all day. Sorcery wasn't enough to cure you completely. Magic never seems to heal the heart of the problem."

He gave her a sad smile. "You have no idea how true that is."

"Lie down. You still look quite ill."

"I didn't feel like fighting gravity anyway." He dropped back onto the pillow. "Cinderella?"

"Yes?"

"You saved my life."

She stared at him for a long moment. "I was so scared."

He looked at his hands, clenching the sheets, and forced himself to relax. "I don't remember falling. Just… flying, then waking in the sand."

"You were unconscious when you hit the water." She walked to the edge of his bed. "I don't want to lose you."

"Why?" he said.

Hurt sharpened her eyes. "Why didn't I let you drown? What kind of question is that?"

"I didn't mean to imply you want me dead. Though my family might find it convenient." He laughed hollowly. "The jinni would no longer be mine. Of course, they would need to find the lamp where it's lost in the desert."

Cinderella's jaw dropped. "Your own family wants you dead?"

"No. Of course not." He stared at a scar on his knuckle, not sure when he had gotten it. "Trust me, I would have been dead a long time ago if that were true."

"Why did they banish you? I can't remember."

He sliced his hand through the air. "Keep your voice down. Nobody knows why I'm back. We *are* under armed guard, which means they must be listening."

"Who sent them?" she muttered, glancing at the door.

"Most likely my parents. They live in the palace at Semarad."

She leaned out the window, her talons curled around the edge. "Are they coming?"

As if his mother and father would rush through the courtyard, run upstairs, and embrace their beloved son. As if they were capable of having a beloved anything.

"Doubtful," he said. "My sister might deign to leave the palace."

"Your sister…?"

"Jawahir. Actually, she could have sent the guards." He glanced in the corner at his pack, which he hadn't lost in the sea by some miracle. "Is it still inside?"

"The Jewel of Oblivion?" She spoke barely above a whisper.

"Yes."

"You never showed it to me. Should I look?"

"Please."

When she opened his pack delicately, the jewel rolled out and wobbled to a halt under the window. Moonlight glistened on the midnight-purple gem.

His stomach tightened into a knot. "Maybe it would be better at the bottom of the Cerulean Sea."

She picked up the jewel. Her claws chimed against its facets. "It looks like it's worth a fortune."

"One of a kind. Dangerous, in the wrong hands. I don't think the Viridian royal family knew. Otherwise, they wouldn't have wasted the jewel in their treasury."

She shuddered and dropped it on his bed. "Take it."

"I can't keep it. Otherwise, someone will know I have it, and will wonder what I've done."

She frowned at the jewel. "You made me forget. Didn't you?"

Guilt coiled in his belly like a snake. "Everyone forgot. Everyone except for me."

"Was that intentional?"

He exhaled hard. "I had no choice."

She reached across the bed and touched her claws to the back of his hand, gently. "Tell me?"

Gods, but if she knew....

But he had told her once before, hadn't he?

"Cinderella." He sounded hoarse. "You don't know me."

"Have you ever lied to me?"

"No."

"Pretended to be anyone but yourself?"

"Never."

Her eyes glittered. "Then I *do* know you."

"But I haven't told you everything."

"Then tell me!"

Gods. He swore under his breath, though it did nothing to solve the problem. "My family banished me for murder."

She didn't jerk away from him, though she gasped. "You're a murderer?"

It was hard to meet her gaze. "I am."

"Did I already know? Before the jewel?"

"Yes."

"And I stayed with you?"

"You did."

She was quiet for a long moment. "Who?"

"My sister's husband," he whispered. "The King of Azurum."

Her eyes flew open wide. "Why?"

"He hurt her."

"And no one remembers?"

He shook his head. "The drunkard king died of a weak heart. Those were the rumors."

"God." The word escaped her on an exhalation. "Sikandar."

"I cursed him."

Cinderella flared her wings like she wanted to flee—or attack. "What kind of curse?"

"If he hurt my sister again, he would die."

"That seems... reasonable."

"Of course, he hit her that night. But he still lived, because my curse was a failure. I was a failure. I didn't specify *when* he had to die. I had to kill him myself."

She braced herself on the side of the bed. "Sikandar, I'm so sorry."

He forced himself to study her face. Why wasn't she glaring or sneering at him? Did it always hurt this much to have someone care? He rubbed the scar on his arm until it became uncomfortable to do so, his skin angry with him.

"Only you know the truth," he said.

"I won't tell anyone."

"The punishment in Azurum would be death. I was lucky to be banished by my family."

She glanced at him. "They knew?"

"They asked me to do it."

"And they still banished you?"

"I disgraced the Zerian name. I nearly implicated them in murder. Jawahir suggested banishment first. And my brothers never argued to the contrary."

"Your parents?"

"My mother always knew there was something wrong with me."

She shook her head. "Wrong?"

He bit the inside of his cheek and allowed himself this sliver of pain. "The jinni's wish proved what they already feared to be true. I was never good enough for them."

"No," she said. "You were too good for them."

He tried to smile, but failed miserably. "I wish that were true."

"You aren't like them!"

"I'm still a Zerian."

"Sikandar," she said, her eyes glittering fiercely. "If your family tries to hurt you again…"

"They won't."

"Why not?"

"They won't remember why I was banished."

"Have they forgotten you? Why haven't they come to the hospital? Why don't they care?"

"I—" He didn't trust himself to speak.

"You don't need to do this to yourself."

She wasn't entangled in the brambles that grew between family, the thorns that dug deep into his skin and held him too close. He couldn't leave without damage.

He inhaled. "I understand why they don't want to come."

"But why?"

"Because I'm still Sikandar. To them, I'm a disappointment."

Cinderella twisted her face, stricken, as if he had exposed a deep and horrifying wound. "But to me—" Her voice broke, and she looked away quickly.

"But to you, I'm also a disappointment. I couldn't break the dragon curse. I couldn't keep my promise to you." His words sounded hollow.

"That's not what I meant!" She whirled on him. "You couldn't be more wrong about how I feel."

"How am I wrong?" He was shaking so hard he couldn't hide it. "Tell me."

"You act like no one should care about you. Not even your own family. Like you believe yourself to be unlovable." Her words had a fierce edge to them.

He said nothing, too afraid his voice would betray him if he did.

"You, unlovable? Impossible." She laughed, almost recklessly. "I'm falling in love with you."

His heart shattered, but it was like ice shattering, leaving him defenseless against a flood of emotion. He pressed his fingers to his eyes, too late to stop himself from crying, not too ashamed for her to see him so vulnerable.

"You're falling in love with me?" he rasped.

He had to ask, as if she might change her mind between one breath and the next.

"Without question." She reached for him, but stopped before touching him. "Even if you don't believe me. Even if you don't feel the same way about me."

He didn't know how he felt about her. Not in a way he could shape into words yet.

"Cinderella, I..."

She retreated. "Don't reply. Please. Not while I'm a dragon."

"But—"

"I just wanted you to know that I care about you. And not out of pity, or wanting your third wish."

"I know."

"I'm glad." She wouldn't look him in the eye, her head bowed. "And now it's frightfully late. I didn't mean to keep you awake, when you need to sleep."

He shrugged lopsidedly, still reluctant to use his scarred arm. "Where will you sleep?"

"With you. On the floor." She sighed. "There's only one bed once again, but I'm a dragon."

He dropped back into bed and let his head sink into the pillow. He wished he had been braver when they had spent the night together before. At the very least, he should have kissed her sooner. Should have tried to admit his feelings.

"Cinderella?" he said.

"Yes?"

"May I kiss you good night?"

"I have fangs and claws."

"Clearly. And yet clearly that won't stop me from kissing you."

She leaned over him in bed. "If only I could kiss you back," she whispered.

He braced himself on his elbows and touched his lips to her forehead. Her pearl-smooth scales warmed his mouth from the fire within.

Did he dare to hope for a future with her?

"Good night, Cinderella."

With the smooth curve of her broken claw, she brushed a tear from his cheek. "Good night."

Dawn broke over Zarkona, coloring the sky a silvery blue, and the sun's warmth promised heat later in the day. Sikandar remained alone, except for the dragon at his bedside and the guards posted throughout the hospital.

His family cared enough to not let him escape.

Cinderella dozed on the tiles, her tail curled around herself, her chin resting on her claws. Sunlight glimmered on her indigo scales and cast scintillations on the wall.

His chest ached when he remembered last night.

She believed he was better than his family. She believed he was someone worth saving.

He swung his legs over the bed, his knees trembling under his weight, and braced himself on the wall. He shuffled to a pitcher and poured himself a glass of water.

Cinderella lifted her head. Wincing, she stretched her wings. She hadn't complained about flying straight to Azurum, though her muscles had to hurt.

"Are you feeling better?" she said.

He downed the glass of water. "Less feverish."

"Thank goodness."

Droplets clung to the side of the glass. He watched them slide down until they fell to the floor.

"Cinderella, I—"

A knock on the door startled them both. But it was just Farid, bringing a tray of breakfast: two bowls of wheat semolina porridge topped simply with butter and honey. On the side, a roll of parchment sealed with wax.

Even without looking closer at the wax, it hit him low in the gut: the royal seal. It had to be.

"Is that from the palace?" Sikandar said.

Farid nodded. "It arrived this morning."

"I knew my family would summon me sooner or later." He took the roll of parchment but didn't open it, instead setting it by his pillow. "Thank you."

"Of course." Farid touched his hand to Sikandar's forehead. "Your fever has broken."

"How much longer will I be in the hospital?"

"It would be safe to heed the royal summons." Farid arched his eyebrows before leaving the room.

Cinderella tapped the tray with her claws. "Will you go?"

"I haven't even read it yet."

"Please, eat. So I won't have to eat alone."

The parchment from the palace had killed his appetite, but as a sorcerer, he understood the importance of keeping up his strength. Grimacing, he spooned some porridge into his mouth. It had been seasoned with cardamom, which evoked eating breakfast in his grandmother's kitchen.

The bite of porridge lodged in his throat like a stone, and he swallowed hard.

"Are you all right?" Cinderella said.

"Yes." He coughed. "I feel well enough to leave."

"And go to the palace?"

"I don't know yet. Gods, let me read the damn summons."

He broke the seal and unrolled the parchment.

Her Majesty, the Queen Regent, requests the immediate presence of Sikandar Zerian at the Palace of Semarad.

Jawahir was the Queen Regent, since her son was too young to rule, but this wasn't her handwriting. Too flowery, when her words bristled like hard and spiky insects.

She hadn't even signed her name. Was he so unimportant?

"What does it say?" Cinderella kept glancing away from the parchment. "I can't read Azuri."

"My sister requests my immediate presence at the palace."

"Is that a good thing?"

"It's not an invitation to teatime. It's a royal summons."

"Oh." She tilted her head. "Will you go?"

Sikandar rolled the parchment until none of the words could be seen. He didn't need to reread them. "We're going to Semarad. But we're not going to the palace."

"If not the palace, then…?"

"The Zarran Desert, where I buried the lamp."

"Won't your sister be angry?"

"My family can wait." He squared his shoulders. "I owe you my life. The least I can do is to bring you to the jinni and break the curse with my last wish."

She bit the corner of her lip. "Thank you."

"Don't thank me yet." He gave her a crooked smile. "Wait until we make our grand escape."

TWENTY-THREE

CINDERELLA

Cinderella couldn't stop glancing at Sikandar. Thank goodness she had brought him to Azurum fast enough for him to be saved. His fever had broken overnight. And after the healing spells, his arm was merely scarred.

Her own confession echoed in her ears.

I'm falling in love with you.

He hadn't returned the sentiment, but he hadn't rejected her, either. And he had kissed her good night, his lips on her forehead, so sweet her heart ached.

"Escape?" she murmured. "When?"

Sikandar hid the Jewel of Oblivion in his pack. "Now."

"Don't forget the royal guards outside your door."

"We aren't strolling out of the hospital, of course. We're flying from the courtyard."

"Flying where?"

"Semarad."

"I don't know the way."

"It's east of here. Toward the sun."

She flexed her wings, her muscles protesting. "How far?"

"Less than a day away." He glanced into her eyes. "I promise."

"I'm a bit sore after flying over the Cerulean Sea."

"I know. I'm sorry." He flashed her a smile. "Semarad's bazaar is famous for its street food."

"Are you trying to tempt me?"

"Is it working?"

She laughed. "Maybe."

"I promise to buy you a proper cup of chai." He swung open the latticed window. "Ladies first."

"Goodness, I'm not sure I will fit."

"If you fold your wings, you will."

"The windows at Knightsend Castle would beg to differ."

He arched his eyebrows. "Did you open them first?"

"Well…"

He stifled a laugh. "Try to save this window."

At least she couldn't blush as a dragon. She flattened her wings against her back and slithered halfway through the window. The courtyard—and the ground—loomed a story below her. Dizzy, she clung to the windowsill with claws.

"Quickly," Sikandar said. "Before the guards see you."

"It's a long way down."

"You have wings."

"Yes, but how will you follow me?"

"Carefully."

She jumped out of the window. The ground lurched up to meet her, but she flared her wings and landed with the grace of a cat.

"I did it!" she whispered.

Sikandar slung one leg over the windowsill. "Come closer."

"Don't fall!"

"Lower your voice."

She lingered under the window. Two royal guards began crossing the courtyard.

"Quickly," she said.

Sikandar slid from the window and landed, hard, between her shoulders. He slipped halfway off her back before catching one of her horns and righting himself.

One of the guards shouted something in Azuri, undoubtedly commanding them to stop.

Cinderella lunged into the air, pumping her wings, and clawed her way into the sky. She just cleared the roof, her belly scraping the bricks. Heat shimmered from the crooked streets of Zarkona and lifted her higher. The courtyard of the hospital dwindled to the size of a postage stamp.

Sikandar shouted over the wind. "Fly east."

She dipped one wing and curved over Zarkona. An old stone wall circled the city, though it had been outgrown by houses on the outskirts. Beyond the wall, the streets of Zarkona yielded to a lush, emerald forest of endless trees.

They followed a serpentine river. Trees thinned into gleaming, water-logged fields. Rice paddies, she deduced, though she had never seen them before. Her reflection rippled beneath her. Farmers stared at her as she flew. There wasn't much to be done about her lack of stealth.

Wind whirled from the land. She rode one breeze to the next, sparing her strength.

A ribbon of farmland braided the river as it twisted inland. Rice paddies dried up, replaced by fields and orchards. This greenery frayed to dust on the edges. Beyond, dust crumbled to sand. That had to be the Zarran Desert.

They flew for a small eternity. The egg-yolk sun slid down the blue bowl of the sky.

At last.

It rippled like a mirage on the horizon: a city of white stone. On the riverbank, an ornately carved palace soared heavenward with roofs of gleaming gold.

"Semarad," Sikandar said. "Circle over the city."

Hope giddied Cinderella. Her shadow rippled over a colorful patchwork of tents and awnings.

"The bazaar?" she said.

"Yes. Land here."

She swooped into a courtyard where a fountain burbled and splashed blue tiles. The crowd scattered under the shadow of her wings, but no one screamed or fled.

Sikandar slid from her back. "Thank the gods we're here."

"Why aren't they running away?"

He cracked the knots from his neck. "Azurum doesn't have dragons. Most Azuri people would be more curious than afraid to see a dragon ridden by a sorcerer."

"How do they know you are a sorcerer?"

"Because I tamed a ferocious beast," he deadpanned.

She snorted. "Of course you did."

"Stay close with me." He smiled. "Pretend to be mine."

Mine. When he rested his hand on her shoulder, her heart skipped a beat. She wished she weren't simply pretending to be a magical beast he had tamed.

She swallowed twice. "I'm thirsty."

"I promised you a proper cup of chai, didn't I?"

"You did."

She followed him through the bazaar of Semarad. Aromas of street food uncurled on the wind. Peddlers stirred rice colored golden with saffron, baked flatbread inside clay ovens, and roasted sizzling skewers of chicken.

Her mouth watered so hard it ached.

"Chai!" Sikandar waved her over to a stall.

A man with an impressive mustache stirred a big pot of milk tea over a charcoal stove. Fragrant steam drifted from the chai and wreathed them all. Sikandar dug a few copper coins from his pack and bought them two cups.

Cinderella smiled shyly. "Thank you."

"Drink it." He was waiting for her, his eyes bright.

She sipped the hot chai. "Oh, that's much better with milk!"

He laughed. "Was my chai that bad?"

"No!"

He laughed again. "You said that awfully fast."

"Sikandar, it was sweet of you to brew me chai when we met."

"It would have been even sweeter if I had more sugar."

She groaned. "What a terrible pun. But I doubt *you* could be even sweeter."

He bit back a smile and shook his head, as if he didn't believe a word she said.

When would he believe she loved him?

Maybe she had been a fool to confess. Maybe he had never thought of her that way.

Even if he broke the curse, he might break her heart.

She finished sipping her chai. The scent of chicken grilling over coals kept dragging her gaze back.

"What are those?" she said.

"Kebabs."

"Can I have one?"

He smirked. "Can I stop you?"

"I have no money."

But he was already walking over to the kebab seller. After a few words of Azuri, he bought them each a skewer. She bit into the meat. Smoky juice exploded on her tongue. She closed her eyes and let out an improper groan.

"I thought you would like that," he said.

It was so meaty and greasy; it was certainly unladylike to enjoy. She loved it even more.

"Still hungry?" he asked.

"A little," she admitted.

"Let me buy you more food. It's the least I can do after you flew from Zarkona to Semarad."

"And from Viridia to Azurum."

"How could I forget?"

They ate the kebabs and kept walking. Sikandar stopped at another stall and bought them each a bowl of rice pilaf spooned from a giant copper pot. It had been cooked with pine nuts, apricots, golden raisins, and fragrant spices.

"Cinnamon?" she said.

Sikandar nodded. "Cinnamon and cardamom."

"It all tastes so marvelous and strange."

His mouth quirked. "Am I marvelous and strange?"

"I didn't mean to imply you were exotic."

"Azurum is ordinary to everyone who lives here."

When she glanced into his eyes, a realization jolted her. He wanted her to see his home. He was detouring from their path to show her a part of him that could have remained a mystery. Even if they never saw each other again after the third wish, she would always have this shared memory.

The sunset burned in a conflagration of red and gold. Night would fall soon. Bazaar peddlers lit brass lanterns, each casting an ornate filigree of light.

Sikandar nudged her with his elbow. "Look, in the shadows."

Royal guards were trickling into the street, trying to blend into the crowd as they advanced.

"Time to go," he said.

"Get on."

When he vaulted onto her back, the guards shouted and rushed through the bazaar. She froze in the middle of the street, the muscles in her legs locked in place. Her stomach clenched; she regretted eating so much street food.

"Go," Sikandar said. "Go!"

Ropes hissed through the air, thrown by the guards, and grappling hooks knocked chunks from the nearby brick building. One of the ropes tangled with Cinderella's wing. Pain shot through her wing, crumpled against her ribs.

"Sikandar!" she cried.

Blue light flashed, dazzling her, as he cast a spell. The rope crumbled into ashes.

"Now!" he said.

When she swept her wings, the downdraft slowed the guards for a few paces. She tilted back her head and blew a plume of fire. The guards shielded their faces from the heat. Screams tore through the bazaar.

The thought of burning anyone sickened her, but scaring them bought her valuable time.

She flung herself into the air, pumping her wings, and hurtled over the bazaar. Guards sprinted below in her shadow until she abandoned them in the maze of streets.

She flew into the desert, not knowing where the jinni's lamp lay buried, until nothing but sand dunes undulated to the horizon. Her muscles trembling, she misjudged her landing and skidded across the sand.

Sikandar tumbled halfway down a dune. He jumped to his feet. "Are you all right?"

She spat sand and blinked her gritty eyes. "I can't keep going. I'm exhausted."

"Gods, I'm sorry." He offered his hand as if to help her stand, never mind she was a dragon.

She rolled onto her belly. The sun's dying light had faded, and the moon's glow turned the desert to silver dust. Stars glittered in the deepening lavender sky.

"Where is the jinni's lamp?" she asked.

"I don't know yet. But the jinni can tell me."

"How?"

He grimaced. "She visits my dreams."

"Do you have time to sleep before the guards track us down?"

"We didn't leave any tracks in the sand. Besides, it might be enough to close my eyes."

"Are you sure this isn't dangerous?"

"No. A jinni is always dangerous."

"Sikandar…"

He knelt in the sand and rested his hands on his knees. When he closed his eyes, he exhaled. All the tension relaxed from his muscles.

"Where are you?" he murmured.

His eyelids flickered as if he were dreaming; his hands twitched on his knees. She swallowed his name, not wanting to break his trance.

"She's here," he said. "Her lamp isn't far from here."

Like a sleepwalker, he lifted his hands and sketched a spell. An orb of white light glowed between his hands. It floated into the sky, not unlike the fireflies he summoned for illumination, until it looked like an overgrown star.

Sikandar opened his eyes. "Follow me."

Luckily, they didn't need to fly deeper into the desert. Her aching wings thanked her as he led her across the dunes on foot. The white orb of magic drifted above them, glowing, until it dove and burrowed into the sand.

They shared a glance.

Without a word, they both began digging. Sikandar cast a spell to freeze the sand, so it wouldn't keep crumbling back into the hole.

A chime rang out.

Her claws on a brass lamp.

"Sikandar!" she whispered.

He pawed at the sand until he bared the lamp, engraved ornately and tarnished with age.

"Gods." He laughed, almost giddy. "We found the jinni!"

A strange voice rang out. "Thank you."

Cinderella spun around.

A woman was watching them. She stood silhouetted against the night sky. Wind tugged at her black cloak, the hood of which half-shadowed her face.

Was this the jinni? She looked so... *human*.

"Who are you?" Cinderella said.

The woman's mouth curved into a blade-sharp smile.

Sikandar's hands curled into fists. "Good evening, Jawahir."

"How rude, little brother. Aren't you going to introduce me?"

TWENTY-FOUR

SIKANDAR

Jawahir lowered her cloak's hood. Kohl darkened her eyes, which glittered with an unnamable emotion.

"How did you find us?" Sikandar said.

"I followed the big blue dragon, then the magic ball of light." Jawahir scoffed. "It lit up the Zarran Desert. You were never any good at stealth, Sikandar."

"You cheated."

"Cheated?" She sneered.

"You sent royal guards after us." He hated how his voice went hoarse when he was angry.

"You refused my summons to the palace."

Cinderella's scales rustled against the sand as she edged nearer. "This is your sister?" There wasn't any scorn in her words, just a hint of fear and admiration.

His sister brought that out in people.

Jawahir inspected the dragon. "This is your… what?"

"Friend," Cinderella said. "Tell me, why hadn't I met any of his family at the hospital?"

"He was hardly on his deathbed." Jawahir said it dryly, as if it were a clever joke.

Like a fool, his chest ached because he allowed himself to care. "You could have come."

"I would have, but you ran away." Her gaze slid to the jinni's lamp, glinting in the moonlight.

He stepped between her and the lamp. "Only because you want something from me."

"You lied to me. You told me you lost the lamp."

"I did."

"But clearly not forever."

"I already spent my second wish on you."

On her wedding to King Ali of Azurum, but of course she didn't remember him murdering her deserving husband. Couldn't remember, after the Jewel of Oblivion.

Jawahir tilted her head. "What will be your third wish?"

"Do you genuinely believe I would tell you?"

A calculating look sharpened his sister's eyes. "She's cursed, isn't she? Your *friend*?"

"How did you know?" Cinderella said.

Sikandar grimaced. "Don't tell her anything."

A slow smile curved Jawahir's mouth. "You were never any good at deception, either. Gods, don't tell me you convinced the dragon you can play the hero?"

"You appear to be auditioning for the part of villain."

"Me?" Jawahir had the audacity to look wounded. "I'm not lying about my identity. Does she know who you are? Does she know what it means to be a Zerian?"

"He told me," Cinderella said, but she glanced between them.

"Wouldn't you choose your own sister over this hideous beast?"

Sikandar lunged and grabbed Jawahir by both wrists. Before she could break free, he dragged her into the space between spaces and teleported from the desert.

They stumbled out at the Palace of Semarad, in her private courtyard garden. Citrus blossoms scented the night air under the cold glow of the moon. Blood-red roses choked the courtyard, so dark they looked almost black.

"No," he said.

Jawahir's lips parted. "No?"

"No, I won't give you the lamp." He refused to blink. "No, she isn't a hideous beast."

"Why are you back in Azurum?"

"Why do you think I left?"

She shook her head, glaring at him, masking her own unease. She had no idea where he had gone, or why he had returned, and it jarred her off-balance.

"The jinni is mine," he said. "She can't even be stolen until I make my third and final wish."

"Or until you die."

His blood chilled. "Are you threatening me?"

She forced out a laugh. "I'm joking, little brother. Don't give me that hurt, innocent look."

"I refuse to give you my last wish."

She shrugged, as if this had never been her goal. "Will you give me the jinni afterward?"

He let a moment of silence drag out between them. "No."

Her lips parted with shock and scorn. "What happened to you? What's wrong with you?

"Nothing."

"Why would you turn your back on us?"

"Because I already spent my first two wishes on family. I couldn't save our grandmother, and I couldn't give you a good husband. Jawahir, I'm sorry."

Her lips thinned. "If he hadn't died of a weak heart…"

"I understand." More than he could ever say. "But the third wish will never be enough. I will never be enough. I'm done trying to force myself to be what you want."

"Sikandar… it's not too late."

If he didn't know better, he might believe that she cared about him. That the broken-glass glittering in her eyes might spill into tears of remorse and apology.

"You're right," he said. "It isn't."

"Wait."

"Goodbye, Jawahir."

He retreated from his sister and teleported away.

Sikandar returned to the desert.

He found the dragon curled around the lamp, as if it belonged to her own hoard of treasure.

"What happened?" Cinderella said.

"I made my choice."

He couldn't deny it any longer. He had been so wounded by his family that he hadn't allowed himself to be vulnerable, but now, in the desert, he forced himself to feel.

"When I kissed you," he murmured, "the truth frightened me."

"Tell me."

"My heart has already chosen you."

"Even if I'm a hideous beast?" Her voice broke.

"No curse could hide your beauty from me." His heart soared on wings of hope. "And I wanted to tell you before the last wish, so you would know I meant it."

Gods, why was she crying? And now smiling?

"Sikandar," she said. "This is why I love you."

He didn't trust himself to speak, afraid his voice would betray him, afraid of echoing the words, *I love you*, as if they would ring false coming from his mouth.

He would tell her later. When it felt right.

Trembling, he dusted sand from the jinni's lamp. Carved letters glinted in the moonlight.

Slake my thirst.

He had packed a canteen. He uncorked it and poured a trickle of water into the top of the lamp. Smoke poured from the spout. The jinni took shape from the darkness, the curves of her body nearly invisible against the night sky, the rippling of golden silk obfuscating her true outline.

The jinni stared at them. "A dragon?" she said in Azuri.

He smirked. "So, you aren't all-seeing." He switched to Viridian. "Her name is Cinderella."

"Pleased to meet you," Cinderella said, as if she were thinking of curtseying next. "Might I ask your name?"

The jinni tilted her head. "Why?" She spoke flawless Viridian.

"Because we haven't been formally introduced yet."

Cinderella never seemed to hesitate on matters of etiquette. When she glanced at Sikandar, his face heated.

"I never asked her name," he said.

"Leyla," said the jinni.

That couldn't be her true name. It sounded so human, as if she could have been a childhood friend.

"Leyla," Sikandar repeated. He gripped the lamp in his hands, sweat dampening the brass. "I want to make my third and final wish."

The jinni—Leyla—sighed. "After an eternity of waiting."

His nerves sharpened his tongue. "I was the one who freed you from an eternity of being lost in the tunnels under the University of Naranjal."

"Only you are lost," Leyla said.

Sikandar shook his head. "Not any longer."

Leyla looked at him with hunger in her eyes. After his third wish, she would no longer be bound to him, though she would still be bound to the lamp.

I wish for my family to love me.

But the words died deep within him. It was an impossible dream, one best forgotten.

Instead, he stared at the jinni with cold certainty.

"I wish for you to break the curse placed upon Cinderella, now and forever, and for you to transform her from a dragon back to her true form of girl."

A gasp, a sob, escaped Cinderella.

"No," said Leyla.

He jerked back as if she had slapped him. "No?"

"The curse runs too deep."

"What are you saying?" Cinderella whispered.

Leyla touched her between the eyes, her amethyst fingers bright against indigo scales. "I can't untangle the dragon from the girl. Not without killing you both."

TWENTY-FIVE

CINDERELLA

Cinderella froze under the jinni's fingertips, even though she wanted to shove her away and scream that she was wrong, and this was a cruel mistake. Her heartbeat pounded like she had been running and only just stumbled to a halt.

"Why can't you break the curse?" Sikandar demanded.

Leyla looked at him with the unfathomable stare of a statue. "Magic in the blood and bone."

"And?"

"Would you wish her dead?" Leyla said it so calmly, as if she found them insignificant. "I could break the curse and kill her, if that is what you desire."

"No!" He spoke through gritted teeth. "Help her. I command you."

Leyla folded her arms, her bracelets like armor. "That is not precise enough to be a wish."

"You dare defy me?"

"No, sorcerer. This is not defiance."

"If you're lying—"

"Sikandar!" Cinderella cut him off. "Stop."

His fingers tensed around the lamp, as if he wanted to reduce it to dust. "Jinn can't be trusted."

"I think she's telling the truth."

"She has to obey me."

Cinderella glared at him. "Not if she can't."

"What's the point of wishes with limits?"

"Nothing is limitless," Leyla said.

Sikandar bowed his head, the lamp cradled in his hands. His shoulders sagged in defeat.

Cinderella's hopes and dreams tasted like ash in her mouth. They had come all this way to Azurum, and for what? The dragon curse could not be broken.

And yet, she couldn't just walk away.

Couldn't leave the jinni bound to Sikandar forever.

Couldn't leave her trapped in the lamp for another eternity.

"Leyla." She met the jinni's gaze. "What is your wish?"

Stars glittered in Leyla's eyes. "Mine?"

"If you could grant your heart's desire."

"Freedom," Leyla murmured, the word nearly lost in the wind.

Cinderella turned to Sikandar. "Give me the lamp."

"What?" His head jerked up. "You can't make a wish, not until I have made my last."

"Then wish for me. Free the jinni."

"No. It's too dangerous. Why are you even asking me?"

"Because it's the right thing to do."

"How can you be certain?"

"Leyla, how long have you been trapped in the lamp?"

"Years, perhaps centuries. I lose all sense of time whenever I slumber in the lamp."

"Sikandar."

His face twisted. "Don't look at me like that! I wasn't the sorcerer who imprisoned her."

"And so you're innocent?"

"I never said that."

Shadows tattered the edges of Leyla's shape. The jinni focused on a faraway place. "I have become little more than a slave. Forced to give magic without consent."

"Gods." He paced across the sand. "Cinderella, we would lose any chance of saving you from the curse."

"The curse can't be broken. Why shouldn't we believe her?"

"Because she doesn't want to help us?"

"She stopped before breaking the curse and killing me."

"Cinderella—"

"Wish. Please."

Sikandar exhaled hard. "Leyla, I wish for you to be free."

Flames ignited on the jinni's skin. Her eyes burned golden, and her hair whipped into a wildfire. Wind howled through the desert, stinging them with sand. Her skin tattered into ashes; her body crumbled into embers.

Leyla vanished into moonlight and shadows.

Sikandar dropped the lamp. Empty, it thudded on the sand. He followed it down. Kneeling, he stared at the palms of his empty hands as if he had lost his sorcery.

"I broke my promise," he said. "I couldn't break the curse."

"No," Cinderella said, fiercely protective. "Not even a jinni could break the curse. I was born to become a dragon. Neither one of us knew this when you made your promise to help me, but you helped me discover the truth."

His dark eyes looked so deep. "We have lost everything."

"We haven't lost each other."

He twisted his mouth into a sad smile. "A sorcerer and a dragon, both penniless and alone."

"Where do we go from here?" She let out a broken laugh, verging on a sob. "I understand if you have changed your mind and would rather say goodbye."

His lips parted. "Why would I abandon you now?"

"Because I'm *definitely* still a dragon."

"Not forever." He dusted off his hands. "Don't forget the potion."

"Wouldn't we have to fly all the way back to Viridia?"

"I kept the ingredients in my pack."

"They didn't fall out into the Cerulean Sea?"

"Gods, I hope not." He rummaged through his pack and muttered the names of the ingredients under his breath. "Everything except void saffron."

"Fell into the sea?"

"No, everything but the saffron is safe."

"Oh, thank goodness! Where could we find the void saffron?"

He pushed himself to his feet. "The University of Naranjal."

"I hate to even ask, but how far away is it?"

He lifted one eyebrow. "Never fear, I won't ask you to fly there. We should sleep tonight."

"In the middle of the desert?"

"I have a better idea."

They flew over the Zarran Desert under cover of darkness.

Sikandar guided her back to the river, though they avoided the lights of Semarad. They landed in an orchard of lemons that reminded her of the apples at Umberwood. White flowers scented the night with intoxicating perfume, and glossy emerald leaves stirred in the warm river breeze.

"Are you sure we can sleep here?" Cinderella whispered.

"Until dawn," he said.

She lay down among the fallen leaves. He rested his head against her shoulder.

"Such sweet perfume," she murmured.

"I would have liked to study the magic of perfume." He sounded sleepy. "Rather than curses, hexes, poisons, and other ways to kill your enemies with sorcery."

"I would still like to run a bed and breakfast."

"Culinary enchantment, then."

"Couldn't we?" She curled her wing closer around him. "Run away and start one together?"

"One what?"

"A bed and breakfast, or a restaurant, or a perfumery."

"Perhaps." He stifled a yawn. "We can dream."

She smiled. "You're halfway to dreamland already."

"I'm exhausted."

"Good night, Sikandar."

"Good night."

But even as his breathing deepened, she couldn't sleep. Perhaps it was the endless sighing of the wind. Perhaps it was the way it sounded like her name.

Cinderella.

"Leyla," she whispered.

From the shadows, the jinni's shape hardened into reality. She walked without footfalls between the lemon trees. Strangest of all, the wind silenced as she advanced.

"Am I dreaming?" Cinderella said.

"Yes," Leyla said. "The sorcerer will not wake."

A knot tightened in Cinderella's gut. She was alone. "Why have you returned?"

"The curse cannot be broken. But it can be bent."

"Bent? What—?"

Leyla's fingers touched the scales between Cinderella's eyes.

Red-hot magic surged through her skull. Pain knocked the air from her lungs. She moaned through clenched teeth as her skeleton bent into another shape, bones and sinews rearranging. Her claws gouged the dirt.

Blue scales faded into pale skin. She lost her wings and fangs. Her claws shrank away. She clung to the dirt with fingernails.

"I'm a girl again?" she whispered.

"Both a girl and a dragon," Leyla said. "I have given you the power to shapeshift."

Shaking, Cinderella hugged herself. "Thank you!"

Unblinking, Leyla tilted her head. "You chose my freedom rather than your own desires. Consider my debt to you repaid."

When Leyla vanished, Cinderella woke with a gasp.

Sickness punched her in the stomach. Blue scales still armored the skin along her hands.

"No," she said. "No, no."

Sikandar jolted upright. "What's wrong?"

Shaking, she couldn't stop staring at her hands. She traced her claws over her scales, resisting the urge to claw at them. "I dreamed that Leyla turned me back into a girl. She told me she gave me the power to shapeshift."

His jaw dropped. "She did?"

"But I'm still a dragon. It was just a dream."

"Cinderella, dreaming of a jinni is never just a dream. Can you try to turn back to girl?"

"Myself? How?"

"I don't know how, but I believe you can do it."

She tensed every muscle in her body, until she began trembling from the strain.

"Girl," she whispered. "*Girl.*"

"Breathe. Trust in yourself."

She allowed herself to inhale. The transformation shuddered through her bones. She cried out. Scales melted away and bared her skin, pale under the moonlight. The dragon retreated from the surface and slumbered deep beneath her flesh.

This time, it wasn't a dream.

It was real.

"Sikandar?" she said. "Hold me."

He tugged her into his arms, never mind that she was naked. She clung to him, shivering, his embrace just shy of crushing. With her face pressed against his chest, his strong heartbeat pounded under her ear. God, he smelled so good.

"Kiss me," she said, "before I die of longing."

"Die?" He flashed her a grin. "That sounds dangerous."

She laughed. "Don't ruin the moment!"

He couldn't stop grinning, so she hooked both hands behind his neck and erased the distance between their bodies. She met him in a fierce kiss, a hard kiss, one that unfurled inside her like a night-blooming flower.

When they broke apart, he looked at her with blown pupils. "That was overwhelming."

She glanced at him through her eyelashes. "In a good way?"

"Yes. Very. You leave me speechless."

She laughed. "I won't ask you for detailed descriptions."

"That might help." Raspy, he cleared his throat. "Cinderella."

"Yes?"

He tucked her hair behind her ear, with infinite tenderness. "I love you."

She clung to him, wondering if she might swoon in his arms, but his eyes anchored her there. A constellation of stars glittered in her chest.

He was hers. This beautiful, dark-eyed sorcerer had given her his heart.

"Tell me again," she whispered.

He kissed her, which was much better than words. His hand stroked her wild mane of hair before fitting the curve of her back like it belonged there. Propriety be damned, she didn't care for clothes right now. Her skin craved his touch.

"Sikandar," she said. "I have a confession."

He smiled, no doubt in his eyes. "Yes?"

"You are my happily ever after."

"And you are mine."

The End

EPILOGUE

SIKANDAR

"What happens after happily ever after?"

Cinderella asked the question as she lay beside him in the orchard of lemons. Dawn gilded the leaves above and shimmered on her hair. She had borrowed some of his clothes, too modest to stay naked for long, not that he had complained.

"I don't know," he said. "The stories always end there."

"Unfortunately, we're still homeless, penniless, and friendless."

"We have each other."

She kissed his cheek. "How sweet of you."

He tilted his head and kissed her on the mouth. She melted in his arms, her hair draped against him like silk. If only they could stay in this orchard forever and survive on kisses alone.

She leaned away. "Where should we go?"

"Viridia?"

Her shoulders tensed. "You know I can't go home. I burned down Umberwood Manor and smashed the windows of Knightsend Castle. Twice. I'm assuming my crimes against architecture won't go unpunished."

He sat upright and reached into his pack. "There's always the Jewel of Oblivion." The gemstone's twilight facets glinted in the palm of his hand.

She nudged a fallen lemon with her toes. "You could make everyone forget?"

"Not everyone. Hundreds of people saw you turn into a dragon at the ball. Hundreds more saw you flying over Viridia. That would require sorcery beyond my skill."

"Is there a sorcerer skilled enough?"

He frowned. "Doubtful." It would take an immense amount of magic.

"Never mind Viridia." She braced herself on her elbows before meeting his eyes. "I would rather explore Azurum with you."

A knot tightened in his gut, but he smiled at her regardless. "Explore?"

"It sounds more exciting than seeking gainful employment," she said dryly.

"The Jewel of Oblivion might still help us."

"How?"

"I can sell it."

Her eyes widened. "After all the trouble you went through?"

"I'm no longer banished. Besides, it might be more trouble than it's worth."

"How much is it worth?"

"Excellent question." He tossed the jewel and caught it again. "We can't stroll into the nearest pawn shop. We would need to take it to the experts."

"Who?"

"We could travel to the University of Naranjal." He rubbed the jewel with his thumb, back and forth over a polished facet. "We could sell it there."

"Weren't you expelled?"

"Yes, and?"

"Won't they wonder why you're back?"

"I expect they will have forgotten why I was banished, just like everyone else in Azurum."

She shook her hair from her face. "So this will be a second chance?"

"A chance to turn the jewel into gold."

Flying to the University of Naranjal on the back of a dragon had a certain daredevil appeal. Besides, neither one of them wanted to trudge across the desert on foot.

Cinderella soared over the sand, riding the heat that shimmered to the azure heavens. Sikandar crouched low against her back, squinting, glad for the wind that cooled his skin. The university rippled on the horizon like a mirage. Onion-domed towers glinted in the sun, tiled in gold.

"Land outside the front gate," he said.

She swooped down, gaining speed, before she flared her wings and landed with a teeth-rattling thump. A caravan of camels bawled and shied away from the dragon. The merchant leading the camels shouted a few choice words of Azuri profanity.

"What did he say?" Cinderella said.

Sikandar jumped to the ground. "I won't translate. It's too rude." He paced back and forth on jittery knees.

"The gate is open," she pointed out.

"I know."

She glanced at him. "Are dragons not allowed inside?"

"Actually, I don't know." He let the breath rush from his lungs. "Let's find out."

"Goodness, I hope they won't incinerate us with magical fireballs."

"Pretty sure dragons are fireproof."

"Sikandar." She gave him a look that was less than amused.

"Follow me."

He strode through the front gate, giving a wide berth to the camels, who looked mad enough to spit. He looked back at Cinderella. She had her wings clamped and a glint in her eyes. He didn't blame her for being afraid.

"Don't worry," he said, "I can protect you."

She nodded, then gasped as they stepped through the front gate.

The University of Naranjal had also dazzled him, long ago, when he first arrived as a student. Ornately carved sandstone arches and towers soared heavenward. Now, he glanced around with dread gripping his gut like a fist. The silver gleam of the oasis reminded him of the day he found the jinni's lamp deep within the underground tunnels.

Gods, the students were staring at them. Whispering. A few of the older students even sneered at him. How much did they remember after the Jewel of Oblivion? He'd had a bad reputation here before he was banished.

"Sikandar Zerian!" a deep voice rang out. A familiar voice that made him sweat.

Aslan Karakhan, the Headmaster of the University of Naranjal, strode across the courtyard. His white robes billowed in the wind. He halted in the dragon's shadow, not a trace of fear in his black eyes. He stroked his salt-and-pepper beard.

"So," said Karakhan. "Why have you graced us with your presence?"

Banishment wasn't an excuse any longer. But his family hadn't been paying tuition, so presumably the headmaster remembered that much.

"My apologies, sir." Sikandar cleared his throat. "I've been away in Viridia."

Karakhan's eyes narrowed. "Vacationing in Viridia? With a dragon?"

"Cinderella," she said. "Pleased to meet you."

Karakhan stared at her for a second too long, his only hint of surprise. "Sikandar, you owe me answers to many questions."

Sikandar gestured at the students lingering around them. "Can we speak without an audience?"

"In my office. Now."

Karakhan turned on his heel and sketched a symbol in the air. He walked through an invisible door and vanished between one step and the next.

Sikandar glanced at Cinderella. Better not to risk teleportation. "We can walk."

"Thank you." She followed him deeper into the University of Naranjal.

Sandstone corridors sheltered the cool hush of shadows. Ancient sorcery permeated the walls with an electric scent like a distant thunderstorm. He hadn't forgotten the way to the headmaster's office, though he hadn't been summoned often as a student.

Confronted by a closed door, Sikandar rapped with his knuckles.

"Enter," said Karakhan.

Sikandar opened the door and stepped into the office. The bitter smell of blackest coffee hit him. Scrolls and books crowded the shelves, packed to the ceiling. The headmaster had crammed enough reading material for a small library into one room. Sunlight sliced through the windows and transmuted drifting dust into gold.

Karakhan waited behind his desk, his fingers steepled on the mahogany wood. "Is the dragon relevant to this discussion?"

"Possibly?" Sikandar said.

"She can wait outside." Karakhan pointed to the chair opposite his desk. "Sit."

Sikandar obeyed. He dropped his pack between his knees. The chair was just as uncomfortable as he remembered.

"What have you done?" the headmaster demanded.

Sikandar swallowed hard, his mouth bone dry. "Aren't you the one who expelled me?"

"After your family refused to pay tuition. Heaven knows why. You were one of our most promising students."

Sikandar grimaced. The compliment was too little, too late. "If you aren't questioning my expulsion, then what are you asking?"

Karakhan lifted a cup of coffee to his lips. "Are you the one who stole the jinni's lamp?"

That wasn't what he was expecting. He had never been caught before, had he?

"My apologies, sir. I meant to borrow it." His stomach clenched. Did the headmaster know he had freed Leyla?

"How did you find the lamp?"

He blinked. "Excuse me?"

Karakhan leaned forward, his elbows propped on the desk. "Tell me."

What punishment would the university devise for his thievery? Surely, a jinni's lamp was considered priceless. Unless…

Sikandar rummaged in his pack, trying to find the Jewel of Oblivion. "Let me pay you back. You might want—"

"Enough." Karakhan lifted his hand. "We believed the lamp to be lost for centuries. Sorcerers much older and wiser than you spent countless years exploring the bowels of the university, but they failed to find even a hint of the jinni."

Sikandar stopped hunting for the jewel. "Sir?"

"Are you aware of the enchantments placed upon a jinni's lamp?"

"Not particularly." Was this a test?

"Intricate, diabolical enchantments," murmured the headmaster, his dark eyes gleaming. "Magic to hide a jinni's lamp at the bottom of the sea, or within the stone heart of a mountain, or in the darkness of the longest night of the year."

Sikandar frowned. "I found the lamp in the tunnels beneath us."

"Yes! When it had been lost for ages. We know of a sorceress who wove a spell into brass and bedrock. She hid the lamp from those who sought to steal it from her, even after her death. Only you could navigate this ancient magic."

The chair creaked as Sikandar leaned back. The headmaster was talking nonsense. "Me?"

"Where is the lamp?"

"I don't have it." He gritted his teeth, bracing himself for his reaction.

Karakhan locked stares with him. "How many wishes did you make? All three?"

"Yes."

"Who has it now?"

"No one."

"Sikandar, I don't have time for cryptic responses to my questions."

Damn, it was hard to resist the urge to apologize and beg for mercy. "I'm telling the truth. No one has the lamp. It's empty."

"Empty? Don't tell me you—"

"Freed the jinni? I did." Sikandar's heartbeat pounded in his ears. "With my last wish."

The headmaster thumped his desk, rattling the cup of coffee. "Gods, Sikandar. You committed a crime even greater than theft."

"Yes, sir." He squared his shoulders. "What will you do to me? Expel me again?"

Karakhan's eyes flashed at his sarcasm. "Expulsion isn't the worst fate that could befall you."

Sikandar said nothing. He curled his hands into fists to hide how much they were sweating.

"As repayment for your crimes, you will find another jinni."

"Another?"

Karakhan gave him a blade-thin smile. "A much more ancient and powerful jinni. One who has been lost for a millennium. One who vanished after granting a wish that ended the Empire. The mother of all she-demons."

Cold rushed over Sikandar's skin. He had heard legends of a jinni with immensely dark and dangerous power. Fragments of warnings carved onto broken statues, and whispers of a terrible villain in children's fairy tales.

Legends. Nothing more.

"Of course," Sikandar said. "You want to punish me with an impossible quest."

Karakhan sipped his coffee before grimacing at the dregs. "You have a gift, Sikandar. You will find what no one else could."

"No." He didn't believe it. Couldn't believe it.

Karakhan laughed, a crackling sound like flame. "And you don't have a choice."

The story will continue in *Sorcerer by Dawn*…

AUTHOR BIO

Karen Kincy writes books when she isn't writing code. She has a BA in Linguistics and Literature from The Evergreen State College, and an MS in Computational Linguistics from the University of Washington.

Find Karen online at:
www.karenkincy.com
www.facebook.com/KarenKincyAuthor
www.twitter.com/karenkincy

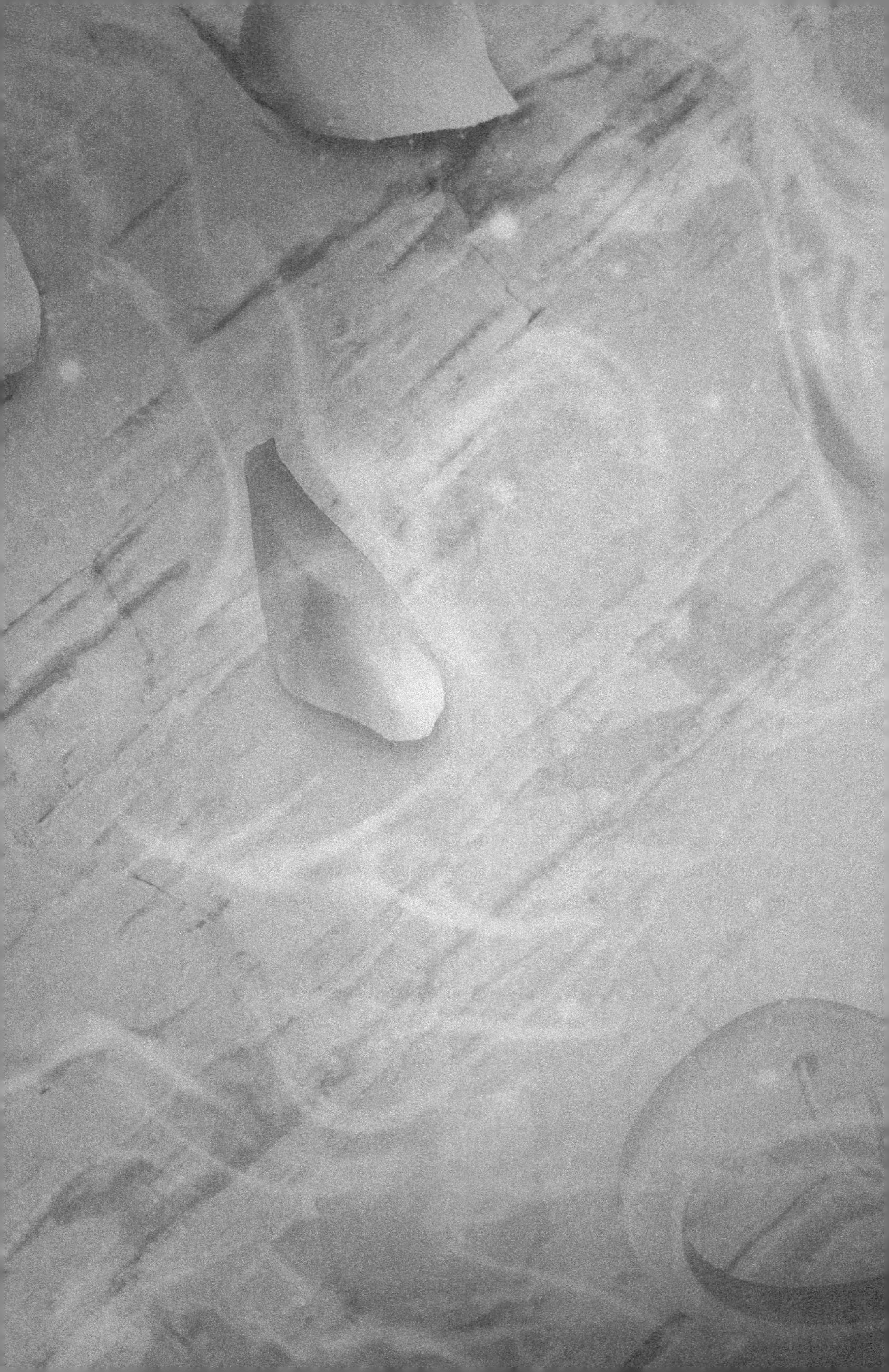

MORE BY KAREN KINCY

YOUNG ADULT FANTASY

Dragon by Midnight

YOUNG ADULT PARANORMAL

Other
Bloodborn
Foxfire

FANTASY ROMANCE

Wildfire in Her Blood
Shadows of Asphodel
Storms of Lazarus
Specters of Nemesis
Clockwork Menagerie

CPSIA information can be obtained
at www.ICGtesting.com
Printed in the USA
LVHW092040241021
701403LV00015B/228/J

9 781737 925101